THE HIGHLANDER'S GIFT

Book One: The Sutherland Legacy

ELIZA KNIGHT

HISTORY INKED
IN DRAMA

THE HIGHLANDER'S GIFT

Book One: The Sutherland Legacy
A Stolen Bride Novel

Betrothed to a princess until she declares his battle wound has incapacitated him as a man, Sir Niall Oliphant is glad to step aside and let the spoiled royal marry his brother. He's more than content to fade into the background with his injuries and remain a bachelor forever, until he meets the Earl of Sutherland's daughter, a lass more beautiful than any other, a lass who makes him want to stand up and fight again.

As daughter of one of the most powerful earls and Highland chieftains in Scotland, Bella Sutherland can marry anyone she wants—but she doesn't want a husband. When she spies an injured warrior at the Yule festival who has been shunned by the Bruce's own daughter, she decides a husband in name only might be her best solution.

They both think they're agreeing to a marriage of convenience, but love and fate has other plans...

More Books by Eliza Knight

Highland Lairds

The Laird's Prize
The Laird's Kiss - pre-order!
The Laird's Guardian Angel - coming soon

Distinguished Scots

A Scot's Pride - pre-order!
A Dash of Scot - coming soon
A Scot's Perfect Match - coming soon

Scots of Honor

Return of the Scot
The Scot is Hers
Taming the Scot

Prince Charlie's Rebels

The Highlander Who Stole Christmas
Pretty in Plaid

Prince Charlie's Angels

The Rebel Wears Plaid
Truly Madly Plaid
You've Got Plaid

The Sutherland Legacy

The Highlander's Gift
The Highlander's Quest
The Highlander's Stolen Bride
The Highlander's Hellion
The Highlander's Secret Vow
The Highlander's Enchantment

The Stolen Bride Series

The Highlander's Temptation
The Highlander's Reward
The Highlander's Conquest
The Highlander's Lady
The Highlander's Warrior Bride
The Highlander's Triumph
The Highlander's Sin
Wild Highland Mistletoe (a Stolen Bride winter novella)
The Highlander's Charm (a Stolen Bride novella)
A Kilted Christmas Wish – a contemporary Holiday spin-off
The Highlander's Surrender
The Highlander's Dare

The Conquered Bride Series

Conquered by the Highlander

Seduced by the Laird
Taken by the Highlander (a Conquered bride novella)
Claimed by the Warrior
Stolen by the Laird
Protected by the Laird (a Conquered bride novella)
Guarded by the Warrior

The MacDougall Legacy Series

Laird of Shadows
Laird of Twilight
Laird of Darkness

Pirates of Britannia: Devils of the Deep

Savage of the Sea
The Sea Devil
A Pirate's Bounty

THE THISTLES AND ROSES SERIES

Promise of a Knight
Eternally Bound
Breath from the Sea

The Highland Bound Series (Erotic time-travel)

Behind the Plaid
Bared to the Laird
Dark Side of the Laird
Highlander's Touch
Highlander Undone
Highlander Unraveled

Touchstone Series

Highland Steam
Highland Brawn
Highland Tryst
Highland Heat

Wicked Women

Her Desperate Gamble
Seducing the Sheriff
Kiss Me, Cowboy

HISTORICAL FICTION

The Mayfair Bookshop

Releasing June 6, 2023
The Other Astaire

Tales From the Tudor Court

My Lady Viper
Prisoner of the Queen

Ancient Historical Fiction

A Day of Fire: a novel of Pompeii
A Year of Ravens: a novel of Boudica's Rebellion

French Revolution

Ribbons of Scarlet: a novel of the French Revolution

A Note to Readers

Dear Reader,

I'm thrilled to be writing in the Stolen Bride series again. And even more excited to be writing Arbella and Magnus's (*The Highlander's Reward*) daughter's story. Get ready for this epic new spin-off of the Stolen Bride series—the Sutherland Legacy. There are currently five books planned for this series, one for each of Magnus and Arbella's children.

A note about some of the history in this novel. My hero in this story, Sir Niall Oliphant, is the fictional son of real-life figure Sir William Oliphant. His brother, Walter Oliphant, did actually marry Princess Elizabeth, the daughter of Robert the Bruce. The meeting at Arbroath Abbey between the clans in this novel is fictionalized, however, in the spring of 1320, a declaration for independence was signed at the abbey, (known as the Declaration at Arbroath) by the Bruce and dozens of Scottish leaders, including the Sutherland and Oliphant chiefs.

Best wishes and happy reading!
  Eliza

Prologue

Dunrobin Castle, Scottish Highlands
Fall, 1306

"I want to be knight for the day." A petulant lass with golden locks crossed her arms over her chest and glowered at the line of grubby lads with their wooden swords tucked into the corded belts of their plaids. For the first time in her short life, she had the chance to prove something.

"Ye canna. Ye're a lass. Go back to the keep and help the maids with their chores." Several of them snickered and rubbed elbows at that.

Snorting, another added, "Aye, go and milk a cow."

"Or knead the bread."

The list of chores typically delegated to females continued on for several minutes. All the while, the young lass's face grew redder and redder, her fists tighter and tighter, until one particular lad stepped forward.

He opened his mouth to say something, but she didn't let him get further than that. She tugged her arm back as she'd seen her brothers do, and let her tiny fist fly, landing hard on his chin.

Zounds, that hurt.

Her knuckles were instantly red and stinging. She thought the whole point of hitting a lad would be to hurt *him*, not herself.

Surprised, the lad stumbled back a few paces, eyes wide. "What the hell did ye go and do that for? I was going to tell these raven-gut idiots to give ye a shot."

She was immediately contrite, but being as stubborn as she was, and feeling more than mildly embarrassed, she pursed her lips in a frown and refused to say anything at all.

The other lads were laughing, doubled over as they slapped their knees and rolled around on the ground, clearly not taking her seriously.

"Ye're on your own then, wee chicken," the lad said, backing away and rubbing his reddened jaw.

"Wait," she whispered, stepping forward and looking at him nervously. "Ye'll really let me try?"

He smirked, green eyes flashing with some emotion she couldn't understand. "I'm not so sure anymore after the way ye just walloped me."

The lass stiffened her spine, knowing exactly what mocking was when directed at her. "Why's that? Ye think I fight like a lass?"

"Nay, just the opposite."

Most of the lads had stopped laughing long enough to listen, surprised perhaps that the older lad had just admitted her blow had hurt.

"What do ye say, lads, are we scared to have her join in our tournament?"

"Scared?" They laughed. "Not on her life."

"All right then," the one she'd given a good smack to said. "We'll let ye join us."

She'd not planned for them to actually allow her. Och, she had all sorts of plans involving revenge and sneaking in dressed as a lad, but not once had she thought they'd welcome her. "And if I win?"

His smirk widened. "We'll let ye be knight for the day."

Thrusting her chin forward, she gave him a righteous smile. The other lads balked, because it wouldn't be right for a lass to be the knight for the day, given that she was...well, a *lass*.

The lad, a little taller than his friends, raised his hand for their silence. "But laddies, ye recall what happens to the knight for a day?"

They narrowed their eyes, unsure what to say, for there was an ominous tone to his voice.

The lass wasn't certain of what he spoke, either. She only wanted to prove she was good enough, show her da she could beat the lads at their own game, that sewing and wearing dresses wasn't all she was good at. To prove that her brothers weren't the only ones who could help defend their castle. But...what else happened?

"The knight has to choose his lady. Who will be your lady?" the lad asked her, his grin growing wider.

Well, she wasn't going to be sucked into whatever trick he was trying to lay on her. Crossing her arms over her chest, she looked at him confidently. "Why *ye* of course."

At that, the other lads fell to laughing once more.

But the older lad she'd addressed only smiled. "If ye can be a knight, then I supposed I shall honor ye with being your lady for the day."

Even the lass had to giggle at that. "Ye're jesting with me."

"Mayhap."

"All right." She beamed a smile at him. "Agreed."

She sauntered away, a skip in her step. Those lads were going to rue the day...

An hour later, she arrived on the makeshift list field. The lads were all covered in iron-studded armor, their wooden weapons thwacking together as they practiced. With the permission of her ma and da, she'd trained with weapons since she could toddle around. And by nine summers, she was skilled with a bow, a sword and hand-to-hand combat. But she'd never been allowed to go up against anyone other than her father, uncles and brothers.

Even still, she was certain these lads didn't stand a chance. Their size didn't matter to her. She trained with grown men who'd taught her how to go up against someone bigger.

The lads snickered at her approach, but she didn't let that bother her. Soon they would see that laughing was foolish.

The children lined up, facing the target that had been erected for the first of the tournament rounds—archery.

In the stands, all the parents and those of the clan sat and cheered the children on. Upon seeing the laird and lady's daughter, a rush of chatter went up. The lass met her father and mother's gaze unwaveringly, half expecting them to rush from their place of honor and physically remove her. But her mother placed her hand on her father's arm, and the two of them simply nodded. With both of her brothers gone off with their uncle for two weeks of training, she was the only one representing their house. And she wasn't going to lose.

"Ready!" The warrior in charge of the event stood to the side, giving only a few seconds for the children to load their arrows. "Sight your mark!"

She blew out a breath, feeling her pulse beat in her fingertips on the strings. The horn sounded for them to let their arrows fly, and she didn't hesitate, watching as her handmade arrow flew through the air, the feather fletching fluttering in the wind. Hers sank home, dead center. Only one other was close. She turned to see whose smile was the broadest, only to realize it was the lad she'd whacked in the face that morning.

He winked at her. Something she'd seen her father do with her mother, and she wasn't certain how to react. So she stuck out her tongue at him, which only made him snicker more. Was this why he'd said she could join him? Because he didn't think he would lose?

"Ye two," the warrior called. "Ready your bows."

She wasted no time in setting hers up, lining it with the target that had been moved at least fifty feet back.

"Sight your mark!"

Again, she blew out her breath and let the sounds all around her disappear.

The horn blew, and she let go, staring without blinking as her arrow and the lad's sailed side by side, fighting for air.

They landed with a *thunk*, both of them dead center, battling for space.

With breath held, the crowd leaned closer, their murmuring like bees buzzing around her head.

"Tie!" shouted the warrior in charge.

A tie. Och, but this was not going her way. She wanted to be the *champion*.

"Seems I should have let the lads have their way," he muttered beside her, nudging her arm. "Else I'd be champion."

She glowered at him. "And yet here we are, with me kicking your arse."

The target was moved another fifty feet back, and before he could comment, they were told to ready their bows once more.

This time, when the warrior called for them to shoot, she waited less than half a second behind her opponent. There was only one way to beat the arrogant lad. And that was to split him in half. Just as his arrow landed in the center of the target, hers came crushing behind it, obliterating the shaft, and sinking into the hole where his arrow had been.

"We have a winner!"

This time it was her turn to smirk at him. "Better luck in the next set."

In the next round, the warrior called for everyone to prepare for hand-to-hand combat. And she could not wait. Her mother had taught her a specific move she'd used on her father early in their marriage—a simple strike at a place on the neck that took a person's breath, and if successful, had them dropping to the ground in a dead faint. The lass smiled wide, for she'd used this move on each of her brothers with success. And she was going to take these rowdy pigs down. They grinned like fools, certain they would be able to take her out of the game now.

Silly lads.

She went through half the other competitors quickly. Many of them were too afraid to fight back, fearing her parents' wrath should they strike her. After that, she taunted the lads into at least taking a swing before she ducked and brought the side of her palm down flat on the fleshy part where their necks and shoulders met. Another one flat on the ground.

Finally, it came down to her and the lad she'd bested at archery. He had a smirk on his face that made her nervous. He'd been watching with interest every time she'd made her move, and she could see now he'd been figuring out a way to stop her, because with each arch of her hand, he blocked her.

Sweat beaded on her upper lip. If she couldn't hit him the way she needed to, there was a possibility he would win this round. And then they would be tied for first place.

She let out a frustrated growl, her arms growing tired.

The lad's smile grew, but he said nothing, just continued to let her swing. Slowly, she started to tire, muscles growing weak. Frustrated, she grew silent. She leapt forward in hopes of shocking him.

The move worked, as he'd been expecting her to keep going, but instead of taking a step back, he stumbled forward, tripping over her feet. He came down hard on his knees beside her, and she thought quickly, kicking out until he rolled onto his back. She rolled over onto him, even though she knew that doing such a thing would mortify her parents.

Too stunned to move, he watched with wide eyes as she brought the flat side of her hand down on the side of his neck. And his eyes closed.

Huzzah! She'd beaten him again.

They would not do a third round—weapons, as she was already the majority winner.

She was tugged up by the cheering warriors to be carted around in the air, and as everyone shouted her name, she saw the lad peek beneath his lashes up at her.

Her mouth fell open in shock. Her move hadn't worked on him. The little rascal had outwitted her! Tricked her. But why?

She started to sputter, but he squeezed his eyes shut. Why was he doing that? Why was he pretending she'd bested him?

They started to put the winning garland around her neck, but the lass refused. "Nay, this belongs to us both."

"Both?"

"The lad. The one over there." She pointed to where he was getting up off the ground.

"Nay, lass, ye beat him fair and square, both times."

"Nay, he—"

They cut her off, with another shout of joy.

But the lass was nothing if not stubborn. She struggled out of their grasp and ran toward him. Hands on her hips, she stared up into his clear eyes the color of grass in spring.

"Why'd ye do that?"

"Fall? Ye hit me." He shrugged. "Ye won."

"I won at archery. But ye let me win just now."

He crossed his arms over his chest. "Ye canna prove that."

She narrowed her eyes. "I wanted to win. I wanted to be knight for a day, but I canna accept if I know 'twas not me who truly won."

"I dinna know what that has to do with me."

"Everything." She stomped her foot.

He chuckled. "Did your mother never tell ye that stomping your foot will get ye nowhere?"

She rolled her eyes. "Dinna bring my mama into this."

"My lady?" The warrior in charge of the event appeared at her side with the garland.

She took the garland from him, and with both hands wrapped around the loops, she tugged until she broke it into two pieces and then handed one to the lad. "For ye, ye sorry winner."

The lad's face reddened, and he shoved it back at her. "This is not mine."

"The lass insists ye are tied."

"There canna be two knights for the day."

"Then 'haps there should be a knight and lady?" the warrior suggested.

The lass pursed her lips in a frown, uncertain if she wanted to agree with that, either.

The lad bent low and gallant. "Sir Niall Oliphant at your service, my lady."

She curtsied and tossed the garland at him. "Lady Bella Sutherland. And according to our bet this morning, ye're to be the lady."

Chapter One

Dupplin Castle
Scottish Highlands
Winter, 1318

Sir Niall Oliphant had lost something.

Not a trinket, or a boot. Not a pair of hose, or even his favorite mug. Nothing as trivial as that. In fact, he wished it *was* so minuscule that he could simply replace it. What'd he'd lost was devastating, and yet it felt entirely selfish given some of those closest to him had lost their lives.

He was still here, living and breathing. He was still walking around on his own two feet. Still handsome in the face. Still able to speak coherently, even if he didn't want to.

But he couldn't replace what he'd lost.

What he'd lost would irrevocably change his life, his entire future. It made him want to back into the darkest corner and let his life slip away, to forget about even having a future at all. To give everything he owned to his brother and say goodbye. He was useless now. Unworthy.

Niall cleared the cobwebs that had settled in his throat by slinging back another dram of whisky. The shutters in his darkened bedchamber were closed tight, the fire long ago grown cold. He didn't allow candles in the room, nor visitors. So when a knock sounded at his door, he ignored it, preferring to chug his spirits from the bottle rather than pouring it into a cup.

The knocking grew louder, more insistent.

"Go away," he bellowed, slamming the whisky down on the side table beside where he sat, and hearing the clay jug shatter. A shard slid into his finger, stinging as the liquor splashed over it. But he didn't care.

This pain, pain in his only index finger, he wanted to have. Wanted a reminder there was still some part of him left. Part of him that could still feel and bleed. He tried to ignore that part of him that wanted to be alive, however small it was.

The handle on the door rattled, but Niall had barred it the day before. Refusing anything but whisky. Maybe he could drink himself into an oblivion he'd never wake from. Then all of his worries would be gone forever.

"Niall, open the bloody door."

The sound of his brother's voice through the cracks had Niall's gaze widening slightly. Walter was a year younger than he was. And still whole. Walter had tried to understand Niall's struggle, but what man could who'd not been through it himself?

"I said go away, ye bloody whoreson." His words slurred, and he went to tipple more of the liquor only to recall he'd just shattered it everywhere.

Hell and damnation. The only way to get another bottle would be to open the door.

"I'll pretend I didna hear ye just call our dear mother a whore. Open the damned door, or I'll take an axe to it."

Like hell he would. Walter was the least aggressive one in their family. Sweet as a lad, he'd grown into a strong warrior, but he was also known as the heart of the Oliphant clan. The idea of him chopping down a door was actually funny. Outside, the corridor grew silent, and Niall leaned his head back against the chair, wondering how long he had until his brother returned, and if it was enough time to sneak down to the cellar and get another jug of whisky.

Needless to say, when a steady thwacking sounded at the door—reminding Niall quite a bit like the heavy side of an axe—he sat up straighter and watched in drunken fascination as the door started to splinter. Shards of wood came flying through the air as the hole grew larger and the sound of the axe beating against the surface intensified.

Walter had grown some bloody ballocks.

Incredible.

Didn't matter. What would Walter accomplish by breaking down the door? What could he hope would happen?

Niall wasn't going to leave the room or accept food.

Niall wasn't going to move on with his life.

So he sat back and waited, curious more than anything as to what Walter's plan would be once he'd gained entry.

Just as tall and broad of shoulder as Niall, Walter kicked through the remainder of the door and ducked through the ragged hole.

"That's enough." Walter looked down at Niall, his face fierce, reminding him very much of their father when they were lads.

"That's enough?" Niall asked, trying to keep his eyes wide but having a hard time. The light from the corridor gave his brother a darkened, shadowy look.

"Ye've sat in this bloody hell hole for the past three days." Walter gestured around the room. "Ye stink of shite. Like a bloody pig has laid waste to your chamber."

"Are ye calling me a shite pig?" Niall thought about standing up, calling his brother out, but that seemed like too much effort.

"Mayhap I am. Will it make ye stand up any faster?"

Niall pursed his lips, giving the impression of actually considering it. "Nay."

"That's what I thought. But I dinna care. Get up."

Niall shook his head slowly. "I'd rather not."

"I'm not asking."

My, my. Walter's ballocks were easily ten times than Niall had expected. The man was bloody testing him to be sure.

"Last time I checked, I was the eldest," Niall said.

"Ye might have been born first, but ye lost your mind some time ago, which makes me the better fit for making decisions."

Niall hiccupped. "And what decisions would ye be making, wee brother?"

"Getting your arse up. Getting ye cleaned up. Airing out the gongheap."

"Doesna smell so bad in here." Niall gave an exaggerated sniff, refusing to admit that Walter was indeed correct. It smelled horrendous.

"I'm gagging, brother. I might die if I have to stay much longer."

"Then by all means, pull up a chair."

"Ye're an arse."

"No more so than ye."

"Not true."

Niall sighed heavily. "What do ye want? Why would ye make me leave? I've nothing to live for anymore."

"Ye've eight-thousand reasons to live, ye blind goat."

"Eight thousand?"

"A random number." Walter waved his hand and kicked at something on the floor. "Ye've the people of your clan, the warriors ye lead, your family. The woman ye're betrothed to marry. Everyone is counting on ye, and ye must come out of here and attend to your duties. Ye've mourned long enough."

"How can ye presume to tell me that I've mourned long enough? Ye know nothing." A slow boiling rage started in Niall's chest. All these men telling him how to feel. All these men thinking they knew better. A bunch of bloody ballocks!

"Aye, I've not lost what ye have, brother. Ye're right. I dinna know what 'tis like to be ye, either. But I know what 'tis like to be the one down in the hall waiting for ye to come and take care of your business. I know what 'tis like to look upon the faces of the clan as they worry about whether they'll be raided or ravaged while their leader sulks in a vat of whisky and does nothing to care for them."

Niall gritted his teeth. No one understood. And he didn't need the reminder of his constant failings.

"Then take care of it," Niall growled, jerking forward fast enough that his vision doubled. "Ye've always wanted to be first. Ye've always wanted what was mine. Go and have it. Have it all."

Walter took a step back as though Niall had hit him. "How can ye say that?" Even in the dim light, Niall could see the pain etched on his brother's features. Aye, what he'd said was a lie, but it had made him feel better all the same.

"Ye heard me. Get the fuck out." Niall moved to push himself from the chair, remembered too late how difficult that would be, and fell back into it. Instead, he let out a string of curses that had Walter shaking his head.

"Ye need to get yourself together, decide whether or not ye are going to turn your back on this clan. Do it for yourself. Dinna go down like this. Ye are still Sir Niall fucking Oliphant. Warrior. Heir to the chiefdom of Oliphant. Hero. Leader. Brother. Soon to be husband and father."

Walter held his gaze unwaveringly. A torrent of emotion jabbed from that dark look into Niall's chest, crushing his heart.

"Get out," he said again through gritted teeth, feeling the pain of rejecting his brother acutely.

They'd always been so close. And even though he was pushing him away, he also desperately wanted to pull him closer.

He wanted to hug him tightly, to tell him not to worry, that soon enough he'd come out of the dark and be the man Walter once knew. But those were all lies, for he would never be the same again, and he couldn't see how he would ever be able to exit this room and attempt a normal life.

"Ye're not the only one who's lost a part of himself," Walter muttered as he ducked beneath the door. "I want my brother back."

"Your brother is dead."

At that, Walter paused. He turned back around, a snarl poised on his lips, and Niall waited longingly for whatever insult would come out. Any chance to engage in a fight, but then Walter's face softened. "Maybe he is."

With those soft words uttered, he disappeared, leaving behind the gaping hole and the shattered wood on the floor, a haunting mirror image to the wide-open wound Niall felt in his soul.

Niall glanced down to his left, at the sleeve that hung empty at his side, a taunting reminder of his failure in battle. Warrior. Ballocks! Not even close.

When he considered lying down on the ground and licking the whisky from the floor, he knew it was probably time to leave his chamber. But he was no good to anyone outside of his room. Perhaps he could prove that fact once and for all, then Walter would leave him be. And he knew his brother spoke the truth about smelling like a pig. He'd not bathed in days. If he was going to prove he was worthless as a leader now, he would do so smelling decent, so people took him seriously rather than believing him to be mad.

Slipping through the hole in the door, he walked noiselessly down the corridor to the stairs at the rear used by the servants, tripping only once along the way. He attempted to steal down the winding steps, a feat that nearly had him breaking his neck. In fact, he took the last dozen steps on his arse. Once he reached the entrance to the side of the bailey, he lifted the bar and shoved the door open, the cool wind a welcome blast against his heated skin. With the sun set, no one saw him creep outside and slink along the stone as he made his way to the stables and the massive water trough kept for the horses. He might as well bathe there, like the animal he was.

Trough in sight, he staggered forward and tumbled headfirst into the icy water.

Niall woke sometime later, still in the water, but turned over at least. He didn't know whether to be grateful he'd not drowned. His clothes were soaked, and his legs hung out on either side of the wooden trough. It was still dark, so at least he'd not slept through the night in the chilled water.

He leaned his head back, body covered in wrinkled gooseflesh and teeth chattering, and stared up at the sky. Stars dotted the inky-black landscape and swaths of clouds streaked across the moon, as if one of the gods had swiped his hand through it, trying to wipe it away. But the moon was steadfast. Silver and bright and ever present. Returning as it should each night, though hiding its beauty day after day until it was just a sliver that made one wonder if it would return.

What was he doing out here? Not just in the tub freezing his idiot arse off, but here in this world? Why hadn't he been taken? Why had only part of him been stolen? Cut away...

Niall shuddered, more from the memory of that moment when his enemy's sword had cut through his armor, skin, muscle and bone. The crunching sound. The incredible pain.

He squeezed his eyes shut, forcing the memories away.

This is how he'd been for the better part of four months. Stumbling drunk and angry about the castle when he wasn't holed up in his chamber. Yelling at his brother, glowering at his father and mother, snapping at anyone who happened to cross his path. He'd become everything he hated.

There had been times he'd thought about ending it all. He always came back to the simple question that was with him now as he stared up at the large face of the moon.

"Why am I still here?" he murmured.

"Likely because ye havena pulled your arse out of the bloody trough."

Walter.

Niall's gaze slid to the side to see his brother standing there, arms crossed over his chest. "Are ye my bloody shadow? Come to tell me all my sins?"

"When will ye see I'm not the enemy? I want to help."

Niall stared back up at the moon, silently asking what he should do, begging for a sign.

Walter tugged at his arm. "Come on. Get out of the trough. Ye're not a pig as much as ye've been acting the part. Let us get ye some food."

Niall looked over at his little brother, perhaps seeing him for the first time. His throat felt tight, closing in on itself as a well of emotion overflowed from somewhere deep in his gut.

"Why do ye keep trying to help me? All I've done is berate ye for it."

"Aye. That's true, but I know ye speak from pain. Not from your heart."

"I dinna think I have a heart left."

Walter rolled his eyes and gave a swift tug, pulling him halfway from the trough. Though Niall was weak from lack of food and too much whisky, he managed to get himself the rest of the way out. He stood in the moonlight, dripping water around the near frozen ground.

"Ye have a heart. Ye have a soul. One arm. That is all ye've lost. Ye still have your manhood, aye?"

Niall shrugged. Aye, he still had his bloody cock, but what woman wanted a decrepit man heaving overtop of her with his mangled body in full view.

"I know what ye're thinking," Walter said. "And the answer is, every eligible maiden and all her friends. Not to mention the kitchen wenches, the widows in the glen, and their sisters."

"Ballocks," Niall muttered.

"Ye're still handsome. Ye're still heir to a powerful clan. Wake up, man. This is not ye. Ye canna let the loss of your arm be the destruction of your whole life. Ye're not the first man to ever be maimed in battle. Dinna be a martyr."

"Says the man with two arms."

"Ye want me to cut it off? I'll bloody do it." Walter turned in a frantic circle as if looking for the closest thing with a sharp edge.

Niall narrowed his eyes, silent, watching, waiting. When had his wee brother become such an intense force? Walter marched toward the barn, hand on the door, yanked it wide as if to continue the blockhead search. Niall couldn't help following after his brother who marched forward with purpose, disappearing inside the barn.

A flutter of worry dinged in Niall's stomach. Walter wouldn't truly go through with something so stupid, would he?

When he didn't immediately reappear, Niall's pang of worry heightened into dread. Dammit, he just might. With all the changes Walter had made recently, there was every possibility that he'd gone mad. Well, Niall might wish to disappear, but not before he made certain his brother was all right.

With a groan, Niall lurched forward, grabbed the door and yanked it open. The stables were dark and smelled of horses, leather and hay. He could hear a few horses nickering, and the soft snores of the stable hands up on the loft fast asleep.

"Walter," he hissed. "Enough. No more games."

Still, there was silence.

He stepped farther into the barn, and the door closed behind him, blocking out all the light save for a few strips that sank between cracks in the roof.

His feet shuffled silently on the dirt floor. Where the bloody hell had his brother gone?

And why was his heart pounding so fiercely? He trudged toward the first set of stables, touching the wood of the gates. A horse nudged his hand with its soft muzzle, blowing out a soft breath that tickled his palm, and Niall's heart squeezed.

"Prince," he whispered, leaning his forehead down until he felt it connect with the warm, solidness of his warhorse. Prince nickered and blew out another breath.

Niall had not ridden in months. If not for his horse, he might be dead. But rather than be irritated Prince had done his job, he felt nothing but pride that the horse he'd trained from a colt into a mammoth had done his duty.

After Niall's arm had been severed and he was left for dead, Prince had nudged him awake, bent low and nipped at Niall's legs until he'd managed to crawl and heave himself belly first over the saddle. Prince had taken him home like that, a bleeding sack of grain.

Having thought him dead, the clan had been shocked and surprised to see him return, and that's when the true battle for his life had begun. He'd lost so much blood, succumbed to fever, and stopped breathing more than once. Hell, it was a miracle he was still alive.

Which begged the question—*why, why, why*...

"He's missed ye." Walter was beside him, and Niall jerked toward his brother, seeing his outline in the dark.

"Is that why ye brought me in here?"

"Did ye really think I'd cut off my arm?" Walter chuckled. "Ye know I like to fondle a wench and drink at the same time."

Niall snickered. "Ye're an arse."

"Aye, 'haps I am."

They were silent for a few minutes, Niall deep in thought as he stroked Prince's soft muzzle. His mind was a torment of unanswered questions. "Walter, I...I dinna know what to do."

"Take it one day at a time, brother. But do take it. No more being locked in your chamber."

Niall nodded even though his brother couldn't see him. A phantom twinge of pain rippled through the arm that was no longer there, and he stopped himself from moving to rub the spot, not wanting to humiliate himself in front of his brother. When would those pains go away? When would his body realize his arm had long since become bone in the earth?

One day at a time. That was something he might be able to do. "I'll have bad days."

"Aye. And good ones, too."

Niall nodded. He longed to saddle Prince and go for a ride but realized he wasn't even certain how to mount with only one arm to grab hold of the saddle. "I have so much to learn."

"Aye. But as I recall, ye're a fast learner."

"I'll start training again tomorrow."

"Good."

"But I willna be laird. Walter, the right to rule is yours now."

"Ye've time before ye need to make that choice. Da is yet breathing and making a ruckus."

"Aye. But I want ye to know what's coming. No matter what, I canna do that. I have to learn to pull on my bloody shirt first."

Walter slapped him on the back and squeezed his shoulder. "The lairdship is yours, with or without a shirt. Only thing I want is my brother back."

Niall drew in a long, mournful breath. "I'm not sure he's coming back. Ye'll have to learn to deal with me, the new me."

"New ye, old ye, still *ye*."

Chapter Two

Dunrobin Castle
Spring, 1319

If there was one thing Lady Bella Sutherland loved, it was a good challenge, which was why she snuck from the castle at dawn to go down to the beach, set up a target and blindfold herself with a strip of plaid.

She was already a master archer. Had been practically all of her life. Her mother and father had both seen to her training, believing that a woman should never be left defenseless. In fact, every woman in her family had some sort of special skill. While Bella seemed to have soaked up each of those skills, her absolute favorite was archery. This was a skill she knew, well...blindfolded.

Some might say she led a charmed life, being the daughter of the Earl of Sutherland and Chieftain of the Sutherland Clan. Aye, her father was a powerful man. A legend, in fact. But she tried not to let that overshadow her own talent.

Bella felt over her shoulder for the feather fletching of her arrow and tugged it out. She nocked her arrow and tilted her head toward the sky, breathing in deeply and feeling the sun as it rose. It gave off an odd feeling of warmth in the brisk winter chill.

With every shot she took, she remembered how she'd proven her skill to everyone as a lass with that simple decision to wait a half second after her opponent, Sir Niall Oliphant. She'd not seen him since that day. Not heard much news of him, either, but she thought of him often.

He was a few years older than her. Had he grown into a handsome man? Had he retained his skill at archery? Undoubtedly. There had not been anyone that rivaled her since him. After they'd tied in the competition, everyone had asked for them to put on another archery show with challenging targets. Bella had wanted him to do so in her gown and she in his plaid, but he'd refused, and she'd not argued the point. They'd gone head-to-head for an hour or so until their arms gave out and fingers were covered in new blisters. She'd not found a suitable partner since.

She focused her energy on pulling the bowstring taut and then let go, leaving herself blindfolded and listening to the whistle of her arrow cutting through the air toward its mark.

Thunk.

She grinned and pulled another arrow from her quiver, nocked it and set her blinded sense of sight toward the target. She let go again, waited for the *thunk,* and repeated the move until her quiver was empty.

Only then did she tug the blindfold from her eyes and settle it at her neck to see her arrows were almost in the center of the target.

"Dretch," she murmured.

Bella sauntered toward the target, her eyes drawn to the lapping water that flowed over the pebbles, shells and sand, creating foamy patterns at the water's edge, only to wash them away. She paused a moment to enjoy the fresh sea-salt air, the gentle spray of water. There was something so mesmerizing about the sea. Something that drew her there again and again. In fact, when she wasn't dragging her target down here to practice, she was sitting on the beach contemplating things like the phases of the moon and why ants worked in groups.

Perhaps after she was done with practice, she'd sneak away to the part of the beach obscured from the castle and go for a swim.

After tugging her arrows from the target and refilling her quiver, Bella marched back fifty feet down the beach and then backed up another twenty-five. What was the point in challenging one's self if it wasn't truly a challenge? She was about to lift the blindfold back into place when she heard her name carried on the wind.

"Lady Bella!"

Tugging the cloth away from her eyes, she scanned the land behind her. One of her father's men stood some two hundred feet away, waving his arms. Grinning mischievously, she lifted the bow *without* an arrow notched and pretended to shoot. He dropped to the ground, pretending to be frightened for his life, but she knew her father's men could block anything hurtled at them. She laughed and put the blindfold back on. The game they all played with her never seemed to get old.

Ordinarily, she would not have been so disrespectful as to ignore a summons, but she had an idea of what that summons was regarding. And she didn't want to be any part of it, so she turned back around to face her target.

Just before retiring to her chamber the night before, she'd walked past her father's study and heard her parents discussing a suitor coming this morning. Even the word suitor left a sour boulder in her belly. She'd barely been able to sleep at the thought of what would happen. Potential grooms coming to see her was embarrassing and awkward. To have a man stand there and tell her all the reasons why he would be good for her and why she should choose him. To have him even go so far as to say why he'd chosen her. For all of them, she gave the same practiced negative response she'd been giving for years, and it was...humiliating. There had been plenty of good ones that had asked, and several she might even have said aye to if not for the one she'd been holding out for.

This was the reason she'd woken before dawn to come down to the beach to practice. She'd wanted to work off some of her angst before the inevitable, while secretly hoping no one would realize where she was and send the man away.

The sea air, the sound of the waves and the exercise often set her mind to rights, but this time it hadn't. And until she'd seen the guard waving his arms around like a windmill, she'd almost forgotten about what was most likely going to happen today when she disappointed her mother and father once more.

Blowing out a breath, she let her arrow fly, imagining the sharpened point sinking into the very desire her suitor had to marry her. Crushing it. Obliterating it. Perhaps if she thought hard enough, if she wished most fervently, whoever he was would turn around on his noble horse and ride away.

"Lady Bella!" The guard was not going to give up.

With a sigh of frustration, Bella tugged the blindfold off and glanced his way.

"Ye're needed at the castle."

She waved one hand and looked away, gazing longingly down the beach. She could run. She could hide in the woods that lined the edge of the beach away from the castle walls. Or she could steal a *birlinn* and row herself out to sea, find some remote isle and live the rest of her days off the land. She knew how to hunt, how to fish. When she was younger, she and her brothers had even built their own shelters out of debris in the woods for fun. She could make it. Though she'd be lonely.

The sound of the guard's heavy footfalls as he jogged toward her sounded from behind while she collected her arrows.

"I'll get the target for ye, my lady."

"Thank ye," she murmured.

They walked silently back to the castle, her steps lagging just a little behind his. Why did it feel like she was marching to her death?

"In his lairdship's study, my lady."

Bella hesitated. "I'll be down shortly. I just want to put these away." She held up her bow and quiver full of arrows with a sheepish smile.

The guard kept his gaze steady, but she could practically read from his body language that he didn't believe her. "I was told to escort ye directly, my lady."

Bella frowned, gave a little huff and a stomp of her foot. "I am not presentable. If ye must escort me, than ye can wait." She didn't normally snap at the servants or her father's men. In fact, it was so out of character for her that her father's man stepped back. "Apologies, Sir Finley," she said. "I but want to put this in my room and...well, I need to...um..."

His face reddened, seeming to take in her drawn-out silence for something more private. "Ye need not explain. I will put the target away and meet ye at the stairs outside your chamber."

"Thank ye." She had the forthrightness to look down with humble gratitude.

"No thanks required."

Without dragging it out further, she nodded and hurried back into the castle. She rushed up the stairs to her chamber with her skirts lifted past her ankles and promptly slammed the door closed and barred it behind her. She was not going to go to her father's study. Feigning a headache or vomiting ought to do the trick. Or maybe she should pretend to have spots. A rare fever.

"I thought you might do that."

Bella whirled around to see her mother sitting on the cushioned bench by the window. "Mama."

"I trust you had a good morning on the beach?" Voice soft and distinctly English, Lady Arbella, Countess of Sutherland, nodded toward the bow and quiver full of arrows. Her golden hair, streaked with white strands that only made her hair shine, was braided into a crown around her head. Laugh lines framed her eyes and mouth. She was without a doubt the most beautiful woman Bella had ever seen, not that she was biased by any means.

"Aye." Bella opened her wardrobe and placed her weaponry on the special hooks that had been designed for them.

Her mother's smile was soft, sympathetic and full of love. She'd never been anything but warm, gentle and supportive of Bella.

"Am I to understand you are hiding from your father?"

Bella pursed her lips and marched toward her window to stare outside over the moors.

"Ah, I take by your silence you also hoped to avoid me."

Bella whirled around. "I know what this is about."

"Do you?"

"Aye. Another suitor."

Arbella nodded, her eyes crinkling at the sides.

"Mama, I dinna want to see another suitor. I want to stay here with ye. The entire process is humiliating and ye know I will only deny the man."

"I used to feel the same way." She smiled nostalgically. "But you're one and twenty, long past the time we should have seen to your future. Meet him first before you decide his fate."

"Please, Mama. Give me more time before ye make me marry." *A lifetime* in order to avoid the inevitable tying down, the taming, and the disappointment when her future husband realized she would not birth him children.

Her mother gazed into her eyes, studying her. Softly, she touched Bella's cheek. "You're so beautiful, clever, so kind and gentle, and yet you have a warrior's heart."

Bella smiled. "Da says I am the perfect combination of ye both."

The countess's smile broadened. "I believe he is right."

"Please, Mama," she whispered. "Send the suitor away."

"I want you to meet him first. If you are not satisfied, we will send him away."

"Promise?" No matter how appealing the man was, even if he gifted her with a golden bow, she would turn him away. Bella could never marry, else her entire family would face the inevitable humiliation when her groom sent her back home.

"Aye, my sweet darling girl."

Bella embraced her mother and breathed in the subtle floral scent of her hair, felt the warmth of her body. Her mother never changed.

"I love ye, Mama."

The countess tugged gently on Bella's long braid. "I love you, too, dear one."

Her mother waited as Bella freshened up, and then they ascended the stairs together with Sir Finley behind them.

In her father's study was a large golden-haired warrior with brown eyes that held a spark of mischief.

"My lady." He bowed low, then stood and flashed her a friendly smile.

Bella nodded but did not curtsy. She never curtsied to the men her da introduced her to. It was her subtle attempt at keeping control and letting whoever sought her hand know she was not a simpering lass willing to drop to her knees and declare her willingness to obey for the rest of her days.

The warrior's smile did not dim. In fact, he seemed to hold back a bit of a laugh and continued to look at her with appreciation. That was different. She wanted to like him, but that didn't matter. In the end, she would always say nay.

"I am Sir Walter Oliphant."

Unbidden, her eyes widened. Oliphant? As in *Niall* Oliphant? She searched his face for any traces of the lad she'd once known, and while there was a likeness, she recalled vividly the green of Niall's eyes. Walter's were distinctly brown. He wasn't Niall, but he could be his brother.

"I am glad to make your acquaintance, Sir Walter." Bella smiled, though she was certain the gesture did not equate to happiness. How many times had she wished to walk through this door and see Sir Niall there?

From behind his desk, her father came to stand beside his wife. The Earl of Sutherland was still handsome, though he was nearing fifty summers. His black hair was still full of luster, though shot with silver now. Because he continued to actively train with his men, he was thick as a tree and as strong as a boulder.

"We shall leave the two of ye for a moment."

Bella started to interrupt, to say it would not be necessary, but her father cleared his throat and gave her a look that said she'd best at least listen before she said nay. She shot her mother a worried plea-filled gaze. Lady Arbella nodded encouragingly, then they were both gone. All Bella could do was pray her mother was speaking to her father about the promise she'd made.

As soon as the door closed, Bella folded her hands in front of her, met Sir Walter's gaze head on and said, "Sir Walter, while I appreciate—"

"My lady, before ye reject me outright, allow me to plead my case."

She winged a brow, speechless. No one had ever interrupted her before.

"Perhaps I am a fool for having come, as I know there have been many men before me that have asked for your hand, but if I didna, then I'd always wonder at what ye might have said."

Bella searched for a more sincere way to turn him down than by simply saying, *Nay, and thank ye for trying.*

"Perhaps ye fear that a husband will not let ye continue your pursuits, but I assure ye, I would be amenable to such things. In all the Highlands, ye and your sisters are the most eligible maidens. The most beautiful. The most clever. I would be a fool not to ask."

Bella drew in a deep breath. "Ye flatter me unnecessarily, sir."

"I have admired ye since the very first day I met ye."

"And when was that?"

Was it the day she'd met his brother?

"At Stirling, 'haps two years back when your father met with King Robert and the other lairds of the north."

Bella nodded. She didn't recall meeting him at all. However, she did remember searching for Niall and feeling foolish because she'd not seen him since he was a wee lad, and lads changed so much when they became men. Alas, she hadn't found him.

Was Walter one of the lads who'd taunted her at that tournament all those years ago?

"As I said, ye flatter me unnecessarily, sir. While I find your proposal to be better than most, I must humbly refuse."

Walter's face grew red. "Refuse?"

"Aye."

"Why?"

Och, why could they never be gentlemanly about it? It wasn't like she set out to bruise their egos, but bruised they'd be all the same with her rejecting them.

"I am...in love with another," she said, squaring her shoulders.

At that, Walter's face grew all the redder, and he sputtered with embarrassment. "I see."

How would he feel if she told him it was his brother she'd loved since she was nine years old?

"May I ask ye a question?" Bella cocked her head in curiosity.

Sir Walter looked ready to refuse her request, but after a moment's pause he nodded.

"Do ye recall a children's tournament here at our castle?"

He looked at her thoughtfully.

"I think it was perhaps a dozen years ago." Och, but she knew exactly how long ago. Had etched the memory on her heart, but she wasn't about to confess that much.

"Aye, there was a lass. A right arrogant one, too..." He trailed off, eyes widening. So, he had been one of the lads to taunt her.

"That was...ye?"

"Aye."

Walter's eyes widened even more, some hint of knowledge sparking in them. "And the man ye're in love with?"

Bella folded her arms over her chest, safeguarding the truth of that statement in her heart. "None of your concern."

He nodded knowingly. "I understand now, and I am not offended at your refusal. But I should let ye know, he is betrothed to another."

How could he have seen so easily through her? And why did she feel as though that truth crushed her painfully, like she'd taken one of her own arrows and pierced her heart with it.

"If ye should change your mind," he mused. "I will not be seeking another bride for some months, in order to heal from this setback." He winked to let her know it did not truly bother him, but that he was merely giving her a chance to change her mind.

Bella tried to smile at him, letting her arms fall away from their crossed position, but there was only sadness inside her. "Dinna wait too long, sir, for I willna change my mind."

She would have never been able to accept Niall if he'd been the one to come asking for her hand, and yet, the disappointment of knowing he never would caused her pain all over again. Since she was a lass, she'd dreamed of him riding into the bailey at Dunrobin, leaping from his horse and demanding the hand of his *knight*.

Whatever fantasy she'd created and built up, worshiped, for all these years had been just that. Pretend. Unrealistic.

"I thank ye for the pleasure of your acquaintance," she murmured.

"And I ye, my lady. Whoever ye do decide to accept will be a lucky man."

Bella nodded once more, unwilling to contradict him, eyes burning with the need to shed tears of mourning for a treasure lost.

In the corridor, she could hear Sir Walter saying his goodbyes to her parents and the regretful tone in her father's voice. Before they could come in and question her reasoning for this refusal, she hurried toward the secret door and clicked the latch that would help her disappear into the castle walls.

She just wanted to be left alone.

Chapter Three

Sweat dripped from Niall's bare back and chest. Muscles burned from the exertion of training, and yet he still didn't stop. He had to fight twice as hard as any other man, and in the months since his brother convinced him to get off his arse and do something with himself, he'd come back nearly to his full strength—though he'd had to learn some new techniques.

Inside his own mind, things were definitely not the same.

Not that he was willing to reveal that to anyone else.

He still planned to resign his position as heir in favor of his brother whenever the time came, and he wasn't willing to listen to anyone tell him otherwise.

Though he could knock every one of the warriors on their arses, that didn't mean he was capable of leading them any longer. Besides that, there was a part of him, a niggling in the back of his brain, that said the men that once followed him into battle weren't fighting as hard as they should when put up against him. That they were giving him favor. Backing down at the last minute, missing a block when they were perfectly capable of avoiding it, and not using their full strength when it came to attacking him. How else could he explain why they were losing to him—a one-armed cripple. The muscles in his shoulder and arm grew exponentially as he trained himself to be able to wield a massive two-handed claymore with only one hand.

With his arm having been removed just below the shoulder socket, Niall wasn't able to hold a targe to protect himself. In battle, this would mean he'd have to be even more aware of oncoming attacks in order to block with his weapon, to dodge any blows, or use his feet and legs in ways he'd not done so before.

As the months went on, he'd gotten quite good at using any means necessary. But he still didn't think his men were bringing the full force of their power down on him.

And he was about to prove it now. Niall let out a snarl. "The three of ye. Stand and fight."

The three warriors he pointed his sword at glanced at each other where they sat on the practice field resting after a hectic morning of training. "Sir..."

"I said stand and fight," Niall burst out in a fit of rage that they would even attempt to argue against his command. "A warrior does not counter a direct order."

The three men nodded wearily. But then Walter appeared as if he'd felt the tension brewing from across the field. His brother had barely been home a day from wherever it was he'd gone before he was breathing down Niall's neck again, constantly worried he might escape into the darkness again.

"What's this? Only three?" Walter teased, rolling his eyes. "Allow me to join in, make it an even four against one."

What was he playing at? Niall shrugged as though he didn't care, hiding his surprise. He'd thought his brother would argue against him, tell him to calm down, placate him as he had been doing these last few months. Well, if this was another bluff, Niall wasn't going to let him get off easily this time. Niall lifted his sword. "Let's do this."

Walter eagerly jumped into the fray. The four of them circled Niall, jabbing forward with their swords and kicking out with their feet, thrusting their targes into his back to shove him toward one another. This was exactly what he'd wanted. It reminded him of many a bailey fight he'd witnessed among the lads, picking on one not as tough as they. Well, to him, this was finally a fair fight.

Niall could no longer block the blows. He had to duck and dodge, to roll out of the way, only to leap up and kick his opponent in the arse from behind.

"Sir Niall wants to be knight for a day," Walter taunted.

Niall was immediately alert to the words. His mind anchored back to the day he'd heard an obstinate mini-wench shout the very same thing. He grinned, always having fond memories of her. In fact, before his father had settled on his betrothal to Princess Elizabeth, Niall had fancied he'd one day come across Lady Bella Sutherland all grown, still just as full of fire, and that he'd beat her at archery.

All the air left his lungs when he realized even if he ever did meet her now, he'd never be able to do that.

That made him falter in his steps, earning him a hard punch from his brother on the jaw. Niall stumbled backward. Strong hands shoved him forward, and he stabbed his sword into the earth, letting go in favor of taking a swing at his brother—who allowed him to connect.

They tumbled to the ground, fists flailing.

"Hit me harder," Walter demanded. "As hard as ye can."

Niall shoved his knee into Walter's chest and wrenched his arm back, prepared to do as his brother requested.

He suddenly paused. "Why did ye say that?"

"Say what?" Walter raised a brow and gave Niall a look as though he'd gone mad.

"About wanting to be knight for a day."

Walter smirked. "No reason."

Niall narrowed his eyes. "Ye're lying."

Walter shrugged. "If ye're not going to hit me, then get off. I'm not used to being ridden by a man."

Niall snorted, smacked his brother on the cheek and leapt back to his feet. The men had pressed the tips of their swords into the ground, seeming to have decided that the fight had ended, and Niall didn't press them to continue.

"Where were ye?" Niall asked suspiciously.

"I had business up north."

"Where up north?"

"Sutherland." Walter picked up Niall's sword and tossed it to him.

"Want to go another round, or are ye ready to wash the stench off in the trough?"

Niall wanted to laugh at his brother's jibe, but he was too busy losing his mind over the fact that Walter had just said. "Ye were in Sutherland?"

"Aye. Have ye lost your hearing as well as your arm?"

"What were ye doing up there?"

"I had some business at Dunrobin."

Dunrobin. Lady Bella's home. Niall's mouth went dry. He licked his lips, his tongue getting stuck for half a second, before he drew in a long breath. "Ye're skirting round my questions like a lad at his mother's gown."

Walter grinned. "What difference does it make to ye?"

Why was his brother toying with him? "I dinna know, ye havena told me a damn thing." Niall waved the men away and picked up his shirt, wiped his sweaty face on it and tugged it over his head. "What's the big secret?"

Walter wiped his brow on his sleeve, eyeing his brother in a way that gave Niall the impression he was trying to decide how much to tell him, if anything at all. "Well, if ye must know, I was there attempting to fetch a bride."

Niall's blood chilled. "A bride? How come I didna know about this?"

Walter shrugged. "I guess father didna tell ye."

"Why did *ye* not tell me?"

"I..." Walter ran a hand through his hair, giving a great sigh. "Father asked me not to."

Niall frowned again. "I dinna understand. Why would he ask that of ye?"

Walter shook his head and picked up a discarded waterskin, draining the contents. "Ye'll have to take that up with him. I merely did as he asked."

"And are ye now a betrothed man?"

"Nay. She rejected me."

"She?" Ballocks, why was his brother being so close-lipped? Couldn't he see the torment in Niall's face?

"Lady Bella Sutherland, the earl's daughter."

The words hit Niall like an arrow through the heart. *His* Bella. The urge to punch his brother was strong.

"She said nay? To ye?"

"Aye. Odd, isna it? I am one of the most eligible bachelors, am I not? I've a powerful father. A brother about to wed a princess." At this, Walter gave Niall a questioning look, as though he knew exactly why Niall was so concerned. "A string of satisfied women behind me. Why should she not want me?"

Niall cleared his throat, forcing his fisted hand at his side to relax. "I'm not certain the latter actually stands in your favor brother. Most women dinna prefer a man with a sordid past, especially if that past can return to haunt them and bring with it their bastards."

Walter shrugged. "Nay matter. She said nay."

"Did she say why?"

Walter looked away. "She said she was in love with another."

"I see." Niall ground his teeth, feeling foolish for even asking. Of course she loved another. They'd not interacted with each other since they were children. Why, she probably barely remembered him.

"Speaking of betrothed, where is your lucky princess and her lovely entourage?" Walter's voice was cheerful, but he stepped away, perhaps expecting Niall to lash out at him. His brother had developed a lust for at least three of Princess Elizabeth's ladies in waiting, and Niall had caught him on more than one occasion in a less-than-prudent position with those same three women. Not all at the same time, though he wouldn't put it past him.

"Dinna be afeared brother, I willna beat ye to a bloody pulp for asking, even if ye could use it." Niall nodded toward the gate. "They went out riding."

"And ye didna accompany them?"

Niall ignored the accusation in his brother's tone. The last thing he wanted to do was accompany the ladies. For one thing, his betrothed, a spoiled princess with a head the size of a hay bale and an ego that could have filled all of Scotland, was not someone he particularly wanted to spend time with.

Though she was pretty enough, she'd never measure up to the

image of Bella Sutherland. He'd seen her a few years ago at a court gathering, but the moment he'd gone to speak with her and ask for a dance, she'd excused herself and not shown herself again.

But what were a woman's looks to him, a one-armed man? Aye, he would be lucky if the hag at the market would have him. Nay, his dislike of the princess was not because of her looks. But rather the attitude she had. The better-than-thou smirk she had permanently plastered on her face. The snide comments she made whenever she got the chance about tasks she thought he might not be able to accomplish.

If there was one thing that was certain—his betrothed did not like him any more than he liked her. Their feelings were a mutual combination of distrust and dislike. Add to that her obvious disgust and his disdain, and it was an all around disappointment.

Unfortunately, neither of them had any choice in who they could wed. Her father was king, and as such, had decreed she should marry Niall.

"I was not needed," Niall said. "She had all of her ladies and a full contingent of men."

"What is going on between the two of ye?" Walter asked.

"I went away to war one way and returned quite another. I suppose I offend her tender sensibilities."

Walter frowned. "She'd best learn to push it aside."

Niall shrugged. "I'll do my duty by her, by the king." Not wanting to discuss it anymore, Niall left his brother to go in search of a cold bucket to wash the sweat from his skin—and hoped it would also cool the frenzied path his mind was taking in regards to a certain lady.

Just who the hell was Bella Sutherland in love with?

LATER THAT EVENING, when Niall entered the great hall, his heart dropped to his toes. Across the hall, Walter was standing with a golden-haired lady. She was tall and curvy in all the right places. Her back was to him, but the tinkle of her laughter sounded across the distance between them as she lifted a bow and pretended to aim her arrow at the boar's head on the wall.

Walter moved to stand behind her, shifted her position and whispered in her ear. And all Niall could think was how dare his brother taunt him. How dare his brother bring Bella Sutherland to Dupplin? She'd denied him. She loved another, so why was she here?

This was an outrage. Niall whirled on his heel, prepared to find the nearest jug of whisky and take it to his room for the night. It had been months since the darkness beckoned, but perhaps it would be best for everyone if just this once he agreed to it. Else he'd march across the great hall and beat Walter to a bloody pulp. Which he couldn't do. How could he begrudge his brother's appeal to women?

No one would stop him if he tried to leave. They were used to him leaving the great hall unexpectedly, as he was often disturbed by something, anything, everything. Though he'd worked hard to recover over the past several months, there was never any clue as to when he might have a sudden attack of rage, of sorrow, or even a phantom pain that drove him to madness.

"Niall." Their father's voice cut into his retreating figure. If he was feeling well enough to get out of bed and go to the great hall, Niall could not abandon him. Laird Oliphant had been ill for the better part of a year. An affliction of the lungs that often gave him pains in his heart.

Swallowing down his anger and frustration, Niall turned to face his father, who managed to hobble forward and press a mug of ale into his hand.

"I'm glad ye could join us."

Niall nodded, believing if he attempted to speak, it would only come out an inaudible snarl.

"Princess Elizabeth's cousin has arrived just this afternoon." His father nodded toward the woman Walter was flirting outrageously with. "Walter, of course, has taken a liking to her. Too bad for him she's already wed to another. One of the king's generals, I think."

More like Walter's lucky day. He loved when a lass was wed. They were the most experienced, he said. And if any bastards were born of their union, he didn't have to worry over it. Niall shook his head.

Just then, the woman turned and laughed at something one of the other ladies said, allowing Niall to see her face. She looked nothing like the Bella he remembered. Her nose was a little too long. Eyes brown rather than blue. Lips thinner, and neck longer. Now that he could see her, he was surprised he'd even thought she could be his Bella at all.

Och, not my *Bella.*

His father murmured something about needing to sit and lumbered off toward a chair by the hearth where Niall's mother sat chatting with a few of the princess's ladies.

"Sir Niall." Princess Elizabeth approached, the impatience in her eyes brilliant. She reached forward and offered her hand for him to kiss, knowing that with him holding his ale, he'd not be able to do so without either setting it down, or bending over to kiss her hand without taking hold of it.

Well, he wasn't going to give her the satisfaction. "Princess," he murmured and ignored her outstretched hand. He took a long swallow of his ale, watching her over the rim of his mug as her face grew red with rage.

The rage subtly changed, transforming into something mean and ugly. "The men have been proposing a tournament. Archery and hand-to-hand combat. But I supposed ye willna be able to join in, given your...unfortunate condition." Her hateful gaze roved over the empty sleeve at his side. "I'll have to choose another champion."

Niall's lips peeled back from his teeth in a menacing smile. "By all means, princess, dinna let me stand in the way of your wanton desires."

Her mouth fell open in shock. Though Niall couldn't be certain if she was more shocked she'd not managed to stir him into a painful rage at her hurtful words, or that he'd dare hint at her being a whore.

Lips drawn and thin, menace in her eyes, Elizabeth looked ready to have an apoplectic fit. "I will speak to my father about this," she hissed. "I refuse to be connected to a man like ye."

Niall could care less. If the good king decided to marry his daughter to another, Niall would drop to his knees and praise the Lord above for answering his prayers. "I hope your conversation goes better than mine did."

Her eyes widened, again seeming shocked at his output. Niall sighed, hating the way he was treating her. Even if she was being a total bitch. Women needed to be coddled. Tended to. Well, most women. This one made it particularly hard. She'd been dragging him down with her insults for days. How much more could a man take?

Again, his mind went to Bella. He couldn't imagine her putting down a wounded man. Was she the type of woman that needed to be coddled?

From the way she'd wailed on him with her fists all those years ago, he was certain the only coddling she'd need was to clean up her bloodied knuckles. But what fun it would be…

The princess, seeing she was getting nowhere with him, stomped off.

Niall found his father by the hearth and begged to be excused. When his father refused, Niall managed to get through the rest of the evening without killing anyone. He sat silently on the dais, managing to swallow a few bites of meat while his betrothed giggled beside him with her ladies, making side-long glances at him. He didn't care what they were saying. In fact, he leaned back to catch his brother's eye around their father's back.

Walter stood and came toward him. "Is everything all right?"

"Ye need a wife. And I need to get rid of one," Niall muttered.

"What?" Walter narrowed his eyes.

"Ye take the princess."

His brother squeezed his shoulder. "I'd never do that to ye."

"Bloody hell, Walter, ye'd be saving me. Ye need a wife, and ye'd be son-in-law to the king."

"I dinna think so." Walter escaped back to his chair and made a point of calling for music and announcing that Niall and Princess Elizabeth would dance.

The clansmen and women leapt from their tables and pushed them to the side, the benches too, making room in the center of the great hall for a rousing night of dancing.

With an irritated huff, Niall pushed back his chair, stood and offered his arm to the princess.

Thrusting her nose in the air, she delicately stood and brushed past him, down the stairs of the dais and to the center of the floor with her ladies. Taking note of the cut she'd just given Niall, Walter somehow convinced her ladies to usher the princess toward Niall, where she stood rigid, lips pursed in distaste.

"One dance," he muttered from the side of his mouth to her. "Then ye can be done with me for the night."

"I wish it were for a lifetime."

"Perhaps both of our wishes will come true."

When the music started, the ladies formed a circle taking Walter's hands, and it was then his brother looked at him with a mix of horror and anguish. The ring dance was done in a circle, all the participants holding hands. Niall would break the circle by only being able to hold on to one.

Niall backed away, swiped an ale from a passing servant and raised it into the air. "Would ye look at my wee brother! I declare him knight for the day, and I'd be honored if he'd take my place."

With that, he marched out of the hall without a backward glance. Come hell or high water, he was going to put off wedding that spoiled brat for as long as he possibly could.

THE FOLLOWING MORNING, when Niall woke, his brother stood at the end of his bed.

"What the hell are ye doing?" Niall asked.

Walter crossed his arms over his chest and jutted out his chin. "I've thought about what ye said."

"What?" Niall rubbed at his eyes, trying to wake more fully.

"About wedding the princess."

At that, Niall sat straight up, the cobwebs of sleep suddenly cleared. "And?" He loved his brother, and considering how much Walter had done for him over the past year, the man deserved a rise in the ranks. Perhaps he would be able to tame the unruly princess, too. But he wouldn't force him if it wasn't what he truly wanted.

"I'll do it. It would be an honor to be so close to the king, and I can see how she's treated ye. I'll not have her hurt ye anymore."

Niall swallowed around a lump of emotion that formed in his

throat. His brother would really do this for him? "How can I ever thank ye?"

"Ye'll need to let me kick your arse every once in a while. I've a feeling I'll have a need to let my frustrations out with my fists."

Niall chuckled. "Anything for ye."

"How will ye arrange to break the betrothal?"

"I've no idea. Maybe I'll start a rumor that my cock isna in working order. That ought to send her running."

Walter burst out into raucous laughter at that. "I'll pay ye a year's wages to do it."

Niall grinned. "I've never been a betting man, but ye've just convinced me, brother."

Chapter Four

Dunrobin Castle
Scottish Highlands
December 1319

Bella had never seen the castle so filled with people. They took up every corner of the great hall, sitting on the wooden benches and lounging against the tapestry-covered stone walls. Extra chairs and stools had been brought in as well as fur rugs to line the floors. Her mother's solar was also packed with ladies, and men covered the bailey like flies on overripe fruit.

Invitations for the largest gathering since the great tournament in 1306 had been issued to the surrounding clans, the Sutherland allies, and King Robert Bruce himself.

Bella's father and mother had not expected everyone to accept their invitation, and due to the unseasonably warm months leading up to this point, they'd not expected a massive snowstorm to keep their guests stranded at Dunrobin Castle for the foreseeable future. Well, at least it felt that way to Bella. Interminably long.

Two days had passed since the first horses and carts arrived loaded with people, but already Bella was willing to beg her father to send everyone on their way.

There seemed to be music and games at all hours, which interfered with her ability to sneak away and shoot her arrows. All she desired was to remain aloof and quiet in the lady's solar, except that too was now in constant use by others. Three extra hands would be required if she were to count on her fingers the number of times she'd gone to the solar to read and found every inch of space covered by a lady other than herself.

It was only by chance that her bedchamber was empty now so she could take just the briefest repose. With all their guests at the castle, she'd been forced to share her bedchamber with her two younger sisters. She let the fur covering over her window drop to muffle the sounds from outside.

Was she a spoiled lass? Some may say so, but she tried to be kind and generous and have a tender, encouraging word for anyone who spoke to her. She helped her mother with the household chores without balking, assisted her father in any duty he might request of her, and even helped her brothers and sisters at whatever task they struggled with—including flirting with the lassies.

Bella had also brought together a number of lasses and lads. It seemed she had an eye for matchmaking. Her mother said was because she spent so much time with the minstrels and bards who passed through Sutherland. Bella copied down their stories and songs, embellishing them and creating her own tales that she regaled the clan with daily. Every one of the legends she wove had a love story entwined, though most of them were tragic.

It was Bella's perhaps not-so-subtle way of informing her parents she was not interested in marriage. Ever. Unless, of course, it ended in her spouse succumbing to an untimely death. Aye, a tragedy to call her own.

She'd made a deal with her mother in the spring for a short reprieve from proposals, which her father had complied with, but there had been a subtle shift in the wind lately that Bella was very aware of. She wasn't certain exactly when the shift had started, but it had been made unpleasantly clear two days ago.

Until two days ago, Lord and Lady Sutherland had not pushed the idea of marriage. However, the notion had not gone by her that her older brother, Magnus, named for their father, had been betrothed last month. Even her younger brother Liam, and her two younger sisters, Greer and Blair, were hoping to soon be attached. But since Bella was second born in the family and first of the daughters, her sisters could not be married until she was. A thought she'd not considered at all until Greer mentioned it—and then looked forlornly off into the distance.

The fact that if she were to wed, she'd likely be set aside soon after, was a point Bella could not make. She was not surprised when two days after speaking with her sister, her father informed her she must choose a husband from the crowds descending upon their castle. When she'd opened her mouth to argue, her mother had spoken up, saying they'd allowed her enough time to come to terms with her future, and seconded the laird's decree that Bella pick one of the eligible bachelors, threatening that if she did not, they would pick one for her.

At least they were giving her a choice, she tried to remind herself. But even having that choice didn't make the task any more pleasant.

Bella did not want to marry. At all.

Throughout her life, she'd looked upon her parents' marriage and known she could never have anything so perfect. They *loved* each other. Appeared to still desire each other, given the looks and kisses they were not too subtle in sharing, which always brought a round of groans from their five children. Their affection was so rare. Bella couldn't possibly hope to replicate it.

Not to mention, the deepest secret she kept buried in her heart of hearts, never shared with any other. In fact, she dared not think it in case the truth of her fears were plainly seen on her face.

Unlike most of the lassies her age—two and twenty summers—she'd never been interested in kissing lads. For certes in her tales, she always talked about a great kiss between a man and a woman, but not once had she wanted to do the deed herself. Perhaps, if not for her secret, she might actually have desired it. But what was the point when a great love would never be hers?

Her mother said it was because the right lad had not yet come along, but her father said he was glad for it, and to keep her lips well away from any of the mongrels that might try to paw at her. Lord and Lady Sutherland did not know her secret. And she could never tell them for fear of disappointing them greatly.

With a begrudging sigh, Bella pushed off the chair covered with thick cushions her sisters and mother had embroidered for her birthday the previous year and marched toward the door. If she was going to have to choose a husband, she might as well get it over with.

The march down the stairs was interminably long, the sounds from the great hall deafening. None of the boisterous lads dancing around and clashing their mugs of ale would do for a husband. So outside she went, where great bonfires were lit to warm the bailey as large clumps of white snow fell. She tilted her face up, closed her eyes and let a few of the icy puffs land on her cheeks.

It was then she heard something most intriguing. An argument. A rather one-sided row. Did that still make it an argument, or merely a ranting?

Curious as always for a new angle to add to a story, Bella crept toward the wall of the keep from where the shrill voice of a young woman sounded around the corner. She paused when her slippers crunched on the newly fallen snow, but whoever was making a ruckus did not cease their squabbling, and so she continued on.

"I will *not* have ye. I should have called the betrothal off months ago." The female speaker was shrill and indignant, and there came no reply. But she must be spouting off to someone. "Ye're not a man. I am the daughter of a king—the greatest king! And I deserve a whole man."

Daughter of the king? Bella's spine straightened, knowing at once who the speaker was. Only one royal offspring was in attendance—Princess Elizabeth.

Bella chewed her lip, considering that perhaps she ought to turn and slink away rather than listen to the dressing down Princess Elizabeth was giving to whomever it was she was betrothed to. And just who was it? This man that was not a *whole* man. She rolled her eyes heavenward, wishing she could be more like her sisters and actually pay attention to who was marrying who, and all that other fluttery nonsense. A whole man... That particular offense rolled around in Bella's mind. What ever could that mean?

Bella's curiosity exploded. There was no turning back now, even if she were to get caught. Pressing her hands to the cold stone for balance, she peered just slightly around the corner of the keep to see Princess Elizabeth, hands on her hips, giving quite the dressing down to a rather handsome warrior. She wore an elegant cloak, lined as well as hemmed with furs and trimmed in gold. Though the cloak was pulled up over her hair, the moon shone on her pale skin and the few snowflakes made her appear to shimmer.

Bella shifted her gaze back to the warrior who towered over Elizabeth. He leaned up against the wall, his great plaid slung over his shoulders. His face was partially covered in shadow. She squinted her eyes, trying to make out every chiseled feature. There was something vaguely familiar about him, but she figured she must have seen him around the castle or at another event.

The warrior shifted forward, coming out of the shadows to crowd closer to the princess. Bella's own heart leapt to think of herself in that position.

Exposing himself to the moonlight gave Bella a chance to examine him more fully. He looked whole enough to her. And much too handsome for his own good, despite the bored expression on his striking visage.

Aye, he was quite good-looking, and the way his golden-colored locks pulled free of the queue he'd attempted to tuck them in gave him a wild look. With chiseled features, albeit a slightly crooked nose, he could have been carved from stone. He towered over the princess. Was nearly as broad as he was tall. A mountain of a man. What was not whole about him? He was standing on what appeared to be two legs. Though his arms were hidden beneath a swath of plaid, they certainly looked to be attached from where she was hiding.

"Are ye calling off the engagement then?" His tone was as bored as his expression, but Bella picked up on the underlying edge of danger, which only sparked her interest more.

Who was the mysterious warrior engaged to the princess? There was definitely something about the eyes and mouth that she recognized. Where had she seen him before?

"Of course that's what I'm saying. I need a man with two arms and —" The princess glanced most improperly in the direction of the warrior's nether parts. "A man with a working member. I have a duty to my father and this country to reproduce."

Heat suffused Bella's face. Had she heard correctly? Was the princess accusing the warrior of not being able to...? Oh, goodness... To be unable to lie with a woman? To...have children?

Not having two arms was not a bother for Bella, and not being able to lie with a woman was even better. Was it serendipity that she'd happened to eavesdrop on this most private conversation? Well, it wasn't as if they'd chosen to have it behind closed doors. No matter that they were hidden around the side of the castle from the rest of the guests, they were out in the open where anyone might hear. Aye, this was not a simple case of eavesdropping at all. She'd just happened to stumble upon this most...intriguing conversation.

Not to mention opportune...

If the princess was going to break off her betrothal to this man, Bella was more than happy to scoop him up. He was perfect. Exactly what she was looking for in a spouse.

"Ye seem to be forgetting one thing, Princess," the warrior sneered. "The alliance between my house and yours."

The princess scoffed, crossed her arms over her ample bosom and tapped her foot. "Ye canna tell me that ye want this marriage."

"I'd be lying if I told ye so."

"Then let us part ways. We shall confront my father together."

The warrior's expression lit up, and he pushed off the wall, standing taller than he'd appeared before, if possible. He could rival the tower of Dunrobin itself. "I have a better idea."

The princess's tapping foot increased its pace. "Well, out with it then."

"My brother just so happens to be looking for a bride, and I promise ye, he is whole in every way."

The princess stopped tapping her foot and glanced up, intrigued. Was it just Bella, or did the warrior's plan seem contrived? Bella narrowed her eyes, studying him. Aye, he was not at all upset about the breaking of the betrothal and was all but tossing his brother at the princess.

Bella frowned. Perhaps he was like her and did not wish to marry, which meant if she were to propose it to him, he might not be amenable to the idea. That would mess up everything. He was perfect for her. Even if she didn't know who he was, everything about him was what she needed in a husband.

Well, no bother. Was she not the best matchmaker in all of Sutherland? Perhaps Scotland? She could make a match for herself without issue. And perhaps his desire not to wed would be the perfect angle to go about it. Then again, her father held sway with the king. Perhaps she'd not have to say anything at all.

"Bella?" Speak of the devil...

"Da!" She whirled around and tossed herself into her father's massive arms, breathing in his familiar comforting scent and then gazing up at him with wide, innocent eyes.

Magnus Sutherland's light hair was also pulled back in a queue, and like the warrior who appeared oblivious to the cold, her father wore only his plaid, no cloak, to ward off the winter weather. Dark-green eyes assessed her suspiciously. He grinned, letting her know she was caught, and that he was amused by it. "Who were ye spying on?" he whispered, making an exaggerated movement to peer around her, as though he would join in with her.

Eavesdropping was yet another talent she'd well-honed. Her Aunt Heather was a master eavesdropper and had often given lessons to Bella whenever she visited.

Bella held back a grin. Saints, couldn't she get away with anything? "No one, Da." She tugged at his shoulder, trying to hold him back, afraid the princess and her mysterious warrior would take notice.

Magnus narrowed his eyes, and his grin widened. "Perhaps, I'll have a closer look myself."

"Nay." Bella pressed her hand to his chest, bit her lip and then whispered, "A warrior. He's just been discarded by Princess Elizabeth. I dinna want them to know I heard such a mortifying exchange."

Her father scowled, peering toward the walls of the castle. "Discarded?"

Seeing as how her father may misconstrue what she meant and think the princess had a lover, Bella was quick to explain, "Her betrothed, Da, nothing nefarious. She's just now broken off an engagement with him in favor of his brother."

Magnus raised a brow, studying Bella's face. "Oh? 'Tis not one of your stories, is it?"

Not yet, she almost said. Instead, she kept her face as serious as the conversation warranted. "Aye, 'tis the truth. And, Da..." She chewed her lip, staring at the pin holding his plaid in place trying to figure out just how to phrase her proposal.

"Ye wish to marry him." 'Twas not a question.

How had he known? Bella jerked her gaze up to meet her father's, her face hot as the rocks that warmed her feet in bed at night. Perhaps Bella was not as inconspicuous as she wanted to be. Though her father always seemed to read her so easily. He claimed it was because she was so much like her Aunt Heather, a hellion in the Sutherland household from the time she was born to this very day. Bella had always taken that as a compliment.

She nodded, sighed. "Aye."

"Do ye even know his name?" Her father sounded skeptical now.

Drat! She knew there was something she was missing. She shook her head.

"And why would ye want to marry him?"

"He is handsome." She shrugged, winged a brow hoping that would do the trick.

Magnus only scowled. "I know ye better than that, my sweet."

Thinking quick on her toes, since her true reasons the earl would never find valid or understand, Bella said, "If he was good enough for the king's daughter, then he should be good enough for me."

"Och, but she has just discarded him. 'Haps her reasons for doing so should be considered by ye, lass."

Bella pursed her lips and crossed her arms over her chest petulantly. "She is a fool." Bella meant it. The man was handsome, well built, and it would appear he came from a good family. Just because he was missing an arm and unable to perform... Well, she supposed she could see why Princess Elizabeth might not have wanted to marry him for the latter reason. But that was perfect for Bella. She'd be happy not to have him perform *those* duties with her.

Magnus Sutherland laughed at that and tapped her on the nose. "Dinna let anyone hear ye say such, else her father might challenge me."

Bella smiled wide. "I promise. Besides, if that were the case, I'd take him on for ye, Da."

"Nay doubt ye would, which is why we must keep such talk quiet, for I'll not have ye starting a revolution of your own. I respect the king, and I know he values me as his vassal."

"There is that," Bella said with a laugh. She pinched her lips and turned an imaginary key.

Magnus grinned. God, how she loved her da. He was handsome, strong, intelligent—but beyond that, he was caring and fun. He didn't attempt to squash her. All he did was encourage her in all of her interests.

"All right, if he is the one ye choose, I shall approach him about forming an alliance."

"Aye. Da, what *is* his name?"

Her father's gaze shifted over her shoulder then. "Sir Niall Oliphant, just the man I was coming to see."

Bella whirled around and came face-to-face with a mountain of muscle. He was even more striking close up. Hard eyes, the oddest shade of gray, almost like metal, glinted in the firelight, assessed her briefly before he looked to her father.

Sir Niall Oliphant. Her childhood fantasy. The lad who'd let her win. Oh, she could have fainted right then and there. Here he was in the flesh, the man she'd dreamed of marrying, and now she just might.

Was this really happening? Her breath grew rapid until it all but stopped.

"My laird." Niall reached out with his good arm to grip her father's.

Bella stared at the long, powerful appendage and forced herself not to reach forward to touch him.

It was then, as his cloak gaped open, that she caught sight of the other sleeve hanging empty by his side. She didn't gasp as some of the vaporous lassies might. So he only had one arm, who cared? Anyone had to take but one look at his impressive physique and know he was still in possession of his faculties. She continued to peruse his shape, finding it pleased her very much indeed. In fact, there was a slight warming in her belly, and her breath caught. How odd. She'd never before looked at a man and found him pleasing in the least, let alone had such a...visceral reaction. She shook that off, taking note of the strength and breadth of him. Despite the missing arm, he looked hale and hearty. Saints, she'd been waiting over a decade to see him again.

"Welcome to Dunrobin," her father was saying. "This is my daughter, Lady Bella."

Niall shot her a look that went from shock to a heated intensity that made her knees knock. Did he recognize her? Remember her at all? If she had to guess, she'd say aye, but he soon shuttered away the interest sparking in his expression and turned back to her father.

"I've something I'd like to discuss with ye, Sir Niall. Would ye join me in my study?"

Niall glanced at her one more time with a slight narrowing of his eyes, as though he wished to say something, and then nodded to her father.

The two men moved off toward the castle, and while she briefly thought it might be a good idea to mingle with those who were celebrating around the bonfires, she quickly dismissed that thought in favor of eavesdropping on whatever was about to happen in her father's study. With an excited skip to her step, she headed toward the castle.

Chapter Five

Prickly numbness tingled Niall's fingertips, and it took everything he had not to turn around and look behind him.

Bella Sutherland. *Bella, Bella, Bella...*

He'd known he would run into her. In fact, Walter had practically forced him to Dunrobin Castle. Ever since his brother had mentioned how she'd rejected his proposal in the spring, the lass had never been far from Niall's mind. He saw her in every golden-haired lass he met. In every arrow. In every tinkle of feminine laughter. In every jest.

Despite his best efforts to put her from his mind, throwing himself whole-heartedly into training like he'd never done before, she surrounded him. Consumed him. And he'd not seen her or spoken to her since he was lad. But he'd built her up in his mind into this mythical, goddess-like creature from that brief glimpse at Stirling several years ago.

Then, there she was, near perfection, the way he'd imagined her. Only better. Beyond. He'd soaked up the perfect lines of her flawless, creamy skin with cheeks and nose reddened from the cold. Bright, amused violet eyes, and hair like soft, spun gold. She was tall, with lush seductive curves, and he imagined legs that went on forever. He'd taken note of the callouses on her fingers when she'd tucked her hair behind her ears. She was still practicing archery. And yet there was something else there, too. Ink stains, and he didn't know what to think of that. Her smile had been bashful but not shy, and the way she'd looked at him, studied him—hell, no woman had looked at him like that since before the battle. There had been interest, desire in her eyes, which had him wondering if perhaps she was...idealistic.

Och, but seeing her only made his heart drop to his feet, made his tongue grow thick. He held back for fear of being awkward.

No matter if she was a few feathers short of a fletching, Bella Sutherland was... Saints, was there even a word to describe her? Stunning, enchanting. If her father had not been standing between them, Niall might have pulled her flush to him and kissed her, if only to slake a hunger that had been pounding in his veins, demanding to get out for months. Years, if he were honest.

Niall swallowed, dread curdling his belly. He wanted to escape, the familiar tingling panic starting at the back of his neck. He flexed his fingers, cracked his neck, tried to pay attention, tried to ignore the tumult of thoughts running through his mind.

Beside him, the Earl of Sutherland was making idle conversation, and Niall attempted to pay attention, but the blood rushing in his ears caused all the noises around him to sound as though he were under water.

Mouth dry, throat tight, Niall worked on forcing the breath from his closed lungs, on counting the paces from where they were to the front of the castle. *One. Two. Three. Four. Five...*

Luckily, whatever Magnus was saying didn't require more than a grunt or two.

A tirade of images and questions tunneled their way through the rush in his head. Why had he not been able to say anything to Bella? To at least make a jest about how the last time they'd met, she'd turned him into a lady. Or to ask if she was still using her bow and arrows? Had she ever been defeated?

From the moment he'd laid eyes on her, he'd been consumed with jumbled thoughts that wouldn't leave him in peace.

He was humiliated at how he appeared now. Maybe he didn't want her to remember him, the lad who had nearly bested her at archery.

The lad whose hand she'd grabbed hold of and held in the air. His left hand. The one that was rotting in some remote forest. Not even a proper burial for the part of his body that was forever dead.

Niall held back a bitter grin at that morbid thought.

At last, they reached the castle and ascended the stone stairs to the arched doorway. Niall choked when he nearly reached to hold the door open with the arm that was no longer present, his shoulder jerking oddly, before his right arm covered his mistake.

It was a good thing he'd not attempted to make any small talk with Bella. As soon as she found out about his disability, she'd turn her cheek just as Elizabeth had. Even as he thought it, he knew it wasn't fair. Bella and Elizabeth were completely different. Well, at least he thought they were. It was entirely possible Bella could have changed from the child he'd known. Perhaps she was addled as he imagined. Perhaps they could help each other—he'd be the mind, and she'd be the limbs.

Bloody hell, I am mad, aren't I?

THE SECRET CORRIDOR that lined her father's study was pitch black, but Bella knew it well. She'd been playing in the hidden passageways since she was a bairn.

The two men entered the study and her father poured them both a drink. She watched as Niall tossed back one cup, followed by another in quick succession. How could she blame him? If she had just gone through a humiliating conversation with the princess, she might have grabbed hold of the whole bottle. No matter that he seemed to have been prepared, that he appeared to want out of the marriage, it was still mortifying to hear such disparaging remarks.

Magnus moved to his desk and leaned back against it, sipping his whisky slower and studying Niall as he stared into his empty cup. Bella bit her lip, her heartbeat thudding loudly enough she was certain they would hear it beyond the wall. She pressed her hands to the makeshift wall and breathed out a long, slow breath.

"Have another, lad." Her father nodded to the sideboard.

Niall set down his cup, took hold of the jug and popped the cork with his thumb. He refilled his cup but didn't drink it though. Instead, he turned to face her father suddenly enough that she gasped and then clamped her lips closed.

"What did ye wish to speak to me about?"

Her father's gaze flicked toward where Bella was standing. *Dretch!* He'd heard her. She bit her lip, praying he didn't point her out or speak to the wall as he sometimes did. Talk about embarrassing.

A poke at her side brought a screech to the top of her throat before she clamped her hands over her lips.

"Bella, what are ye doing?" The whisper came from her sister Blair, a beautiful lass with dark hair, and just coming into womanhood.

"Shhh..." Bella warned. "Da is speaking with...a warrior."

"And why's that so interesting?"

"Because, 'tis the warrior I wish to marry."

Blair let out a *whoosh* of a breath that was probably accompanied by a wide grin. She grabbed hold of Bella and hugged her. Bella squeezed back, smiling into the dark. This was a monumental day. Not only for Bella, but for her sisters, too.

The two of them were silent then, paying attention to what was happening beyond the wall.

"'Tis a simple matter really," Magnus said, still leaning casually against his desk. "I am prepared to make ye an offer."

"What sort of offer?" Niall's shoulders stiffened, causing a ripple effect down his entire body. Bella had the distinct impression he was ready to bolt.

Stay. Listen. Say, aye.

"My eldest daughter's hand." Magnus shot a glance at the wall then, a warning look on his countenance. When he started to walk toward them, Blair let out a screech, giving away their position and leaving Bella no choice but to run. "I heard ye, Blair," Magnus called after them, and Bella breathed a sigh of relief that he'd not mentioned her name.

STARTLED by the question rather than the spying child behind the wall, for Niall knew Blair to be the youngest daughter of the Earl and Countess of Sutherland, he braced himself, feet planted wide and knees locked. Had he truly heard correctly? Marry Bella?

The lass wanted him for a husband? Or was this something her father had designed and she would yet balk at. Aye, she'd been kind to him in the bailey, but kindness did not equate to aligning herself to him for the rest of her days.

And why would Magnus be stupid enough to think his daughter deserved a poor wretch like him? He felt like waving his empty sleeve in the man's direction, forcing him to look and see that Niall was not whole, to remind him that as of less than an hour ago, he'd been betrothed to the king's daughter, but that spoiled lass had broken it off before she tied herself for a lifetime to a man who would never measure up.

"Your daughter—Lady Bella?" Niall glanced toward the door, as though he expected the golden-haired beauty to appear, but it remained firmly closed, making him feel trapped.

Unquestioningly, Bella was the most beautiful, enchanting woman Niall had ever encountered, perhaps the most lovely in all of Scotland. What other woman could claim to have beaten him at archery and then made him into her lady? What other woman would he have bowed down to and done such for? None. She was special, and even as a youth, he'd known it.

Indeed, he'd admired her for over a decade, and yet when coming face-to-face with her after all this time, he'd been left speechless.

And it wasn't because she hadn't winced like every other woman when she looked at him. Oh, how she intrigued him—all of the bits and pieces of her put together. And she could possibly be his wife?

Was this a trick? A jest put forth by the princess to humiliate him further? And if it were the truth, how could he possibly go through with it? How could he burden beautiful Bella with him as a husband? How could he ever give her what she needed and deserved when he was only a shell of himself? He had nothing to offer a woman. And yet, the idea of his dream coming true—oh, it was a cruel jest to taunt him with something he couldn't have.

"She has chosen ye as the man she'd like to wed, Sir Niall."

Another blow. *She* had chosen *him*. How? Why?

Niall studied the powerful man before him, trying to ascertain if this was some elaborate jest meant to humiliate him. Tall and still just as commanding in his middle age as he'd likely been when he was Niall's own age, the great earl and chieftain of his clan stood unyielding and firm. One did not contradict Magnus Sutherland. One agreed. The powerful earl was not one to play jests on others. He was revered throughout the country for his intelligence, his mercy, his bravery. Not cruelty.

But how the bloody hell did the Earl of Sutherland know of his betrothal contract being broken already? It had just happened.

Unless...he and his daughter had spied Elizabeth's rejection. Niall glanced toward the wall then, the way Magnus had openly outed a spying child. It was not outside the realm of possibility that they'd spied him with the princess. Another man might have been mortified to realize that, but oddly enough, Niall wasn't. The princess had been rather ugly in her tantrum, and Niall wasn't the least bit upset about not being attached to such a spoiled lass. And if Magnus and Bella had witnessed the quarrel and decided Niall should marry Bella instead, was it out of pity? Shame for him?

"Have another drink, lad." Magnus handed him the cup he'd filled with a dram of the strongest smelling whisky he'd ever inhaled. "Bella overheard the conversation between ye and the princess."

Ah, well, that was what he'd thought. Niall nodded, resisted the urge to snort at Sutherland having read his mind. Still, he did not answer, wasn't certain he even could. His tongue not only felt thick, but numb. Any words he formed might come out in a foreign-sounding tongue.

But he would have to speak, for he could not agree, though he was flattered they would think of him in so highly a manner.

The truth was, even though he'd once wished to marry Bella, Niall could not marry her now. He sipped the whisky and then tossed back the contents, reveling in the burn in his throat. But the liquor did not ease his anxiety over just being rid of one bride in order to gain another.

"My eldest daughter has been reluctant to marry. And I gave her the option of choosing a man during this festival, or I'd choose a man for her," Magnus explained.

Niall gritted his teeth, unhappy with what he was about to do. "I am not the man ye would have chosen." Niall saw no reason to dance around the obvious. "So why did she?"

Magnus eyed him shrewdly, and then nodded. "Bella is...unique. She needs a man who can...live up to her vigor." The earl glanced at the empty sleeve on Niall's left. "A man who can fight for her. Give her children."

Niall grunted. Since the battle that had taken his arm a year ago, he'd kept up with his training in private, not wanting anyone to witness his lameness. Only Walter, his trainer and a few select warriors were allowed to work with him. No one knew this as he'd sworn them all to secrecy. His trainer had been the same man who taught him how to handle a sword as a lad, and he was loyal to a fault. Aye, despite his debility, he could still kick his brother's and his men's arses. Why should he shout out to all of Scotland that he could still wield a sword?

Magnus's words echoed in Niall's mind. *A man who can fight for her. Give her children...* Pride made the words sting all the more, and a sudden urge to prove the man wrong thrummed in his veins.

"I can manage." A phantom pain twinged in the arm that was no longer there, making Niall grit his teeth.

The past year had been rough. He'd wanted to die. Had hoped he would when they'd cauterized the stump where his arm had been, when they'd doused him with whisky and herbs to make him sleep. He'd wanted to die when he'd woken and learned all over again that the nightmare of that sword hacking away at his limb had been real. Wanted to die when he'd had to relearn to dress himself with only one hand. To feed himself. To climb a ladder. Hold a sword. Piss. Everything had had to be relearned.

Even now, he wasn't certain he wanted to live. Knew he'd be no use to a wife. No use to a beautiful, vibrant lass like Bella Sutherland. Aye, he wanted her. Aye, he'd seen her the moment he arrived, tried to ignore her but kept feeling his gaze roam back to wherever she was. Listened to her tell a story to a crowd of children that had them all wide-eyed and just as mesmerized as he was. She'd captivated him. So much so, Niall had searched out the man she must certainly call husband and had been surprised to find she was not yet wed. And then mentally kicked himself for wondering.

"Did ye enter in the tourney?" Magnus's question pulled Niall from his thoughts.

The tourney. The last tourney he'd fought on Sutherland lands was the one where he'd gone up against Bella. The one where he'd told the other lads she should be allowed to fight and then had let her beat him. Well, only halfway let her beat him. The archery she'd done all on her own. She was one hell of a shot. What could she do now? Niall shook himself from the memories, trying to focus on what Magnus was saying.

On the morrow, men would fight in the snow for placement in the king's guard. The thought of entering had never even crossed Niall's mind. "I dinna wish to be a part of the king's guard," he answered bluntly.

"Why not? Your father is legendary for his service to the crown."

"While I am proud of him, I am not my father." *And I've already given up enough for the king. My arm. My future.*

Magnus's green gaze settled on his, staring him down so hard he thought the man might be able to see straight into his soul. "How will ye protect your clan?"

"The same as ye, my laird. My father is still chieftain, and my brother will follow in his footsteps. With the king as his father-in-law, my clan will be safe."

"Enter the tourney." Magnus refilled his cup.

Without sipping, Niall answered, "Begging your pardon, my laird, but if I decline?"

"Then I will find another husband for my daughter. One who will pick up his sword for her."

Niall grimaced, feeling the prick to his pride. "I have not agreed to marry her. Nor did I say I'd not pick up my sword if it were to protect her."

"After being spurned by the king's daughter, and by refusing me, do ye think there will be any other offers?"

Niall straightened. He didn't care if there were any other offers, but he knew a warning when he heard one. "Are ye threatening me, my laird?"

Magnus raised his glass. "Let us call it a recommendation."

Niall grunted. "'Haps I want to spend my life alone."

"Then what are ye doing here?"

The man had a point. He could have remained at Dupplin Castle in Aberdalgie. He'd known before arriving in Sutherland that he didn't want to marry Princess Elizabeth. Had he hoped that he'd find some way of breaking it off with her while he was here? Why else had he come? Deep down, he knew it was because he was searching for a reason to go on. Because he'd hoped to see Bella one more time. Hoped to prove to himself she was not the lass he remembered, not the fantasy he'd created. That she was a heathen with horns and no teeth and a voice that could curdle milk. *Ballocks!*

Maybe the tourney was the opportunity, the sign, he was looking for. The test of whether or not he was worthy of life. Of happiness. "And if I prove myself?"

"Then I will gladly gift ye a future with my beloved eldest daughter."

Niall didn't hesitate this time in drinking down his whisky in one swallow. Was he really going to do this? A tournament? Make a spectacle of himself... That was the last thing he wanted. He'd been happy to lay low, to sink into obscurity. To wallow in the grief of missing his arm and let the world believe him disabled and weak.

He could hear his brother now. *If that be true, then why do ye keep training?*

Niall didn't know why, but perhaps he'd soon find the answer. This was a chance to prove to everyone that he was worthy, not just to everyone, but to himself. He needed a wife. His father had been begging him, even going so far as to say he wished Niall to marry before he passed on to his great reward. If anything, marrying would dispel his parents' fears of him being alone forever, and remove suspicion regarding the rumors he'd spread. But he wasn't certain he was ready to be a husband in more than anything but name, to reveal his wounds to anyone. His true self. Yet the convenience of it would certainly lay to rest many of his current irritations—namely his brother, his parents and any bastard who would dare take Bella from him.

He cleared his throat, looked Magnus in the eye and said, "I am honored, my laird."

The earl's eyes sparked with something that looked a little like pride. "I'd verra much enjoy seeing ye prove everyone wrong."

Niall was surprised by the words. "Why?"

Magnus shrugged and raised his cup, swallowing the spirits. "My daughter sees something in ye that the rest of the world doesna. I want to know what it is."

"I'll do my best." Niall gave the earl his thanks, then walked out of the study and followed him into the great hall, where he entered his name into the tournament.

Needing to feel the cool night air on his overheated skin and to hide the trembling in his hand, Niall attempted to make his escape outside. But before he could, the grand double doors swung open and the sound of Princess Elizabeth's voice came echoing through, sending him backward up the closest flight of stairs to hide. *Ballocks!* The princess was now ascending, her voice growing closer.

Mo chreach, *can I nae escape her?*

Chapter Six

Niall ducked into the first door he found, closed it and sagged his forehead against the wood paneling. Too late, the floral scent of a woman reached him. Niall whirled around, fearing he'd stepped into a lady's bedchamber. He found himself both relieved and panicked to realize he was in a solar, without a bed in sight.

Lady Bella was perched on an ornate chair with a thick sheaf of parchment in her hands. Golden candlelight glinted from the glorious golden curls framing her face, and violet eyes taunted him. Her rose-red lips quirked in a teasing grin.

"Well, sir, this is most inappropriate. Our betrothal has not even been formally announced." Saints, but her voice and the way her lips moved when she formed words took his breath away.

"My lady." He bowed, swallowed hard and then managed to find his tongue. "How can ye be so certain I have accepted our betrothal?"

She pursed her lips. "Have ye not?"

He shrugged, and at that noncommittal movement, the mirth that had filled her eyes dimmed slightly.

"What are ye doing here in my solar, Sir Niall, if not to find me?"

Ballocks, but he'd not meant to offend the lass. He glanced toward the door. The sounds of feminine laughter filtered through, and for one fearful moment, they seemed primed to enter, but then they passed. There was no use but to be honest with Bella. "Escaping."

He glanced back at her to gauge her reaction and was glad he did. She winged a golden brow, and he had a similar response to his blatant honesty. The lass seemed to tear down his defenses without him even realizing it. He could have told her anything, like how his heart was pounding or that he was glad to see her.

"From whom?" she asked.

"The princess..." But his throat tightened, and he found himself unable to finish his sentence.

She waved the papers at him in dismissal of his words. "Say no more. Come and sit. I will tell ye a story."

Sit with her? Nay. There was no way in bloody hell he was going to get closer to her. Just being in the same room made him feel witless. Besides, even if he had agreed to fight in the tournament to prove himself to Magnus and accepted the challenge in order to win her hand, they should not be alone together. "I canna."

"Why not?"

Why did her voice have to be so smooth and melodic? "As ye said, my lady, 'tis most inappropriate."

That taunting smile remained. Not much had changed from when they were young, and he wanted to slink closer to sit beside her and tug her onto his lap. To ask her all of the things he wanted to know about her. To kiss her.

"Did my father speak with ye?"

Niall cleared his throat, trying to clear his mind of his improper thoughts. "Aye," he barely croaked out.

"And?" Her eyes bore into him, seemingly reading every thought that dared cross his mind.

Niall leaned his back on the door and considered barring it from anyone who might want in. He considered charging forward, crowding her space, pinning her there and pressing his lips hard to her taunting mouth. "If I do well in the tourney, we shall wed."

She frowned, clicked her teeth with a fingernail. "Ye may not recall, Sir Niall, but I've seen ye fight before. I've every confidence ye will please my father on the morrow and we shall be wed, so sit." She tapped the arm of a wooden chair to her left.

Niall glanced at her, a little surprised at her certainty of his doing well. He was also warmed by the fact she remembered him. There appeared to be no doubt in her mind of his skill, and he found it unnerving. How could she believe in him when she knew full well he was missing an arm—the limb that should protect him from a blow when his other was on the assault? But rather than ask, he simply said, "Nothing is guaranteed, my lady."

She uncurled her legs from beneath her, tiny slippers touching the bearskin rug before her chair. "Well, there are some things that are guaranteed, such as we all die sometime. And that I will not relent on ye listening to my story."

How effortlessly she changed the subject. How easy it was to be with her. He wanted to shout with joy and run with fear. "Ye're a stubborn lass." Still, he didn't move, though he did find himself smiling.

Bella grinned widely, leapt to her feet and dipped into a mocking curtsy. There was such vibrancy about her it made him want to laugh. A feeling he'd not had in a long time. In fact, he couldn't remember the last time he'd smiled.

She was making it so uncomplicated. As if his being in her solar was an everyday occurrence. The chair beside her beckoned, and her scent tugged him forward. For the first time in over a year, Niall's mind skipped over his weaknesses and leapt right into flirtation. "Verra well, my lady, what will ye give me if I sit and listen to your story?"

She sat back down and pursed her lips at him, those golden arched brows dancing upward on her forehead. "I didna realize I had to give ye anything. Is my story not entertainment enough?"

"We shall see," he teased, the corner of his mouth quirking into a smile.

"And if it is not, what will ye demand of me?"

Och, but that was a loaded question, one he could not help give a goaded response to, one that shocked him even as it left his mouth. "A kiss."

Violet eyes widened in surprise, but not with disgust. Nay, in fact, her gaze held a hint of interest. "It will be *verra* entertaining then, I assure ye."

Oh, what a clever tease. The sound of his laugh was foreign, as though hearing something from a long-lost friend. He even startled himself when he did it. But Niall couldn't help but chuckle at her certainty, and what it meant—that she didn't want to kiss him, or perhaps she was afraid to, for there had been interest sparking in her gaze. Curious, considering she had requested her father arrange for them to be wed. What did she hope to gain from the union?

The lass gestured for him to sit, a stern look on her face. Just as when they'd been younger, Niall was loath to disappoint her. On legs that were sturdier than an hour before, he crossed the room. She smiled up at him as though she'd won a battle, and his chest squeezed in response. Her floral scent was all the more powerful now he was standing this close to her. In the candlelight, he could see her creamy skin was perfection, and he had to fist his hand to keep from reaching forward to touch her and see if it was as soft as he imagined.

Saints, when her father said she was unique, he might have also mentioned how bossy she still was. Niall wouldn't quite call her a shrew, because she was charming as she dictated what she wanted. Just as she had been when they were children. The insight brought on another smile—as he realized the woman he'd dreamed her to be was also just as commanding.

"Can I get ye a glass of ale or wine?" Lady Bella's voice sounded deeper, throatier, and the arch of her cheekbones had taken on a pink twinge.

Niall bit the tip of his tongue and then muttered. "Nay, I thank ye."

"All right." She cleared her throat. "Then so we shall begin." Again, she indicated for him to sit, and he did so swiftly, without taking his eyes from hers.

"I'm all yours, my lady."

She raised a brow at that, and he winked. Dear God, he was flirting. The lass had opened up a whole ocean of emotion and desire he'd keep locked up tight and threatened to never see again.

The delicate blush creeping over her cheeks deepened at his wink. "Well, then, I shall begin. Listen carefully, and prepare to be entertained. On a dusky morning, a warrior returned from battle, hardened by the things he'd seen and wounded by his enemy's blade."

Niall frowned, gaze locked on hers as he realized she wasn't reading from the parchment but staring straight into his soul. It was unnerving. And yet he couldn't tear himself away. Her face was full of admiration, and it made him want to run once more.

"This warrior's name was Strength."

Niall shook his head. "'Tis not a name, but a trait."

"Shh," she admonished, reaching forward and tapping him where he rested his elbow on the arm of the chair, "Let me tell the tale."

"Verra well." His skin sizzled where she'd tapped him.

"Strength had been tested. He'd been pushed to his limits and still did not falter, not even when his enemies took parts of him that would never heal."

Was the lady taunting him? Throwing his wounds back in his face? He frowned, moving to cross his arms over his chest and nearly breaking down when he realized the position was rather awkward with only one arm. It was a wound he wished away, a wound he knew would forever make him lame in the eyes of all. In her eyes. Gritting his teeth, he stood and marched to the window, her voice trailing behind him as she spoke of the empty village mirroring the emptiness in the warrior's heart.

"With all his prospects hanging in the balance, his lost love dead in a siege, Strength was certain he'd not the will to go on."

Niall wanted to hate her. Wanted to go back in time and instead of letting her thump on him in hand-to-hand combat, to lay her on the ground and pin her there, where she couldn't beat him.

"But a fairy came to him, beautiful and golden, she rose majestically from the mist and offered him a different future."

Niall turned around then, leaning against a tapestry, the thickness of it not hindering the biting chill of the stone beneath it. He narrowed his eyes and glanced at her with all the pent-up frustration he had inside. What, did she think she was his savior? He had thought briefly in her father's study that the proposal might be one of pity, and now he was almost certain. "Let me guess, the fairy offered him marriage?"

She cocked her head to look at him, interest in her eyes that he'd not seen from any woman since he'd lost his arm. Interest and something deeper that had him questioning his theory on pity. "Nay. She did not offer him marriage, for what marriage could they possibly have? Instead, she offered him a truce."

"A truce?" he asked mockingly.

"A wish," she countered with a delicate shrug.

"A penance," Niall growled.

But Bella only smiled. "The fairy was in need of a protector, and the warrior was in need of—"

"I dinna need anything, lass."

Lady Bella tsked. "How conceited of ye to think this story is about ye, Sir Niall." She pushed out her lower lip in a pout.

"Isna it?" He hated the harshness in his tone and admired her all the more for being seemingly immune to it.

"Nay. Any similarities are merely a coincidence." Again, that hint of a smile.

He laughed harshly this time, not mirroring at all the joy in the sound earlier. "I am *not* entertained."

Lady Bella harrumphed from across the room. "Well, that is indeed a shame. I was trying to be clever."

"About?"

"A lady never divulges the inner workings of her mind."

"Humor me."

"If ye insist."

"I do."

"Fine." Bella shrugged and set her parchment aside. "I was merely trying to give ye my reasons for wishing a marriage betwixt us in a more interesting fashion than blurting them out like milkmaid."

"I'm a warrior, not a child, lass. I dinna need fairytales, I need facts."

She twirled a lock of hair around her finger, and he had the sudden urge to be the one doing so. To grab her. To shake the truth out of her. To rail at the world for the loss of his arm and this mocking lass.

"Believing in a little magic now and then never hurt anyone." Her soft words put a dent in his anger.

"It wouldna have saved me, either." He glanced down pointedly at his empty shirtsleeve.

"Perhaps it will now." Her voice was soft, having lost all the sarcasm she'd dared imbue earlier. There was a sweetness that drew him in. It made him want to lay his head in her lap and feel her stroke his hair. *Och, but I'm so weak.*

"Tell me why, and be done with it," he demanded. "I dinna want your pity, and I dinna need saving."

She let out a great sigh and locked her gaze on his. "I am in need of a husband, Sir Niall, though I dinna want one. Ye're in a need of a wife, and given your reaction, or lack thereof, to being rejected by the princess, ye dinna *want* a wife—but whether ye want one or not, ye need one. Ye're the heir to the Oliphant Clan."

He shrugged, still frowning. "I'll pass that title on to my brother and his wife."

"Fine, then for your own pride."

Again, that bitter laugh escaped him. "I've verra little pride left."

"I dinna believe ye." She'd straightened her shoulders, and her teasing eyes were replaced by something stronger, that resolute lass he'd first met.

He ignored her. "Why would ye choose me when ye can have any man ye want?"

Bella let out a short, sarcastic laugh and stood. He watched the gentle sway of her hips as she approached him, feeling an ache of desire deep inside.

When she stopped in front of him, the answer she gave was like an arrow straight to his heart, and it hurt like bloody fire. "Because ye canna be a true husband to me."

He narrowed his eyes. "What is that supposed to mean?"

She gestured to his arm. "With your injury."

"What has that got to do with being a true husband?" Och, but she had the power to ignite every emotion inside him. Anger. Desire. Compassion. Humor. Fury. Humiliation.

Her face flamed with color and she avoided his gaze. "Ye know what I mean."

"Do I?"

Uncertain eyes met his. "Dinna toy with me, Sir Niall."

"I fear I am lost," he ground out.

"Then let me save ye." There was a slight tremor in her jaw that showed she was vulnerable behind the strength and the teasing, too. But how? Why? "Now go ahead and kiss me."

"Kiss ye?" He stared at her lush lips, wanting more than anything to do what she asked.

"Aye. I did not entertain ye. Take your prize."

Niall stared down at her creamy face, her wide blue eyes, and felt his body stir. She was so beautiful. So cunning. So ornery. Lord, but he wanted her. Wanted to fight to prove he could have her. To prove to her he wasn't broken. "A kiss from ye is not a prize, but a gift."

"Then accept your gift," she whispered.

Accept his gift. Accept the thing he'd dreamed about for nearly a decade. Niall bent and brushed his lips over hers. At the sudden contact, she sucked in a breath through her nose, and he instinctively tried to retreat, but she leaned into him.

"This time, I'll need ye to be my lady," he murmured.

"And ye will be my knight," she whispered.

Tentatively, he touched her elbow, sliding his hand down to hers, entwining her trembling fingers with his. He breathed in the heady, sweet scent of flowers and herbs. Her lips were soft, warm and pliant. Sweet.

When had he last kissed a woman? He wasn't certain. A year or more? And the kisses he'd shared had never been as sweet or tender as this. What was it about Bella Sutherland?

He shook with restrained desire, madness even. Wanting to deepen the kiss and knowing it was too soon, Niall pulled away.

She blinked her eyes open and stared up at him. Dazed. "Will ye fight tomorrow?"

"I will, but not because your father made a marriage between us contingent upon it. Not because ye asked me to."

Bella nodded, all seriousness as she watched him. "I know."

"What do ye know?"

Her hands pressed to his thumping heart. "I know ye're a warrior."

"I *was*. But I am no longer."

"Ye are still. Ye were born to it. When I first met ye, ye were the only one confident enough in your abilities to let a lass fight ye. Confident enough to let a lass name ye her lady."

"Ye say confident. I say foolish."

She smiled. "Just because ye're impaired does not mean ye're weak. If there is one thing I know about men, having grown up in a house full of them, 'tis that once a warrior, always a warrior."

Niall grunted. "Why do ye care so much?"

Bella blinked and then flashed him a radiant smile. "Just a little encouragement."

He shook his head. "From what I know of ye, my lady, if I had to guess, I'd say ye dinna do anything only a little."

She laughed. "Ye flatter me, Sir Niall." She tapped his chest. "In that case, I think we shall get along splendidly.

Chapter Seven

"Will ye stop rolling around? The bed will collapse if ye keep it up."

Bella flopped her arm over her eyes, ignoring her sister Greer's complaints. She couldn't sleep. Aye, she had been tossing and turning since they'd blown out the candle and gone to bed a couple hours before—and with good reason. The bed felt abnormally lumpy. She was hot. She was cold. She was tired. She was wide awake. All because of what had happened in her solar.

She'd had her first kiss today. Not just any kiss. Not just any man.

Niall... She relived over and over the brush of his warm, soft lips on hers. The way his breath had been sweet with whisky and cinnamon. The way he'd smelled earthy and like fresh snow. How his sun-kissed hair had fallen over his brow, making him look virile and devilish. The slide of his mouth on hers had been a dream. Wondrous and brilliant in its heat. How was it possible that such a small gesture, something millions of people did all the time, could seem so poignant to her in that one moment? She'd never wanted to kiss before. Found it dull and sappy. And yet, if he burst into her chamber right here and now and asked if she wanted to kiss again, Bella would throw back her covers, leap to her feet and declare herself his for every kiss, any time, anywhere.

Oh, Niall...

The very man she'd been dreaming about since she was a lass. The very man she'd thought would never be hers. Somehow, perhaps even through divine intervention, he was going to be her husband, and she could kiss him every day for the rest of her life.

Until Walter had proposed to her several months before and told her Niall was to wed another, Bella had never thought about how devastating that news was. Oh, how she'd sulked the past few months. So it could be nothing short of a miracle that the stars had aligned, for here he was. And he was no longer attached, having agreed to be her husband, and he'd kissed her. Delicious and charming.

Bella flopped once more on the bed, curling into a ball and ignoring the irritated huff from her sister.

Oh, how that kiss had stirred her, still stirred her. It had made her blood burst into flames, and the embers were still burning somewhere deep in her belly. Niall's kiss had the power to make her heart sing, had a thousand stories multiplying in her mind, and had her editing the epic kisses she'd written about in all her tragic tales. His kiss had shown her all she'd gotten wrong with kisses before, both in thought and theory.

And what was she to do with these new feelings? What was she to do with him and his kiss?

Och, but was this a romantic tale doomed to end in tragedy? Aye, didn't they all? She was deathly afraid it might.

And not because she feared that Niall would not be able to fight in the tournament on the morrow. Quite the opposite. She was certain he would win, for she knew him to be one of the greatest warriors in Scotland. Before his accident, he could have fought any man blindfolded. She had every confidence in his ability. That wasn't what had her concerned. What she wasn't certain of was whether or not the gods and fey would allow her this happiness. Was it just a tease? A way to taunt her? A wretched jest to dangle what appeared to be the most perfect union. For all of her life, aye, she'd been privileged, but not in this. For all the years she'd known about what it took to be a woman, she'd known her failings in that regard. Bella would fail any husband who wished for an heir. She was barren. Knew this for a fact. How was it that she should find a man so equally afflicted?

"Bella!" Greer's voice jolted into her thoughts. "What is going on with ye?"

Bella rolled to her other side and faced her sister in the dark. "Something's happened. Something...unexpected, and yet utterly amazing."

"Out with it, ye canna just say that and keep it in." Greer's voice bubbled with excitement. She loved gossip, especially anything that might prove to be scandalous."

Bella smiled, shocked that their youngest sister, Blair, had not gloated to Greer that she knew a secret. There was no point holding it in, she was fairly bursting with the need to shout it out. "I am to be married."

Greer sat straight up in bed, her shadowy form outlined by the dim light coming from the banked fire. "Married? To who, and why did ye not say something earlier? No wonder ye've been flopping abut like a fish out of water."

Bella laughed, reached forward and squeezed her sister's arm. "I canna say anything yet as father has not spoken to me formally about it. But *he* spoke to me last night...and he kissed me!"

"A kiss? Tell me everything. Tell me now." Greer clapped her hands.

"'Tis a man I've dreamed about since I was a wee lass. A man who respects a woman with a bow, and isn't afraid of a woman being herself."

Greer shifted on the bed, sitting cross-legged. "Oh, Bella. I think I know of whom ye speak. The lad from the tournament, aye?"

Bella smiled in the dark. "Aye, how did ye know?"

"I might have been a wee one then, but I'd have been blind not to see it. All the clans saw. In fact, they were taking bets on when the two of ye would be betrothed."

"Really?"

"Aye. Da got verra upset about it, saying no daughter of his would be married off at such a wee age."

Bella laughed, wondering what her father thought now that she'd asked to marry Sir Niall, if he even remembered the tournament from all those years ago. She'd have to ask him.

"Well dinna lay there like a leg of mutton," Greer shook her. "Tell me everything!"

Bella told Greer about hearing the princess berating someone, and how Niall had scoffed and told her to marry his brother instead. How the princess had attempted to humiliate him, but instead he'd sounded bored and tired of her. That his self-confidence was catching, and gave Bella boldness stronger than what she'd already possessed. "Da said he could have me if he proved himself well in the tourney, which I know he will, so I am all but officially betrothed."

"And ye're certain he'll do well?" Greer's voice dipped with uncertainty.

Bella pushed up to sitting. "Aye. The man's built like a fortress, and he'd not have agreed to fight if he didna think he had a shot at winning."

"But what of his arm?"

"What of it?" Bella felt herself immediately defensive. Protective.

"'Tis missing."

Bella rolled her eyes, thinking this was a conversation she might have to have often with any number of people. "'Tis not missing, Greer. 'Twas cut off by an enemy."

"Exactly. How's he to fight like that?"

Bella laughed. "Ye know nothing. Have ye not listened to any of my stories?"

"What have your stories got to do with anything, especially with a man with a missing arm?"

"When a man is perceived to be less than he is, that is when he is in fact most valuable. Besides, the man has drive. There's more life in him than any of these other dullards. I bet if we tied his other arm behind his back, he'd still be able to kick their arses."

Greer giggled at Bella's use of profanity. "If ye believe in him that much, I shall, too."

"Good." Bella hugged her sister tightly. "I want everyone cheering him on tomorrow."

Greer nodded. "I will make certain they do."

Even as Greer fell back asleep, Bella lay awake, staring up at the canopy that covered their shared bed. Tomorrow was going to be the first day of the rest of her life. The first day of something new and different, and soon she'd be asked to leave her home and go with Niall to his castle, and then what? A sudden dread filled. Och, but leaving home was not something she'd thought about before, and the idea of parting from her family, of not feeling Greer's warm body sleeping beside her, had a pain stabbing miserably at her chest.

Because she and Niall would not be man and wife in truth, they wouldn't share a bed. How would she stay warm at night and keep the sheets heated with just her own body heat?

Loneliness gripped her.

How could she leave them? And with a virtual stranger? Aye, she knew Niall, had been acquainted with him since she was a lass—but did she really *know* him? What was she thinking? Perhaps she should have convinced her parents to let her wait a little longer. Bella bit her lip, knowing that was impossible, and truly, if she was forced to wed anyone, Niall was by far superior.

Besides, her parents had given her an ultimatum. Choose a husband, or they'd choose one for her.

She'd chosen. And until this moment, she'd believed wholeheartedly that she'd chosen well. This was just a bit of pre-marital jitters. Aye, she'd witnessed it from her aunts and a few ladies of the clan. All brides seemed to have a moment of doubt. Perhaps when she arrived at his home, she would see the right of it.

Oh, dear heavens, she didn't know where they'd be returning to. What was his castle, and in what part of the country? *Dretch*, but why had she not thought of that before now? She'd only been to a few places beyond Dunrobin.

She'd been with her father to Stirling once, and to Edinburgh as well. She visited her cousins, but those were the extent of what she knew of the Highlands. Why had she not paid better attention? What a fanciful fool she was. How could her father have let her walk this path without at least giving her some guidance?

She looked over toward her sister, about to shake Greer's shoulder and tell her that perhaps there wasn't cause for joy, that she needed to run. But there was no use in causing her sister undue worry. This was her problem, and one that would be easily solved. She'd simply have to ask her mother where it was she was headed and when exactly she'd be allowed to come home.

Or better yet, she could ask Niall if he minded overmuch if she simply stayed put. After all, it wasn't as though they'd be able to consummate their marriage, given the fault with his...well, never mind, the princess had adamantly stated he could not lie with a woman, so what use was it if she returned to his castle with him? None that she could see.

Aye, that was the way this little worry of hers could be solved. Niall would be happy to have a wife, and she a husband, but that didn't mean they had to live as such. She could remain here with her parents, and he would be free to go back to doing whatever it was he liked to do.

With that notion in mind, Bella tucked the fur blankets more tightly around herself and fell into a fretful sleep.

When daybreak was upon her, she felt a none-too-gentle shove at her shoulders from Greer and Blair.

"How is it that Blair knew about the proposal before I did?" Greer accused.

Bella rolled over and groaned. "She was spying with me."

"Ye failed to mention that last night," Greer said, arms crossed over her chest.

"Are ye jealous?" Blair laughed. "Jealous of little old me?"

Greer rolled her eyes petulantly. "I am not jealous."

"Then why do ye care?" Blair said before sticking out her tongue.

Bella took her pillow and plopped it over her head so she didn't have to listen to them argue another minute about it. The two of them could argue for hours, even coming to hair pulling and slaps if someone didn't intervene. Bella was too tired to be that person today.

"I dinna care."

"Then stop blubbering on about it."

All right, maybe she did need to regulate, if only to get them to be quiet.

"Both of ye," Bella groaned, tossing the pillow at them. "Quit your griping. We've a lot to accomplish this morning."

"Aye," Greer said, clapping her hands, the row forgotten.

Blair was already running to Bella's wardrobe. "Ye'll need your finest dress."

"And your hair will need to be done just so." Greer reached forward to tug a lock of Bella's hair.

"And jewels. Ye'll need to borrow Mama's best necklace." Blair spun in a circle after opening the wardrobe.

Bella swung her legs over the side of the bed, trying to muster energy and wishing she could somehow harvest it from her sisters. "I'll not be needing any of that. My best dress will not keep me warm in this wintry weather, and with my hair done up, the wind will slither down my neck and freeze any of the fancy jewels ye imagine me wearing." She stood and stretched, reaching high and feeling the kinks in the muscles of her back stretch out. Knowing the castle would be full of people, she'd trained extra hard with her bow a few days ago and still felt the ache of it in her upper back, shoulders and arms.

"Oh, ye're not any fun," Blair pouted, slamming the wardrobe closed.

"Aye, ye're like a glass of sour milk," Greer added with a look of utter distaste. "What will ye be wearing, a thick woolen gown that could double as a grain sack?"

"And your hair in an unflattering plait?" Blair mimicked Greer's tone.

"As a matter of fact—" Bella started, but both of her sisters cut her off with shouts of disapproval.

Their mother chose that moment to enter, eyes twinkling with amusement at her two daughters standing with their hands on their hips and glowering at Bella as though she'd eaten all their sweets. "What is going on? The three of you were making enough of a ruckus that I heard you two floors down."

"Bella wants to dress like a scullion," Greer accused.

Lady Arbella winked at her eldest daughter before turning her attention to the two younger ones. "Oh, aye, dress like a scullion. Now that is an idea. She'll make a statement that I think will go far amongst the clan, do you not think it so?"

"What kind of statement," Blair put out. "The kind that says she is not good enough to marry Sir Niall?"

Arbella gasped. "Why, Blair, since when did anyone's self worth depend on the clothes they wore?"

Greer and Blair turned matching incredulous looks on their mother. "Since the dawn of time," Greer said with an annoyed tone so typical of lassies her age.

Arbella giggled. "I say we should allow Bella to dress any way she wishes. It is not the clothes she wears that has drawn her match to her."

"Then what is it?" Bella asked, wondering if Niall had mentioned something to her father after she'd fled the secret passage.

"Why, your charm, dear. Your wit. Your acceptance."

"Hmm. Perhaps." Bella went to the basin filled with cool water and splashed some on her face. "But I maintain he has agreed because he is in need of a wife, and one who will not bother him. Which, Mama, brings me to a question. Greer and Blair, will ye go down to the kitchens and fetch my breakfast? I'm starved."

Her sisters glowered at her, about to argue, when their mother concurred. When the door was closed behind them, her mother spoke. "Ye know, when I was preparing to wed, my maid, Glenda, told me the oddest things that scared me half to death."

"Like what?" Bella imagined all kinds of crazy things and was glad her own dear maid, Mary, was more sympathetic—and also a mute.

"Just how awful it would be. How messy. How—"

Bella cut her mother off there, having a very good idea where her mother was going with this conversation, and not wanting to hear a syllable more. "Never mind that, Mother, we can discuss it some other time. Closer to the time of well, me needing it." Which she fully expected to put off indefinitely given the circumstances and the lack of bedding that would be occurring in her own marriage. Thank the fey for small favors. "I but wanted to ask your opinion on whether or not it would acceptable for me to remain at Dunrobin?"

Her mother's mouth fell open in surprise. "Why ever would you do such a thing?"

"I am not ready to leave."

"Aye, but a wife's place is beside her husband. I do not think Sir Niall will be amenable to you staying behind. He will need his wife at the castle. His father is unwell and his mother cares for him, not leaving much time for her duties as mistress. You will be instrumental in helping him there. He needs you."

Bella waved away that line of thinking, for the Oliphants had managed long enough without her, they could manage a while more. "And if he was amenable? Would ye and Da allow it?"

"Well, I suppose if Niall wished it..." She tapped her lip. "Though that would be very odd. Has he said something about it?"

Bella shook her head. "Nay, nay, nothing like that, but I had thought to bring it up."

Her mother's face was clear of any censure, though Bella could tell from the way her eyes were partially widened she had much to say on the subject that she was keeping inside. "Well, my advice would be to bring it up after you wed."

"Why?"

"Because if he knows before he says his vows that you wish to remain at home, that may sway him to not agree."

"And so ye think I should lie?" Bella was incredulous. She couldn't lie to him.

"I did not say that. Obviously, if he asks you about living arrangements, you should be honest. Lying never got anyone anywhere."

Bella chewed her lip, feeling as though omitting the truth was just as bad as lying. "Perhaps I should discuss it with him. Find out what he expects of me."

"That is probably a good idea, but try not to be upset if he expects you to go home with him. After all, his castle will be your castle." Her mother approached and tugged Bella into her arms. "I've always believed you to be a clever and kind, lass. I trust in you and I love you very much."

"I love you, too, Mama."

Arbella held her at arm's length. "And he is the one you want? Out of all the men?"

"We share something special." Bella smiled. "He let me be knight for a day."

"Oh," Arbella gasped. "I had not realized he was the lad from the tournament. How romantic." She sighed and pressed her hands to her heart.

Then her mother began brushing her hair, chattering on about the day, not once bringing up the fact her betrothed was bereft of an arm, never judging, and making Bella feel more excited by the minute. Her sisters returned with breakfast, and they ate excitedly as they pulled ribbons and dresses from the wardrobe, parading around in what they thought Bella should wear.

In the end, she allowed her hair to be styled in something other than a plait. In fact, she left her hair loose around her shoulders save for strands on either side that were braided and looped like a crown around her head. She settled on a practical, warm, and yet still stylish gown of blue wool. When she started to tie on the Sutherland plaid, her mother stopped her.

"If you are to announce your betrothal today, do you think it wise to do so in your father's colors?"

"I am a Sutherland and proud of it," Bella answered. "Any man who marries me should be proud of it, too, and know that my family means everything to me. He is not only marrying me, but joining with our entire clan."

Arbella smiled. "As always, you are the voice of wisdom."

Behind their mother's back, her two sisters stuck their fingers into their mouths to imitate gagging and rolled their eyes. Rather than be annoyed at their antics, Bella laughed, flopping back onto the bed in a fit of giggles.

Everything was falling perfectly into place, and the sun had barely risen.

Chapter Eight

"Get up ye fool." A sharp kick to the back along with roughly spoken words woke Niall from a deep sleep.

He rolled over and glared up at the ogre standing tall in the barely lit barracks. The man's face was covered in a scraggly dark beard, his hair looked to have come straight from a thatch of weeds, and the front of his shirt was stained with last night's supper and Lord only knew what else.

"What the hell was that for?" Niall wished to hell he could pummel the whoreson for stooping to such a low blow. But he had to conserve his energy for the tournament.

"Just a taste of what's to come."

Niall's eyes adjusted enough so he could see the man barking like a rabid beast was, in fact, Eòran MacGregor, another of Princess Elizabeth's spurned beaus. Though there had never been any chance the man would have been accepted by her father as a contender, that didn't seem to cause Eòran any less ire toward those who'd been more successful. The man had lost all sense of pride and bodily upkeep since she'd brushed him aside.

Rolling his eyes, Niall nimbly leapt to his feet, coming within an inch or so of the man's face, showing none of the cowardice he supposed this bastard had expected. "She's all yours, ye filthy maggot. Kick me while I sleep again, and ye'll wake without a foot to stand on —if ye wake at all."

An ugly laugh fell from the lecher's mouth. "Ye're amusing, Oliphant, but not amusing enough for me to waste my time on."

With that said, the man faded into the barracks where men had started to wake and dress for the tournament that was to start after the household had risen and broken their fast.

Niall, too, prepared himself, fully armed, and walked into the dawn light. The bailey of Dunrobin Castle was in full working order with servants and clansmen alike running this way and that. A few chickens chased by a...goat? How odd.

He made his way into the great hall to look for his brother and found Walter breaking his fast at one of the long trestle tables. The crowd was even louder, if at all possible, than they'd been the day before, the excitement over the tournament causing the volume to rise unpleasantly. A cursory glance did not reveal Lady Bella, though her mother sat beside Magnus on the dais. The lady cast him a warm smile, and the earl nodded, his expression unreadable.

Walter patted the bench beside him, but Niall shook his head. Instead, he reached for the bread and a thick slice of bacon, and then walked back outside away from the cacophony. He needed to get right in his head before the tournament began. And that required quiet contemplation. The kick in the arse from Eòran MacGregor had put him in a dark, brooding mood, and flashes of the battlefield, with sharp, glinting swords hacking at his body threatened to take him down. Perhaps fighting in the tournament was a bad idea. He'd not gone up against anyone but his brother, trainer and a few trusted men, since the fateful day that took his arm. What if the past came to the forefront and took over when he was on the list field?

He blew out a frustrated breath and then bit hard into his bread as he marched around the back of the castle to get away from everyone. Aye, he needed to withdraw. What did he care about proving himself to Magnus and the others? He was going to tell Walter he didn't want to be laird anyway, and he didn't need a wife, regardless of how sweet and charming Bella was, or how much his parents wanted him to get married. She deserved a better man than he—a whole man. One who always appreciated her stories and wit. One who could protect her. That man was not him. When he wasn't tucked inside his soul, he was raging on the outside. He ignored the fact that being alone with her last night had brought out some of the old parts of himself he thought dead. That maybe she was good for him.

"Sir Niall." The voice of an angel—or should he say fairy—broke into his internal diatribe.

Niall turned to see Bella approaching, her cheeks rosy in the morning cold. She was wrapped up in a thick, fur-lined cloak with the hood pulled up over her golden hair. A smile curved her lips, and there was excitement in her eyes.

He swallowed his bread and bowed. "My lady, good morn to ye."

"Aye, I do believe it will be a good morning." She glanced at his half-eaten bread and bacon. "I see ye've already begun to break your fast. Are ye prepared otherwise?"

Niall grimaced. "I'm afraid—"

Bella held up her hand. "Dinna say it, warrior. Ye're going to hold your sword with pride."

His gut tightened as he took in the determined look on her face. "I dinna understand why ye care so much. Ye can find another husband. I've no stake in the tournament. No stake in the king's guard."

There was a flicker of something on her face, quickly replaced by that jovial twinkle in her eyes and a smile that said no argument would be accepted. "I dinna care to find another husband. Besides, my father said I had to pick a man—and ye are he. As for a stake in the tournament, well, I think ye're mistaken. I've heard it told Eòran MacGregor has been boasting that even a bairn could beat ye in a fight."

Niall shook his head in disgust. His appetite fading, he passed the bread and meat to a hovering hound and then turned to face the woman who was starting to become the bane of his existence. He was going to make a fool of himself. Choke up.

Even knowing that whoreson was talking about him behind his back didn't help, though it made him angry.

"My lady." He shrugged his left shoulder, showing her the way his sleeve flowed forever vacant. "I must withdraw. I'll only make a fool of myself, and ye by extension. Ye've been verra kind, and I am flattered, but..." His words faded as her face paled.

"I need ye, Sir Niall. Please dinna walk away from me." The knuckles of her hands whitened in front of her as she clutched them at her middle. "I simply canna marry any of the other fools here. I need ye to be my knight for a day."

The words lobbed at him were unfair, and she must have known they would affect him. Well, he wasn't going to play the jester for her. "And I'm just the right fool for ye?"

She shook her head, smiling nervously. "Nay. Ye're not a fool. And ye're braver than ye're allowing for. I, on the other hand, am not so brave. And any other man will no sooner marry me than turn me out."

The lass looked ready to collapse, the vibrancy he'd seen in her quickly fading, replaced by vulnerability she had hidden so well before. He didn't like seeing her like this. This was not who she was. "Why is that?"

She bit her lip and shook her head. What had her so fearful?

"Ye see my affliction, lass, plain as day in this empty sleeve. I wear my weakness in full view of everyone. Tell me yours. Tell me why this means so much to ye."

Bella glanced from side to side then stepped closer to him, her gaze toward the ground as she whispered, "I've never told anyone before."

"Ye can trust me."

The lass looked ready to burst into tears, gripping some part of him that wanted to reach forward and comfort her.

She wrung her hands between them, chewing her lip so hard he feared she'd bite it clear off. Then she nodded.

"I do trust ye. I have since we were bairns, and that is why I chose ye. I am..." She sucked in a ragged breath. "I am barren."

Niall narrowed his eyes. "Ye've been wed before?"

Violet-blue eyes flicked to his, wide as the moon and begging for secrecy. "Nay, but trust me in this. I know it."

What game is she about? "And what makes ye think I would accept a barren wife when another man would not?"

Her gaze jerked up sharply, and she stiffened, growing taller. The redness that touched her cheeks was more than just from the cold. "Because of your...condition."

Ballocks, did the chit truly think that just because he didn't have an arm, he couldn't make love to a woman? He grunted, not wanting to get into the specifics of it with her, as she was obviously very naive. While he'd not made love to a woman in his new condition, he was certain he'd be able to figure it out just fine. Och, but the very thought of bedding her had blood rushing from every limb to his groin. Why did she have to put such thoughts into his mind? He imagined what all that creamy flesh would look like. The way she'd responded to his light kiss in her solar... The lass would be excitable in the bedchamber, bringing all that energy and enthusiasm to the act. Pleasures upon pleasures they'd have. It was enough of an appealing thought to have him marching early to the list field and demanding an opponent.

"I see, my lady. But ye know, as my father's heir, I must have children."

The lass blanched. "But...your condition. And ye said ye were giving up leadership to your brother."

Niall was enjoying watching her squirm. "'Haps I want to keep it."

She squared her shoulders, and though she tried to hide her disappointment and her fear behind an icy veneer, he could see well beneath it. "Well, that is your choice, Sir Niall."

What would she do if he continued to goad her? Would that veneer shatter? Would she slice a sharp edge into him? He kind of wanted her to. "Aye, 'tis."

"And I see ye've made it." She stepped away from him.

Bloody hell, but he wanted her. "I have."

She cast her gaze to the ground, nodded solemnly and turned to walk away. Niall reached for her, his fingers grazing her elbow before he pulled back. Bella stilled, looking over her shoulder at him, so many questions in her eyes. Those around them had stopped what they were doing to watch the exchange. Hell, he hated being the center of attention—though once he'd loved it.

"Ye didna wait to hear my answer," he murmured.

"I assume ye're denying me. Why would I wait to be humiliated?"

The last thing he wanted to do was humiliate the lass. "Five minutes ago, I would have denied ye."

"And now?"

Ballocks, this was a struggle for him. "Ye've sparked something in me."

"Have I?" She whirled to fully face him, that fire and ice back in her gaze.

"Ye're different, my lady. I've known that from the first time I met ye. And never have I met another like ye in all my life. Ye...ye're changing me."

She shrugged. "One person canna change another." She pressed her hand to her heart. "That comes from within."

"Aye. But knowing there is someone who believes in me, even if I dinna know why, seems to make a difference."

"I am just a woman, what does it matter what I believe?"

Niall grinned, heaven help him, but she brought out a side of him he'd buried deep. She made him want to prove to her, to the world, and to himself, that he wasn't a failure as a man. "It matters, trust me, lass."

"All right. Then I shall see ye out on the field." She glanced down at his empty sleeve. "And ye may want to tie that up so it doesna get in the way."

He nodded, his throat tight that she would have thought of it. When he trained, he always tied it. He wasn't sure why he continued to wear shirts with two sleeves to begin with. Perhaps so as not to draw too much attention to the fact that one was empty.

Bella stared at him a moment longer, her expression not revealing what was going on behind those wide blue eyes, and then she spun toward the castle. He watched her go, his stomach tightening with nerves.

The next few hours were going to determine the rest of his life. Was he ready for wherever that road led him?

Chapter Nine

If her nerves didn't calm down soon, Bella was going to chew right through her bottom lip. She sat under a tent, warm stones beneath her boots, and thick fur blankets on her lap. To her left was her mother and father, and to her right, her younger sisters. Her brothers stood with the other men, preparing to fight. Her father would be joining the men before the tournament began.

The king and Princess Elizabeth also joined them under the tent.

They all sat in a line, watching the warriors as they warmed up for what would be a rousing few hours of showing off their skills and strengths.

Warm, spiced wine and sweet treats were being passed around the crowd, with the Earl and Countess of Sutherland having made certain there was enough for everyone in attendance.

But Bella had no stomach for anything. All she could do was search the crowd for Niall Oliphant. And then she spotted him.

The man was as big as a mountain, standing at least a head taller than most of the other contestants, just as he had as a lad. His wheat-colored hair had been pulled back in a tight queue. The empty sleeve had been tied off. Iron-studded leather covered his chest and wrist. That was the only armor and defense he had. His missing arm would have held a targe like the other warriors had to block blows. Instead, he carried a massive claymore that had to be longer than she was tall, the point in the ground, and the hilt near his shoulder. Strapped to his leather belt were a war hammer and a wickedly curved dagger.

The sudden urge to leap up and demand he put down his weapons, that he withdraw, that she couldn't chance him getting hurt, pulsed through her. To hell with this rash spectacle of manhood. Had he not been through enough already? How could she force him to do so again? How could her father? Nay. She'd run away with him. Elope. Force her mother and father to see that Niall was the only man for her.

Bella leaned forward, swiveling to face her father, but Magnus reached over her mother and took hold of Bella's hand.

"He needs this, daughter." Somehow, her father had read her mind.

Bella shook her head, squeezed her father's warm, calloused hand. "He'll get hurt. I canna allow it."

"All warriors can get hurt, love. Niall Oliphant used to be the best warrior in Scotland—bested even your brothers and me. Losing that arm was like losing his life. He needs to know his life isna over."

Bella looked at her father with new eyes then. How was it possible her father had been able to glean all that information? She glanced back out toward the list field and the warriors gathered there. Niall was watching her. His expression was guarded, but even from this distance, she could see a fierce spark in his eyes. She raised her hand, inclined her head to him and smiled. He nodded in return. A man approached him, saying something that caused Niall's grip to tighten on the hilt of his sword. His expression turned deadly, and for a fleeting moment, she could imagine what he must have looked like on the battlefield, and how it must have terrified his opponents.

"I trust ye, father," Bella said quietly.

"He'll be fine, love. Better than fine if I've read him right." Her father stood and approached the field, speaking to the men about the rules of the matches. She couldn't have heard even if she wanted to with the buzzing in her ears. Why had she encouraged Niall to do this? Why hadn't she fought her father on it? Why hadn't she volunteered to take his place?

A few of the men smirked in Niall's direction, and she wanted to leap from her perch and pummel them into the dirt. To show them they were not indestructible. Though some smirked, just as many nodded to him with respect.

Niall was called first against one of the men who'd been smirking at him, the one who'd said something irksome to him just a few moments ago. Eòran MacGregor. The one who'd been attempting to assassinate Niall's reputation all morning. Had her father seen the exchange and wanted to start Niall off with a man who angered him? Didn't he always say that fighting angry left a man weak?

Oh, God...

Bella sat forward in her chair, glad she'd not eaten anything, as she was certain to toss it all up now if she had. Her heart pounded, the buzzing in her ears seemed to have gotten louder, perhaps stemming from the horde of butterflies in her belly.

Back straight, head held high, Niall entered the center of the list, dragging his claymore through the snow, giving off the impression that he could not lift it. And for a moment, she feared he might *not* be able to, even heard a few men call out to him to take up a smaller sword. But then a horn was blown, and he lifted the claymore and swung it in a wide arc before letting it point toward his opponent, to the excitement of the crowd. Not every man could do such with a sword that large. The men circled each other, swords raised. Once. Twice. Three times. Eòran lunged forward, but Niall dodged to the right, surprisingly quick for his large size. This exchange happened half a dozen times. Eòran growled like a beast, but something miraculous had happened to Niall—he was grinning. Confidence oozed from his stance, from his eyes. He was toying with Eòran. Bella found herself grinning, too.

The crowd was starting to cheer for Niall. Not once had he swung his sword or had to block a blow, but he appeared to be taking Eòran on a merry chase. His opponent looked to be tiring as he lunged, swung and missed every time. Sweat wet Eòran's brow and hair, but Niall did not look winded in the least as he dodged this way and that.

At Eòran's next lunge, Niall twisted to the right and kicked out his foot, tripping the warrior. Though Eòran was just as surprised as the crowd, he did catch himself on his hands and knees before his face hit the cold earth. However, that didn't matter, because Niall was right behind him to kick him again, and this time, Eòran did hit the ground and got a mouthful of snow and dirt.

The warrior rolled over quickly, sword swinging and vulgar words spilling from behind his grimace.

Niall laughed and taunted the man by asking who was getting a kick in the arse now, which seemed to make Eòran rage all the more.

When he'd regained his footing, Eòran started swinging his sword wildly. Niall didn't try to duck. Instead, he attacked, arcing his sword and bringing it down with a powerful force. Eòran blocked at the last minute, the sound of steel hitting steel resounding in the quiet. Sparks were generated at the power of the blow. Back and forth they went, and if Bella didn't know that Niall was missing an arm, she would have never guessed. He was more than holding his own.

With a final swing, Niall knocked Eòran's sword from his grip and sent it flying toward the rowdy crowd. Then Niall kicked him to the ground and held his blade at the man's throat. The crowd grew silent, and the whistling of the Highland wind was the only sound besides the beating of Bella's heart.

"Surrender." Niall's voice was surprisingly strong—and eerily calm.

Eòran held up his hands and bared his teeth, letting out a little growl.

"Say it. Say, I surrender," Niall demanded.

"I surrender."

Niall removed his sword from the bloke's neck and took a step back. The crowd erupted into cheers, and Bella leapt to her feet, and the furs fell to the ground. There was a cheer on her lips, and she clapped her hands.

Niall slammed the tip of his sword blade into the frozen earth and marched purposefully toward her, making her heart flip with the look of determination on his face. Oh dear... What was he going to do? He had every right to claim her now, didn't he? Was that not the agreement between him and her father?

Behind him, Eòran came to his feet and made a lunge for Niall's sword in the ground.

"Niall! Behind ye!" Bella shouted, her warning drowned out by the rest of the crowd also calling out their own caution.

Niall jerked around in time to witness Eòran gripping the hilt tight and yanking, but it was stuck. And it didn't matter besides. Niall was on him in a second, pulling his arm back and plowing his fist into Eòran's nose. The crunch of bone filled the air. The warrior stumbled backward and blood gushed as he fell to the ground unconscious.

Bella didn't stop then, she clambered out of the furs tangling around her feet and leapt into the snow, rushing toward Niall in the center of the field. A crowd of warriors had gathered around him, slapping him on the back and gripping his arm with respect. Her father cleared his throat, and the men parted.

"Ye've proven ye're still a worthy adversary. And a worthy man for my daughter."

The crowd began to murmur at that, looking in confusion toward the Bruce, who sat in the stands with his daughter, Princess Elizabeth.

Tears sparked in Bella's eyes. "Sir Niall," she said softly from behind him.

He turned around slowly, a renewed light in his eyes. "My lady."

"I shall soon be proud to call ye husband."

A low murmuring sounded in the crowd, but no one moved to correct them or question it.

He grinned down at her. "And I call myself a lucky man."

Bella's smile crinkled her eyes, and she forced her belly to calm. "Ye did well."

He looked ready to argue with her but then seemed to think better of it and said, "Thank ye, my lady. Your praise is well received."

She stifled a chuckle at how formal they were being when she knew she could speak more candidly with him than anyone else. "Come and sit with me in the tent to watch the rest?"

"I should remain with the men," he started, his gaze flicking toward the tent where Princess Elizabeth and the king sat.

"Nonsense," her father cut in. "Go and sit with your betrothed. Ye'll not be needed until the second round."

But Bella had seen the line of his gaze going toward Princess Elizabeth and knew why Niall hesitated. "I dinna mind joining ye with the men if ye prefer. With your permission, Da." Perhaps she'd even tease a few by declaring that she'd decided to join in the fight.

Magnus narrowed his eyes, then seemed to understand her meaning and nodded. "Of course." He turned and shouted orders, and the servants immediately snapped to attention and brought her chair, a chair for Niall, and the furs and warm stones to the other side of the field where the men waited their turn to prove themselves.

Niall bowed low to Bella, making her heart skip a beat. When he rose, he held out his hand to her. "My lady."

"Sir Niall, when will ye call me Bella?"

"When ye call me Niall."

She slipped her hand in his and smiled. "All right then, Niall. Lead the way."

"My pleasure, Bella."

Oh, if she thought his bow would make her heart skip a beat, hearing her name on his lips was another story. She found herself staring up at him—at his *lips*. They looked warm and soft, yet firm. And she knew they would be, from that simple kiss he'd given her in the lady's solar. And for the first time in her life, she found herself wanting a kiss. But not just any kiss. Niall's kiss. This was the yearning she spoke about in her stories. What had kept her up all night.

But kissing, touching, all of those things led to lying with a man for the sole purpose of procreating.

And she couldn't have children. She'd not been lying when she told Niall she was barren, for it was the truth. Her woman's courses had never come. And when the midwife her mother called had examined her at age sixteen, he'd found nothing wrong with her physically but warned her mother that Bella was indeed barren. Had explained that it happened to some women and not to be overly upset about it.

Her younger sisters had pitied her, until their courses came, and then they, wished to be barren, too, if only to stave off the unpleasantness. Every once in a while, her mother had asked if there'd been any change.

By the time six months had passed from the physician's barren sentence, Bella had grown tired of the questions, the embarrassment.

So to keep everyone from asking, she'd pricked her finger and smeared it on the bed. The excitement that had ensued had caused her to not want to disappoint anyone again. So Bella had grown creative. She'd stolen the bowl of cock's blood from the kitchen, and a few times, she'd done the unthinkable and stolen her sister's rags before they made it to the laundress.

A woman who was barren was broken. Reviled.

She didn't want to be ridiculed.

Glancing up at Niall as he led her toward the chairs, she was suddenly struck with the knowledge that she'd confessed her limitation to him—that he was the only one in all of Scotland who knew her secret. And he'd not scorned her. Had not shied away. He'd said he wanted children, but it hadn't changed his mind about marrying her, because he couldn't lie with a woman anyway. Though he'd not confessed the latter, she suspected he'd been trying to save face by not mentioning it. Princess Elizabeth and the many rumors Bella had heard stated as much though. He'd not been with a woman since he'd lost his arm, and when prodded by the men, he'd told them he couldn't. At least that was what she'd heard.

They were perfect for each other, in her estimation.

"I hope ye dinna mind, my lady, but I will stand beside ye." Niall's voice broke through her thoughts as her father's men set up places for them to sit.

Bella nodded, knowing that for him to sit would put him on a different playing field than the other men, and she'd never ask him to do that. "I'd be proud to have ye stand beside me."

Sitting down, she pulled the furs over her legs, already feeling the biting cold. She blew on her hands and glanced up at Niall, who was watching the next battle taking place on the field. He was so still, only his eyes moved with every exchange. He stood to her left, his right hand resting gently on the back of her chair, silently claiming ownership.

The men did not smirk in his direction anymore, but every once in a while, they would cast approving glances his way.

When it came time for Niall to prove himself in the second round, he was paired against Bella's youngest brother Liam, and the smile left her face.

Chapter Ten

The walk out onto the list field seemed longer than the one Niall had taken when he left the sanctuary of the dark at Dupplin Castle.

Bella's brother Liam grinned at him, but it was a tense smile that didn't quite reach the lad's eyes. They'd gone up against each other before, though it had been prior to Niall's injury. The lad had far more talent than Eòran. Even still, Niall feared hurting him.

Sir Liam was well built, resembling his father's dark looks and size. Though Niall was a few inches taller, they were roughly the same strength—well, they were when he'd had both of his arms. Now, Liam would be a tough adversary to beat, though Niall was fairly certain he could win if forced.

"Want me to go easy on ye?" Liam smirked.

Niall knew this game. Cocksure talk to hide nerves. "And get your arse annihilated?"

"For Bella, I would take a sword or axe to the chest." Liam was serious. Niall knew this, because he, too, would do whatever it took to keep those who depended on him safe.

Bella was one of those people—had been since the day he'd taken up her cause at the children's tournament. "As would I."

"Ye barely know her." Liam spoke the truth.

"'Haps, but I know her strength. She's been with me since the day she named me her lady."

Liam looked at him oddly, perhaps he'd been too young to remember. A horn was blown, and they both raised their claymores. Niall with one hand, and Liam with two.

"We fought against each other in a children's tournament some years ago. I've thought of her ever since." His words faded, and he wasn't certain how to admit that she'd touched him in some way.

Liam nodded. "Ye need say no more. She has that affect on people."

Niall raised a brow, circling the lad. "She'll kill me if I hurt ye."

"Likewise."

The crowd was shouting for one of them to make a move. Bloodthirsty bastards. Niall tuned them out. The only sound was that of his deep breathing. He focused on Liam, watching the subtle change in the muscles of his face, and the twitch of his fingers on the hilt of his claymore. The muscles of Niall's right arm had almost doubled since he'd started to train to handle the massive sword without the use of his left arm.

When he'd been a whole man, he'd fought with both arms, just like Liam. Usually with a claymore and targe, or two broadswords. Maybe a battle-axe and a war hammer. Whatever would bring maximum damage to his enemies. Claymores were massive and meant to be used with two hands. But one of the challenges Niall had put to himself was the ability to use the massive weapon with only one arm. A challenge he'd met head on. Fighting the whoreson who'd woken him up with a kick to the back that morning had been easy. That bastard was too full of fury and self-importance to strategize. He'd underestimated Niall, and as a result had been easy to beat.

But Liam was smart. Niall could see it in the lad's eyes. Besides that, he'd been trained by one of the best warriors in Scotland. Magnus Sutherland had fought beside William Wallace. Robert the Bruce had many a battle to thank the Sutherlands for. And Liam was nearly as accomplished, if not more so, than his father.

Suddenly, Liam dropped to his knees, held his sword over his heart and loudly proclaimed, "I concede to Sir Niall Oliphant, my beautiful sister Lady Bella's betrothed. After watching the way he kicked that bloke's arse, pardon my language ladies, I'd rather keep my pride intact."

Niall grunted, letting the tip of his sword fall to the snow. This was probably for the best. He didn't have to lay hands on his newly betrothed's brother, nor did he have to lose face if Liam beat him. Likewise, Liam wouldn't suffer his sister's wrath, or a few new scars from fighting a one-armed warrior.

Niall returned his sword to the baldric on his back and held out his hand to Liam. "I accept."

He hauled Liam to his feet, grinning when the lad was surprised at his strength. The crowd let out a raucous cheer, and the two men embraced, pounding each other on the back.

When he turned around, Bella was beaming at them both.

"Thank ye," he murmured to Liam. If he was really going to marry the lass, then it was best they not start out with any animosity between them.

"Dinna thank me. Make her happy, else I will call ye out, and next time, I willna concede."

"Ye have my word." And Niall hoped he could keep it.

When Niall reached Bella, he knelt before her, took the hand she offered and pressed his lips lightly to her knuckles. They were cold, and so he breathed on them to make them warm and was rewarded with the slight tremble of her fingers. "My lady."

"Well met," she whispered.

When Niall glanced up into her eyes, something inside him shifted. She smiled down at him, blue eyes twinkling, and he realized in that moment, that to him, she was a guardian angel. His savior. Before meeting her, he'd been perfectly happy to return to Dupplin Castle and spend the rest of his days in a darkened room drinking away his unhappiness. But she'd given him something to live for. His heart warmed, and a sensation flowed through him that he'd never felt before. It was quite unsettling.

Niall stood, not able to take his gaze off her as he did so.

"Walk with me?" she asked.

Niall nodded. "'Twould be an honor." He still held her hand, and she slid her palm up his arm to clasp his elbow.

The heat of Bella's touch, the possessive grip of her hand on his elbow, nearly had him undone.

Once upon a time, he'd taken his position as a bachelor to the extreme. Training hard and cavorting even harder with his comrades and any willing female. Nearly a year ago to the day, he'd been left broken and wishing he'd died in the battle that took his arm. There hadn't been a day that went by when he didn't feel the pain of losing his limb, or the unsettling feeling that he couldn't go on. Until he'd found her again, he realized with a start. Not once today had he had those dark, disturbing thoughts, that doubt that he could succeed or should even at least try at life, any life.

As they walked away from the list field, snowflakes fell from the sky and melted on his cheeks, forming pretty white diamonds on Bella's lashes.

"Ye look beautiful," he found himself saying. There was something profound about complimenting a woman and truly meaning it.

"Thank ye." Her creamy cheeks blushed rose-red, and lips twitched into a soft smile. "Ye were most impressive on the field. I thought ye strong before, but seeing the way ye took down Eòran, I must say, it rivals the strength of my brother and father."

Niall grinned, pleased she'd noticed. His chest puffed a little with pride. "Ye flatter me, lass."

"I suspect that is why my brother did not wish to fight ye."

"I have ye to thank."

"Me?" She stopped walking and glanced up at him with surprise. "I did not train ye."

"But ye encouraged me to go out on the field. Before ye, it is not something I would have done."

"Dinna discount yourself so much. Ye kept training for a reason."

A reason he wasn't sure of. Fighting in secret with those closest to him had been a way to release his anger, to beat the melancholy that surrounded him. He was a warrior, a leader of men, and to have lost half of what he used to protect himself and his people, he might as well be a warrior going into battle without a weapon. And he'd only picked up his sword after—

"I..." He trailed off and then cleared his throat. "There was a time, a verra dark time, that I'd not have come out here today. There might still be dark times to come."

"What do ye mean?"

Niall stopped walking, his legs heavy, and the confession on the tip of his tongue making everything, even the falling snowflakes, appear to slow. "I wanted to die."

"In battle?" Bella searched his face without judgment.

"Aye, and after."

She nodded, understanding rather than pity in her blue gaze. Her grip on his elbow tightened. "Ye thought ye had nothing to live for—after the loss of..."

"Aye."

"And now?" There was hope brimming in her eyes, which sparked the odd sensations running through his chest.

"The future looks brighter."

She chewed her lip. "When ye said there still might be dark times to come, that is what ye meant, living or dying."

Niall drew in a deep breath, contemplating just how to explain it to her. "Aye, sweetling. Today I feel...hopeful. But what's to say tomorrow I will not wish for the...darkness. I understand if ye dinna want to keep yourself tied to me. I will go. All ye need do is ask."

Bella's expression had turned serious. "Nay. I still want to marry ye, and not because I'm afraid my rejection will push ye into despair." There she went worrying that lower lip again. "I, too, feel a bleak melancholy sometimes. But with ye, I feel something, Niall." She tapped his chest. "And it touches me here." She tapped her own chest. "'Tis odd. I've never felt it before." She shook her head and let out a short, disbelieving laugh. "But ye bring me hope. Hope that I'll not have to traverse this life alone. The two of us, we can battle the abyss together."

The place he kept locked up and buried deep suddenly burst open, demanding he accept his fate. The sensation took his breath away, and when he spoke, his voice was tight, "I'd like that."

"Promise me ye'll talk to me if ye feel the darkness coming."

"Ye have my word. And ye, too."

"I vow it." They resumed walking in silence, Bella still clutching his arm, perhaps a little tighter than she had before. Leaning on him for strength.

For the first time since the slash that had changed his life, Niall felt a connection, that someone truly understood him.

He might have lost his arm, but Bella... She had thought to be alone the rest of her life, had been told she'd be alone before she could truly understand what that meant. He was happy he was able to provide her with that little bit of hope, and he wanted to be there for her. Just like she'd been there to push him onto the field of battle again.

When her hand slid down his arm to clutch his fingers, he entwined them in his and brought them to his lips. So slender compared to his and oversize hand. He ran a thumb over the calloused part of her fingers from using a bow, smiling at her bravado.

"I'm a lucky man, Bella Sutherland."

She giggled and rested her head on his shoulder. "Nay, Sir Niall, 'tis I who am the lucky one."

BELLA SHIVERED at the touch of his lips on her fingers. The warmth of his skin, his breath, spread through her. She sighed, her heart doing a little flip as sensations she'd never known coursed their way through her—starting at the place where his lips had touched.

A tenderness.

And the other...feelings, the ones rushing around making her belly tighten, and her blood spark, they seemed like what she sang and wrote about—desire, yearning, tenderness.

Most puzzling was how she could *desire* him? It wasn't supposed to work that way if one was barren. Was it? And did he desire her? Was that even possible in his condition?

Bella chewed her lip, more confused than ever. Why hadn't she paid attention or asked the questions that needed asking? Every time her mother had tried to talk to her about what happened between a man and a woman, Bella had shooed her away, not wanting to know about something she would never need to experience. Being barren had been her whole existence. And barren women didn't lie with men. And men who couldn't...didn't.

And until now, she'd never actually believed she'd end up wed.

But here she was, walking beside a towering giant who made her heart skip a beat and had not only agreed to marry her, but had stepped away from his own darkness and faced his fears in order to prove he was worthy of her. A man she'd pined after since she was a lass.

"Niall." She stopped abruptly and turned to face him once more. "Thank ye."

"I appreciate your gratitude, lass, but for what?"

"For agreeing to marry me, when the last thing ye want or need is a wife."

Niall cupped the side of her cheek, brushing his thumb gently back and forth. Unbidden, she found herself leaning into him.

"Och, lass, but do ye not see? A wife may have been the last thing I wanted, but ye, ye're everything I could have ever dreamed of. I think I do need ye. I think I've known that since the moment we met on the battlefield. Ye're beautiful, strong-willed, and one hell of a storyteller. Ye had the uncanny ability to pull me from my melancholy when no one else could. Do ye know when the princess was denying me, I was not offended, but relieved, because I knew if I was married to her, I'd never be able to live up to her standards. I was—" He clamped his mouth closed, silencing whatever confession had been about to cross his tongue. When he spoke again, his voice was taut, gravelly with emotion. "'Tis I who should be thanking ye, sweetheart. Ye saved me."

Instinctively, she drew nearer to him and then glanced around. They'd walked well away from the tournament and were encased now in a copse of trees. She tipped her head back and rose up on her tiptoes to brush her lips over his.

The day before, she'd wanted to marry him out of convenience, and today—

Today, she simply wanted to marry him, to spend the rest of her life looking up into the eyes of a man who saw her for more than a vessel for bearing children. For the first time, the idea of remaining here at Dunrobin without him seemed bleak. Perhaps she should give living with him a try. She just might find joy having him with her that she'd not known before.

"I want to make ye happy, Niall. I dinna want to disappoint ye."

"Do ye not see? Ye already have made me happy." And then he deepened the kiss, threading his fingers in her hair.

Bella clung to him, curling her fingers in the leather of his armor. All hardness pressed to her soft curves. She gasped when he slid his tongue over her lower lip. He nibbled there, pressing that velvet heat forward into her open mouth.

"Oh," she gasped at the frissons of heat that swelled and surged at his kiss.

How could a kiss make a woman feel this way? Was it wicked? It had to be...didn't it?

"Ye make me feel alive," Niall murmured, sliding his hand down her spine to press against her lower back. "Ye make me want to live."

Nay, it wasn't wicked. Couldn't be. If her kiss gave him the will to live and made her feel like she was flying, then it had to be heaven sent.

All of the sudden, a surge of affection, of tenderness, swept through her. She couldn't have fallen so fast for this man, and yet she was almost certain that she had.

"Oh, Niall," she murmured against his mouth. "I am yours."

Chapter Eleven

The following morning, after breaking their fast, Niall and Bella were wed in front of their king and countrymen. They stood nervously side by side. Her hands trembled so hard that she squeezed them together until they were numb, and beside her, Niall swayed enough times that she worried he might actually lose consciousness.

When it came time for the priest to say, "Ye may kiss the bride," Bella had lost all sense of feeling in her hands and was pretty certain her lips were numb, until she felt the brush of his lips on hers. They were warm and somehow steadied her. Her trembling eased, and his swaying ceased. Bella melted against him then, reaching to grab hold of his shirt when he abruptly ended their kiss, leaving her unbalanced until he gripped her elbow to right her.

A fierce blush covered her cheeks then, and she turned to smile at her parents, seeing them beam with pride. Niall's brother, Walter, was there also, nodding at them with approval, and when she met his gaze, he winked.

A feast followed, with dancing and games. She was too nervous to do either, and luckily, Niall agreed they should sit and watch everyone else anyway, though she had a suspicion he chose to refrain for other reasons. When the sun began to set, Bella was ushered reluctantly upstairs by her mother and sisters, who wanted to help prepare her for bed. The day had been such a whirlwind she barely had time to think. But now that she was in the quiet of the bedchamber she'd had since she was a lass, the reality of being a married woman set in.

They helped her into her night rail and a thin robe, kind enough not to comment on how cold her hands were, or on the shivers that passed through her. Not because she would have to go through with the marriage bed, but because she had no idea how to tell her mother it wasn't going to happen. And what exactly would Niall expect? He'd not spoken to her about it. In fact, when she'd been brought upstairs, he'd promised to be up shortly. Why?

Her sisters took turns brushing her hair and giggling the whole time as they whispered. Finally, Bella took the brush and shooed them away. Their mother, taking note of Bella's anxiety, pushed them out the door.

"Bella," she started, leaning against the door.

Heat rushed to Bella's face, and she was suddenly exceedingly embarrassed at her naivety. "Mama, ye needna say...anything about..." She shifted her gaze away, not wanting to even say the words *marriage bed* to her mother.

"Oh?" Arbella kept any surprise she might have been feeling from her face and tone.

Bella shook her head glancing down at where her hands were folded in her laps. "Niall canna... He is..."

"Oh..." Her mother blushed, speaking softly in her English accent and hurried forward to pick up the brush and run it through Bella's hair that already crackled. "How do you know?"

With her mother no longer looking at her, speaking was a little easier. "I heard Princess Elizabeth say so. 'Tis why she refused him."

"I see. And does your father know?"

Bella shrugged. "I didna tell him, but if the princess knows, I'm assuming most everyone must, aye?"

"Hmm. I did not know, and he did not mention it. I would think..." Her mother paused, a sigh on her lips. "Never mind." Her mother waved away whatever she was about to say. "And this is why you chose him, because you fear the marriage bed? There is nothing to fear, darling."

Bella thought her face might burst into flames, and she nodded and then shook her head, confused as to how to answer.

"Darling, your marriage must be able to produce children, to carry on the line."

"Ye have Strath and Liam for that, and Niall has Walter."

"Oh dear. Your father will not be pleased. We could arrange to have the marriage annulled if you wish."

Bella shook her head vehemently and gripped her mother's hands. "Nay, mother. Niall is not the only one who...canna. I am..." Oh, confessing to her mother about her lie was painful. "I am barren, mother."

Arbella let out a nervous laugh and set the brush down. She put her hands on Bella's shoulders, massaging gently. "Nay, my darling, you merely came into womanhood late."

Bella shook her head, wishing her mother's touch would calm her as it usually did. She turned to look up at her mother. "I was pretending. I have never had my woman's courses."

Lady Arbella blanched. "Oh, my dearest child." Her mother tugged her into her warm embrace, and Bella breathed in her familiar, comforting scent. Like baked honeybuns and roses. She closed her eyes and felt tears gather but pushed them away.

"Dinna pity me, Mama, I couldna live with that."

"I just want you to be happy, and...well, being able to lie with your husband..."

"We will be happy, even without that. I know it in my heart. Please dinna tell Da. Dinna annul my marriage. I wanted him, Mama. Please."

"All right." Her mother pressed her hands to Bella's cheeks and swiped at the tears that dripped. Before she could say anything more, there came a knock at the door and the sound of men singing. "Your husband has come."

"Make them go." Bella was quick to wipe the rest of the tears away with the sleeve of her gown. I dinna want them to...stay."

Though it was customary for the guests to put the groom and bride to bed, since there would be no consummation, and Bella did not want anyone to know that, her mother agreed.

Niall came into the room towering over everyone and grinned at Bella with pride. "My beautiful wife."

"My handsome husband." She blushed from the top of her head clear to her toes, and smiled like a bride who was excited about what was to come next.

Lady Sutherland shooed all the men from the room when they tried to squeeze in.

"Good night," her mother said with a soft smile.

She closed the door and their singing passed down the hall. Bella was relieved for the reprieve from a time-honored tradition. Neither one of them needed the crowd to witness the embarrassment of a husband and wife who could not consummate their marriage.

Well, it was best to get this over with. To rush through the formalities and go to sleep. Perhaps a goodnight kiss would be hers to have. They'd not had a moment alone to kiss beyond the brief press of lips at the ceremony, or since the day before when they'd hidden in the trees. "There is no need for ye to sleep on the floor," she murmured.

Niall raised a brow. "The floor?"

"Aye. I had assumed that was what ye'd do." She wrinkled her brow in confusion. "But since neither of us can..." She waved her hand toward the bed. "Then what harm can it do for us to share a bed?"

"Neither of us can what?" Niall raised a brow, looking so incredibly handsome and roguish at the moment her knees knocked together and her belly fluttered.

Bella cleared her throat, trying to sound completely unaffected. "Have children."

"I've no proof, not like ye, lass, but what does having children have to do with it?"

No proof? Were the whispers she'd heard untrue?

She swallowed hard around the lump that had formed in her throat, trying to concentrate as she watched Niall unpin his plaid and belt. The fabric of his plaid slowly unfurled, leaving him to stand in his leine, the shirt coming to just above his knees.

He sat on a chair and started to unlace a boot.

Bella rushed forward and knelt before him, as she was certain a wife should, and took over the task. He smelled clean, as though he'd bathed right before coming to her. In fact, his hair was still a little damp, droplets sprinkling on her hands. An image of him bathing, muscles rippling as water sluiced over his skin, suddenly invaded her thoughts. She bit her lip at the wicked contemplation and the sudden tightness in her chest, and a shiver seemed to make her skin come alive. *Where did that come from?*

"I heard what Princess Elizabeth said to ye..." Why did her voice have to come out so squeaky?

"About?" he prodded.

Bella tugged off one boot, marveling at the sheer size of his foot. It was easily twice as long as her own. She started to work on the other as he untied the garter around his upper calf and let the hose sag down his muscular leg. She'd have to be blind not to appreciate the beauty of his body. Again, that racing in her heart, the prickles along her skin. And...what in blazes? There was a tingle between her legs, her breasts, too. Her nipples grew taut, and she felt...breathless. And hungry. But not for food. She longed for him to touch her. Wanted to climb into his lap and kiss him. Hard. And with tongues.

"About ye not being whole," she finally managed to say through the tightness.

Niall raised a confused brow. "My arm?"

"And your..." Her gaze fell to where his shirt gathered at his middle, where a bulge had begun to appear. The place where a man had his...

"Ah. Ye thought me to be missing my—"

She was quick to cut him off, already feeling faint, and certain him saying *that* would push her over the edge. "Ye needna say the word. But aye, I believed ye to be...barren, too."

"Did ye now." Humor danced in his eyes and laced his words.

"Aye. I thought that was why ye didna mind having a barren wife."

Niall grinned. "I assure, ye, lass, I am still a whole man where it counts."

"And ye can...have children."

"As I said, 'tis not yet been proven."

"I see." She chewed her lip, sat back on her heels and stared down at his feet planted on either side of her knees. "Ye'll want to try then. With other women."

"What?" He sounded exasperated, and she jerked her gaze back up to his.

"Ye'll want to see, if ye can...with others...so your line..."

He cupped the side of her face and looked at her earnestly. "Lass, if I cared about my line, I'd not have married ye when ye told me ye couldna have children. I wanted to marry ye. And I'll not stray from our bed."

Her heart skipped a beat. "Our bed... So ye expect me to..."

"To lie with me, aye."

"But I canna. I am barren." What was that breathy tone her voice had taken on? It sounded foreign to her own ears.

"That doesna mean ye canna lie with me, Bella." He stroked the side of her face, and she bit the inside of her cheek to keep from sighing.

"Just lie with ye. Beside ye." She swallowed hard when the image of them lying beside each other and him turning to kiss her flashed before her eyes.

"Under me. Over me. Beside me... It doesna matter. I'll have ye anyway."

"Oh..." She did sigh then. "But why? If I canna have children..."

"Men and women dinna just lie together to make bairns."

"Why else would they?" Again, she regretted not allowing her mother to give her further instructions.

Niall leaned down and brushed his lips over hers, and the tingles that were already forming on her skin sprang to life once more, making her shiver as he pressed hard, swiping his tongue over the seam of her lips. He trailed his fingers over her ribs, tickling her, but she didn't want to pull away. If anything, she leaned in closer, wanting his touch.

"Oh my..." she murmured and then gasped at having said the words aloud.

With his lips still on hers, he whispered. "What did ye feel just now?"

"I felt...so many things." *Want so many more.*

"Pleasure?" This he said with his warm mouth trailing over her jawline toward her ear.

"Oh, aye... I like this. A lot."

He chuckled as he scraped his teeth over her earlobe, sending another tawdry shiver through her. "That is why men and women lie together, love, besides for making bairns. For pleasure."

"Pleasure?" She tilted her head to the side as he trailed kisses down her neck. Oh, aye, that was what she was feeling. Her mind was a whirl of incoherent thoughts, but one thing came out loud and clear—she was enjoying his kisses and touch very much, and she didn't want him to stop.

"Aye. I want to make love to my wife."

Saints! Bella gulped, swallowing hard and finding it equally difficult to breathe. "I...dinna know what to do."

A gravelly chuckle came from his lips where they toyed with her neck. "But I do. And I will show ye."

"Oh..."

He trailed his hand down her spine and then circled around her ribs, and if she thought she felt heavy and weak before, that was nothing compared to now.

Niall reached around front and plucked at the ribbon tying her robe closed. The fabric gave way, and Bella shrugged it off her shoulders and let it pool on the floor behind where she knelt.

"We are really going to..." The words evaporated from her mind.

Niall grinned wolfishly, and that look of want in his eyes made her shiver all the more. "Aye, love. We're really going to."

Next, he tugged at the ribbons on the front of her night rail and slid a single finger down the opening between her breasts, making her shiver at the warm contact of his finger on her bare flesh.

"Your skin is so soft. Softer than mine."

Without thinking, Bella reached for him and touched the exposed skin at his throat and unlaced his shirt to touch his chest. A sprinkling of hair covered the exposed skin, and his shirt fell open to form a V over his heart.

"Ye're warm."

He chuckled, the sound like a caress, then pressed her hand to his skin, stopping her from removing his shirt. "So are ye." He bent to kiss her, speaking softly against her lips. "And before this night is through, we'll both be verra, verra hot."

Bella let out a whimper as he snaked his arm around her back and stood, pulling her up against his hard body while deepening their kiss. The feel of his linen shirt against her bare breasts was more sensual than she would have guessed, and she longed to feel herself skin to skin. But when she tried once more to lift his shirt, he stilled her hands. He wasn't ready yet to reveal himself fully to her, she guessed, and she wasn't going to push him, but would rather wait until he was ready.

She wrapped her arms around his neck, on tiptoe now, and press herself tighter against him, gasping at the heat of their bare skin and at the spark of need and hunger it caused.

With his palm at her back, he started to scrunch up her night rail with his fingers, lifting the fabric slowly over her legs until her buttocks were exposed to the evening air.

Bella gasped, thinking at first to pull away, never having been so exposed to a man in her life, but Niall pulled his lips from hers, gazed into her eyes and said, "Do ye trust me?"

Slowly, she nodded, realizing that she absolutely did trust him. With all her heart.

"Take off your night rail. Let me see ye."

Bella took a step back from him, slid a sleeve off one shoulder and then the other, letting the fabric fall around her feet. She stood there completely naked, firelight dancing over her skin, watching as his gaze devoured her.

Prickles of desire rose up on her flesh, and she trembled, but not from cold or from nerves, but with the need to feel him against her, to have his lips on hers, his hand on her back.

"Ye are so incredibly beautiful." Niall's voice was tight, his throat bobbing as he swallowed. "I still canna believe ye wanted me for your own."

"I did, I do. More than a husband in name only. I like the way ye kiss me... I want us to..." She flicked her gaze toward the bed. "Have pleasure."

Niall groaned and reached for her, sliding his fingers over her hip as he drew her back to him. He covered her mouth with his, kissing her deeply. Bella breathed him in, shocked at the contact and delighting in the clean, woodsy scent of him.

He backed her toward the bed, and when her knees touched the mattress, she sat down and scooted back as he covered her with this body. He rolled to the right side of her, her arm cradled behind his back. She drew gentle circles on his spine, wondering at the rippling muscles. Niall trailed kisses down her neck and along her collarbones. The backs of his fingers moved gently up and down her leg, over her waist, then up her ribs to her breast. He cupped the flesh and kneaded it gently, and she moaned, never having guessed that a man touching her would feel this good. His kiss traveled lower, mouth hovering over the opposite breast, tickling her skin, and teasing her tight nipple. When he flicked his tongue over its tip, she arched her back and cried out, not having expected him to do such a thing, nor expecting the sharp tremor of pleasure that went right from that spot to between her legs.

"I love the way ye respond to my touch," he murmured before flicking his tongue out again.

"I..." But she couldn't speak, nor could she even form a thought.

His fingers had moved from her breast to her hip again, and now he trailed them gently over her belly and down over her pubic bone and back.

She instinctively clamped her legs shut, but every time his fingers came back toward her center, she found her legs falling open, beckoning him to touch her in her most sensitive and secret of places.

Still, he taunted her, going back and forth as he laved at her breast and then kissed her hard on the mouth, building a tension and pressure within her until she finally grabbed his hand and pressed it firmly between her legs, gasping at the sensation that shuddered through her, at her own boldness and the feral growl that issued from his throat.

"Och, Bella... Ye're so wet..."

Wet. Was that good? He seemed to think so. He slid his fingers between her folds and found a knot of flesh that pulsed and quickened every time he brushed the pad of his thumb over it. He kissed her again, murmuring against her lips about how much she pleased him. And she hadn't even done anything. He moved back to her breast, sucking her nipple and pushing a finger inside her, and she arched her back again.

Moans and sighs escaped her, and she found herself completely surprised at her reaction to him and wanting more and more.

Niall's fingers worked magic between her legs, caressing and sliding in and out, she writhed with his ministrations, her hips moving up and down of their own accord. Then that fiery tension that had been building and pulsating sharpened into a point, concentrated in her center and exploded outward.

Bella nearly came off the bed, eyes flying wide, fingers digging into his back.

"That was incredible," he murmured against her mouth. "I want to see ye do that again."

"Can I?" She breathed out.

"Och, aye, ye can. Over and over." And he proceeded to show her, stroking her into a fiery passion once more until her body bowed on the mattress.

Except this time, he came over her, supporting himself on his elbow. "Wrap your legs around my hips."

She did as he asked, feeling the plush tip of something hard press to her still-pulsing center. The part of him she'd believed he didn't possess. And oh, how he possessed it. She reached between their bodies and stroked a finger down the long, velvet hard length of him.

Niall's eyes bulged, the muscles in his jaw clenching. "God, lass, if ye keep doing that, I'll not last a breath. 'Twas hard enough watching ye writhe from my touch."

"I want to see ye do the same."

"Oh, sweetheart, I will. Guide me in."

She swallowed, suddenly nervous again. "How?"

"Slide the tip of me between your folds."

Bella did as he instructed, gasping at how it felt when the head of his erection stroked over her sensitive flesh. As she guided him from that knot of flesh downward, he pressed his hips forward, notching himself at her entrance.

"Good, lass. Ye can take your hand back."

"But I like the feel of ye."

He grinned down at her, catching her lips and kissing her deep, his hips pushing forward, the tip slowly entering her. She kept her hand wrapped around him, their hearts pounding against each other.

"This might hurt," he whispered, "but only for a second, and I promise it willna hurt again. Do ye trust me?"

Bella's eyes flew open at the mention of pain, and she gazed into his eyes and nodded. "I trust ye."

"Move your hand. Hold on to my shoulders."

She did as he instructed, holding to the muscles of his strong shoulders beneath his shirt tightly, her legs clutching his hips. Keeping their gazes locked, he surged forward. There was a pinch of pain as he passed through her maidenhead and filled her up, stretching her. The discomfort was not acute, but she still felt invaded and wanted him to move away. All pleasure seeming to evaporate with that one plunge.

"Are ye all right? Did it hurt a lot?"

She blinked, realizing tears had gathered in her eyes, and she contemplated shoving him off. But already the pain and discomfort seemed to be easing. "Not too bad."

"Tell me when it stops hurting."

"Already it fades." And it did. She shifted, getting used to the size of him, and she felt a spark of that heated tension that stirred in her when he touched her with his fingers, only intensified.

"Och, sweetheart, ye feel so good. I'm going to move."

She nodded, and he pulled out of her slowly before pushing back in. Bella had thought when he touched her with his fingers that she'd never felt such pleasure, but with him inside her, there was a whole new amount of euphoria that threatened to consume her.

"Feels...good," she murmured between gasps of pleasure.

"So good." Niall kissed her again, an erotic tangling of tongues. A possessive, demanding kiss.

Bella was a quick learner, lifting her hips to meet his thrusts. She braced her legs higher around his hips, stroking her hands up and down his back, tugging his shirt up so she could touch his bare skin. Even daringly, she roved her caress over the hard, yet soft swell of his buttocks. The man was a god.

That same tension spiraled into her center, threatening to unleash its power, and Bella gave herself over to it—to *him*. Niall led her to a magical place that had pleasure coursing through her, around her, over her. She couldn't think, couldn't breathe, could only feel.

She cried out at her release and felt him shudder over her as he, too, rumbled his pleasure.

When the trembling within them subsided, Niall rolled to the side and tugged her with him. She lay in the crook of his arm as he drew circles on her back and pressed a kiss to her forehead.

"What did ye think?" he asked, a measure of uncertainty in his voice.

"I think I canna believe anyone would say ye couldna...or didna have..."

Niall chuckled. "I pleased ye then, lass?"

"Oh, Niall." She leaned up on her elbow and kissed his chin, not daring to tell him she was now more certain than ever that Princess Elizabeth was a great fool. "Ye pleased me verra much. Taught me even more. And did I please ye?"

"More than I could have ever dared hope for." There was a light in his eyes that she'd never seen before, and it warmed her through and through.

"Are we allowed to do that any time we wish?" she asked, eager to join with him once more.

"Aye," he winked, pinching her bottom. "We are married, after all."

Bella squealed. "Then I wish to do so again."

In one move, he climbed over her, parting her legs. "And I will endeavor to make your every wish come true, Bella."

Warmth spread through her at his words. Oh, but the world seemed to be complete at that moment.

Bella sighed, leaning up to kiss him on his very beautiful lips. "And I ye."

Chapter Twelve

"I wish ye could stay longer," Greer pouted.

"Me, too." Bella pulled her sister in for a hug. Bella had asked that they remain at Dunrobin for another sennight, but given Niall's father's failing health and the many weeks he'd already been gone, they had decided to leave for Dupplin right away. Not to mention that since the weather was clear, Magnus had advised they leave as soon as possible before another Highland winter storm kept them from traveling.

The journey to Dupplin Castle from Dunrobin was going to be a week if they didn't run into any weather problems, which was wishful thinking given that it was winter in the Highlands. But if they were lucky, they might only have to deal with a day or two delay. They had extra blankets and provisions in case anything happened. Niall was well acquainted with the route they'd travel and several inns along the way they could take shelter in each night so as not to camp out in the cold.

"Ye're not far," Bella said when her mother and father approached and tugged her into their arms.

"Not far at all. Come spring, we'll come to Dupplin," her father said, beaming down at her with his soft-gray eyes. Oh, how she was going to miss his morning hugs and the way he challenged her.

"Truly?" Bella glanced up happily at Niall, who had a grin on his face.

"Aye, love," her father said. "We'll make a nice visit of it, and then ye can come to Dunrobin for Beltane."

"We would be honored," Niall said. "My brother will be wed to the princess in the spring, we shall celebrate together there as well."

"Aye."

Bella felt a little better knowing she was going to see her family every few months or so. Besides, after last night with Niall...marriage had taken on a whole new meaning.

They walked out to the waiting horses, Walter and Niall's men, their feet crunching on the snow that covered the bailey. The sky overhead had only a few clouds marring its blue landscape. Walter stood with the princess, and it looked as though their goodbyes were more heartfelt than Bella would have guessed. Princess Elizabeth actually had a genuine smile on her face, and Walter leaned to whisper something in her ear that made her laugh.

How funny the way things had turned out.

Not wanting to drag out the rather somber idea of leaving her family behind, Bella mounted her horse with Niall's help, biting her lip at the feel of his hand intimately pressed to her thigh. Her mother caught her gaze, gave a half smile and winked, as if she knew without Bella telling her that all had gone quite well in the bedchamber. Well, she supposed her mother would have been told about the blood on the sheets, proving that the marriage had been consummated, as witnesses were key in case there was any dispute.

Bella blushed a deep scarlet and waved goodbye to her family, blowing them kisses as she followed the line of horses beneath the portcullis and down the long road to the outer walls. As she went, she breathed in the scent of the ocean air, the pine trees and the crisp smell of winter, trying to memorize exactly the way it looked right then and there. All white and beautiful, with icicles sparkling on the bare branches of the massive oak trees and making the green of the fur needles sparkle.

The clan's children ran behind their caravan, waving and shouting goodbye until their parents called them back.

Tears stung the backs of Bella's eyes. She'd never left the castle without one of her parents, or at least a sibling. And now she was leaving forever. Visiting the castle would never be the same as living there. A brief moment of panic set in. Was she making the right decision?

"Are ye all right, lass?" Niall's soft voice called to her from her left, and she glanced over at him, immediately calmed by his presence and the smile on his lips.

Locking eyes with him, she knew she had nothing to fear. In fact, she had everything to look forward to. He could have been a total stranger, but instead, she was riding off to live with a man she'd been infatuated with since childhood.

Though cold, the ride for the next several hours was pleasant. Niall kept their pace slow enough so as not to jar her, which at first she didn't understand, but soon she became sore in her nether area and knew she would have been quite uncomfortable at a faster pace. Besides that, the roads were covered in snow and icy patches, and to have gone any faster would be a danger to the horses, not to mention themselves. Though the conditions were not ideal, many had traversed the way before them, so their horses where able to trod upon already trampled surfaces, which made the journey easier. In any case, given the circumstances of the road, Niall made mention that they might end up taking a day or two longer than when he'd journeyed to Sutherland lands previously.

"How are ye holding up, my lady?" he asked some time around noon.

"Well, but I think I've a need to stop soon." She blushed. How did one tell their husband that they needed to make use of a chamber pot or bush?

Niall frowned, then his eyebrows rose as he seemed to catch on to her meaning. "Och, aye, I should have thought of that."

"That doesna mean I am weak," she was quick to point out. "Only that I should have perhaps not had that second glass of watered ale this morn."

Niall chuckled. "At least it is not because ye're uncomfortable from...last night." He winked, and she felt her face grow even hotter.

THE HIGHLANDER'S GIFT

Even more shocking, her body reacted instantly to that devilish wink, and yearning coursed through her veins.

She was in fact suffering some minor discomfort, or she had been an hour or so again. Her rear and nether regions had long since gone numb from cold, so she supposed she had the weather to thank for that. Despite that, she wouldn't mind if they found a nice cozy tavern where he could take her to bed and show her once more how much of a man he was.

Niall sent a scout ahead to find a place where they could stop and water the horses. As soon as the scout returned, Niall led them off the road behind the man, and then called for them to pull their horses to a stop. Along with her maid, she found a private spot behind some bushes. She bent side to side, and then reached up trying to stretch out the kinks in back. She shook her legs out, wriggling her feet. Then in an attempt to restore warmth to the rest of her, she sidled up close to the heated mount. Suddenly, she felt another heat behind her, and turned to see her husband towering behind her. Oh, how she wanted to curl against him, to soak in his warmth, and press her lips to his... How was it possible that just a day or two before she'd been completely naïve to the pleasure that could be shared between a man and a woman? To have thought she could never...

"Would ye like anything to eat, lass?"

Bella shook her head, trying to toss away the wanton thoughts and sensations. "Nay, we can carry on a bit longer."

He slid his hand over her arm, absently rubbing. "Good. I was hoping to make it a little farther than this before we made our first stop. If ye're in need of a bite, ye could eat something while we ride?"

Bella again declined, her nerves were such that she didn't want to eat anything while they were in motion for fear of seeing it returned.

"Are ye certain?" he asked.

"I'll be fine."

Niall studied her a moment, as though he were trying to gauge whether or not she spoke the truth.

Bella smiled at him. "I promise."

"All right then." He took her hand in his as naturally as the sun rising, and the warmth of his grasp seeped into her frozen fingers. The leather gloves she wore had long since seemed useful, and since she was riding her own horse, stuffing them into her warm cloak was out of the question. Why hadn't she opted for the thicker ones her father made her wear in winter, instead of this more delicate pair? She chalked it up to nerves.

"Ye're hands are freezing. I can feel it through the leather."

Bella smiled and waved off his comment. "I brought the wrong gloves. I'll live."

"Ride with me for a little while. We can share our warmth, and we'll stop at an inn for the night before the sun sets, where I'll be certain to find ye a seat before the hearth to melt your bones."

She glanced at her maid. "Thank ye, husband. But I could not take such comfort in your offer of sharing warmth for the remainder of the ride if my maid is to ride on her own." She straightened her shoulders. "I am ever conscious of those I mean to care for."

"As am I." Niall whistled to Philip, the warrior closest to him besides his brother. "Take Bella's maid up on your horse."

Without question, the man obeyed, offering to help sweet Mary up. Mary was somewhere between Bella's age and that of her mother, but no one was certain. She was docile as a lamb and quiet as a mouse. She'd been found in the woods alone when Bella was a wee lass, and her parents had taken her in, cleaned her up and cared for her. Immediately, the two of them had formed a connection. Mary had followed Bella around, tried to protect her from anything and anyone, and as Bella had gotten older, she'd naturally fit into the position of her maid. Although she was more of a close confidante. They'd developed a way of communicating together, and were quite close. If she couldn't have her sisters and parents with her at Dupplin Castle, then at least she would have her lifelong friend.

Mary wriggled her brows in Bella's direction and mouthed *handsome* with a nod in the warrior's direction. Bella had to suppress a laugh.

"Will your maid be all right?" Niall asked.

"Och, I'm certain Mary will be just fine." Bella bit the tip of her tongue to keep from laughing or saying anything that would reveal her maid found Philip to be to her liking.

Bella put her foot in the low-hanging stirrup of Niall's horse, smiling at how much lower it was than her own because his legs were so much longer. She reached up to grab the pummel and felt his hand land on her hip and slid lower over her bottom to hoist her up. The heat of his touch seeped through her, which was ridiculous, because there was no way she could actually feel the warmth of him through all the layers, but singed was what she felt all the same.

She bit her lip, glancing down at him to see his intent stare locked on hers as he hoisted himself up behind her, the warmth of his hard body pressed to her back. He lifted her onto his lap and reached around her to take the reins, and she had to suppress a shudder. The sudden full body contact was delicious, and she hadn't realized how much she craved to feel him against her.

"I feel warmer already, what about ye?" he whispered against her ear.

"Immeasurably," she answered, no longer able keep the little shudder at bay when his breath skated over her skin.

It brought back memories of the night before, the way he'd kissed her, touched her, put his tongue to her breasts, his fingers between her legs, the way he'd moved inside her. The very wicked way she'd kissed his torso, flicking her tongue over his nipples just the same as he'd done to her.

How innocent all her stories of love and romance seemed compared to the way he'd taken her in their bedchamber. Niall was a master. She shivered again.

"Shall I get ye another blanket?" Their horses moved back out onto the road.

"Nay, 'tis not that." She bit the tip of her tongue, wishing she'd just accepted the blanket as it wouldn't be a hardship to wear it over her lap anyway.

"Are ye nervous?" Again that whisper of breath on her neck.

"Nay, 'tis not that, either." Oh, dretch! Could she not just lie?

Niall tugged her closer. "What then? Tell me."

"I was but....recalling something." Nope. Not a single lie. All the truth. Every last little bit of it was apparently going to come out of her mouth.

"Oh…" His chest rumbled against her back, and her nipples hardened. "Tell me in a story whatever it is going through your mind."

"Oh…" Bella gasped, knowing she certainly could not do such a thing. "I couldna."

Niall chuckled. "Naughty thoughts ye were recollecting then."

"Aye," she squeaked. If she were able to see her reflection, she was certain the red in her cheeks would match the red of a cherry.

"That is a story I'd like to hear from your lips, but 'haps later on. When we're alone."

Oh, dear heavens—his tongue. The velvet heat of it tickled the shell of her ear, and he chuckled at her stiffened spine.

"What do ye say, wife?"

Bella was having a hard time finding her voice. Speaking seemed an impossibility at the moment. "Perhaps when we're old and gray, I'll have enough gumption to recite it without fainting."

Niall laughed. "Och, lass, if ye can dare any lad to best ye on the field, I've no doubt ye'll do just fine."

"That was a long time ago."

"Ye mean to tell me ye dinna practice now?"

Bella glanced beside her at her horse, now riderless, the reins in Walter's hands, with her bow and quiver tied to the saddle. "Would ye believe me if I said I carried them for sentimental reasons?"

Niall let out a belly rumble of a laugh. "Nay. Especially not since I heard from your brothers that ye still sneak down to the beach in the mornings to shoot."

She grinned. "Then, aye, I still practice. No use pretending I dinna. And ye, do ye shoot?"

Niall stiffened behind her, and she realized the error in her question. But certainly there were plenty of warriors who bore the scars of battle and were still able to shoot? If he'd trained himself to hold a sword, could he not also train himself to steady a bow?

"Not in a while," he finally answered. Then he went quiet and closed off. His laughter died away, and the way his body curved around her seemed to even grow stiffer.

Asking about shooting had upset him, and she could understand why, but no amount of coaxing, no amount of changing the subject or commenting on their surroundings seemed to pull him from the darkened mood her comment had put him in. She would have to be content with soaking up his warmth and not having to pay attention to where she was leading her own mount. In time, perhaps he would return to her.

They stopped near a mostly frozen stream, and the men broke the ice with the hilts of their swords so they could top off their water skins and the horses could drink. They built a fire to warm the riders, and ate a meal of cold chicken and bread, compliments of the cook at Dunrobin.

All the while, Niall stood on the outskirts of the caravan, leaning against a tree and brooding. His brother approached him, said a few words she couldn't make out and then went back to the men. Bella tried several times to catch his attention without success, and when she'd finally had enough, she carried her bread over to him and leaned against the opposite side of the tree, content to wallow with him.

"Who are ye planning to murder?" she whispered, overly conspiratorial and making exaggerated eyes at the men in camp.

"What?" he blanched, jerking his gaze toward hers.

"Ye've a murderous look in your eye. Who is it?" she teased.

"I'm not planning to kill anyone." He frowned, though he did uncross his arm from where he'd had it rooted in place over his chest.

"Are ye certain? Because I'm certain I heard the men taking bets." She jabbed him in the ribs with her elbow. "I want to win the bet, so if ye tell me, I'll wager him, and then we can split the coin."

"Are ye mad, woman?" He turned an incredulous look on her, and Bella burst out into a laugh.

"I'm jesting with ye, husband. Have ye never heard of sarcasm? Here ye are looking as though ye want to skin a man alive. I only wanted to cheer ye up."

Some of the fierceness left him, though he didn't quite smile. "Ye'd best get back to the fire and warm up, my lady."

"Does that mean ye dinna want company? Ye might as well just come out with it, *sir*. I'm not a docile lass in need of my feelings being protected."

"I dinna not want company." He shifted slightly closer, though still keeping enough distance that she wasn't entirely certain of his meaning.

"That's confusing, using the double negative like that."

Niall sighed and turned to face her, the furrow in his brow making him devilishly handsome.

"Ye're vexed." She winked.

"Ye're driving me mad." He dipped his head close to hers, close enough that if she were brave, she could lean in and kiss him.

Well, she wasn't brave enough to do that, so she resorted to her continued baiting instead. "Am I?"

"Did no one ever teach ye to let a brooding dog alone?"

"Nay, canna say as they have." She tapped her chin as though pondering his comment very seriously. "We didna have very many brooding dogs. Not one, in fact."

Niall rolled his eyes. "Ye'll not leave me alone."

"Not likely."

"Well then." He grabbed her arm and whirled her around the back of the large tree trunk, obscuring them from view of their party.

"Och, I see. It's me ye want to skin alive." Bella giggled.

"Ye, and your skin are exactly what I want, but I want ye very much *alive*." He traced a finger over her cheek. "I want to feel your heart beat against mine, and your breath heavy with wanting on my neck."

Bella swallowed hard at the image he conjured. "Then ye'd best kiss me afore I heed your previous demand and return to the fire."

Niall didn't waste time wrapping his arm around her waist and hauling her up to his solid length. A shock of heated desire raced through her at the contact. The sheer size and power of him took her breath, but the look in his eyes—hunger, madness, lust—it made her heart stop beating altogether.

"Ye'll do no such thing. I'm not going to let ye go." And then his mouth was on hers, crushing her, his tongue demanding entrance.

He claimed her with that kiss, made certain she knew just who she belonged to, and how much he could make certain it stayed that way. Bella was ready to fling off her gown and lay on the solid, cold earth while he ravished her in the snow, but he held her still against him, turning her back to the tree as he pressed his solid length against her.

"How is it possible ye can do this to me?" he asked.

"Kissing ye?" she murmured, boldly biting his lower lip. "I'm certain ye've been kissed before."

"Nay. Not like this. Ye make me lose my head. Make me want... Make me feel out of control."

"Oh," she sighed, knowing very much of what he spoke, for she felt the same way. "I fear we will be each other's undoing then, for I dinna want to stop. I want ye out of control, and I want to lose my head. I *am* losing my head."

"Who will save us from ourselves?" he asked, kissing along her jaw, his hand cupping her breast. "Who will stop us?"

"No one. We are on our own. Just ye and me, and this. Oh...Niall, I want ye."

He growled against the pulse point at her throat, and she lifted her leg around his hip, encouraging him closer still.

"Riders," came an urgent warning from one of the men in the camp.

All at once, the hypnotic heat that had enveloped her melted, and Niall was reaching for the sword at his back. "Stay hidden."

And then he was gone.

Chapter Thirteen

The sensation ripping through Niall's chest was not one he'd been familiar with in over a year. Intuition told him exactly what was happening—ambush.

Terror. Dread. The need to shed blood. All of it warred inside him.

The riders, and from the way the ground rumbled there had to be many of them, were approaching at a frantic speed. An unsafe speed. An ambushing speed.

His men had drawn their swords, their backs to each other, and Bella's maid's once sweet face transformed into a silent scream as she ran toward him. It was enough to make his heart skip several beats.

An arrow fired through the trees, narrowly missing one of his men.

Every inch of his body leapt into action.

"She's behind me. Stay with her," he told Mary before searching out Walter, who was shouting orders to the men.

Several squires had the horses and were running to get out of the way as arrows whizzed through the air and struck haphazardly into trees, the fire, a leg, a horse's neck. And then men were leaping from the trees, the MacGregor colors bright on their plaids. Red as the blood they wanted to shed and green as the envy in their hearts.

Ballocks!

Eòran McGregor was out for revenge after their fight in the tournament, that was evident. Niall had wounded the bastard's pride.

Niall hacked at one man after another—and another, and another. En masse, the men attacked him, bypassing the other Oliphant warriors in favor of striking at Niall. It was as if they'd picked him out of the lot to fight, either at MacGregor's order or because they saw his missing arm and figured him for a good target. The reasoning behind it didn't matter at the moment, and as he kicked one man in the chest, shoving him into the bloke behind him, he bellowed in their faces like a madman.

If they thought they'd found a victim in him, well, they'd chosen wrong, for Niall was not going to die this day. If he was to meet Death, it would be by his own hand or by God's grace, not at the end of some ambusher's sword. Not by bloody Eòran MacGregor, who didn't even have the decency to show his face at an ambush he'd clearly organized.

Walter and the other men fought valiantly and with more heart than their enemies, but what Niall wanted most of all, besides victory, was his wife's safety. This wasn't her fight, and there was no way in hell he was going to let her get hurt because of some idiotic vendetta a madman had against Niall.

As he fought, he tried to keep an eye on where their enemy was going, what they were doing, to keep his awareness on the tree where Bella and Mary hid. But with so many of them coming at him, doing so became harder and harder. Sweat dripped from his brow into his eyes, but he fought through it. He didn't have the ability to wipe it away unless he wanted one of the men's blows to land where they aimed.

Then a woman's scream rent the air.

There was only one woman who *could* scream—Bella.

Niall cut through the men in front of him, barreling into those in his way as he charged toward where he'd told his wife to remain hidden. His men swarmed the MacGregors who attempted to stop him, and just before he made it to her hiding spot, a warrior took off at a run from behind the tree, carrying his wife over his shoulder. It was not Eòran, but that made little difference, he could have been a bloody ghost for all Niall cared—nobody was taking her away from him.

Poor Mary lay splayed on the ground, blood seeping from a wound on her forehead. She was unconscious, and Niall called for one of the squires to come get her and keep guard. The MacGregors were thinning out, their ambush objective now obvious. They'd wanted to steal Bella.

"Walter," Niall shouted as he ran after the retreating man. "They've got Bella!"

Bella screamed again, beating at the man's back. Her golden locks had fallen out of the neat plait and waved wildly in the air as she hit the warrior again and again.

Good, lass. Keep fighting.

Niall wanted to shout every obscenity he could, to threaten the man with the most heinous death, but to shout would be to waste the air in his lungs, and he needed to save it all to run as fast as he could.

Bella's gaze, wild and angry, met Niall's as he charged forward, making his heart tug painfully in his chest. She was terrified, and with good reason.

Not once back at the camp when he'd been under attack had he seen Eòran, which meant the rat bastard had sent his men ahead with express orders to ambush them and take the lass, where he would then make his escape with her. Bride stealing was rare nowadays, but not all that unheard of. Usually, it was done before the wedding or shortly thereafter, not after the marriage had been consummated, but Niall was certain that wouldn't make any difference to Eòran. He'd likely make the argument that Niall was incapable as half the country probably thought at this point.

The sound of Walter's steps behind him sent a renewed burst of energy through him, and he picked up speed. From the sounds of it, Walter was not alone. There had to be at least four other men with him. The rest would have remained behind to take care of the MacGregors who had not already fallen or fled. Once done, most would come after Niall to make certain there wasn't a bigger ambush ahead, while others would remain behind with the horses and Mary.

The six of them charged through the snow, slipping on slick parts, but always keeping the MacGregor warrior in their sights. Inch by inch, Niall grew closer. He wanted the bastard's blood so badly he could taste it.

Bella continued to scream, to fight. She was no simpering lass, and he couldn't have been more proud. What she never did was call out to him—even though she kept her eyes locked on him. Maybe she hoped her captor wouldn't turn around and see the Oliphant warriors gaining on him, though the imbecile had to hear them coming. Their footsteps crunched through snow, and they all grumbled and growled like wolves seeking their prey.

So close...

The bastard took a dizzying turn to the right and started to slide on both feet toward a tree. He grappled with the air and let go of Bella, who in her shock was silent, arms outstretched as though she could see the fall happening before it did. All of them could see it. Niall cried out, shooting forward as though he might be able to catch her before she fell, even though it was impossible. The man lost his balance completely then, his fight for purchase leading him nowhere but down. He fell flat on his arse with an *oomph* and a curse.

Bella's head hit the snow hard, bouncing up and then down, her eyes rolling back before they were covered by her hair, and then she lay very still.

Panic rose in Niall, tightening his chest. "Bella!" he shouted.

A breath later, she started to scramble away from the man who'd turned onto his belly and was grabbing for her ankles.

Too late for him—that fall was his end—because it gave the men all the time they needed to catch up with him.

The Oliphant warriors wasted not one second, hacking his hand off where he grabbed at her, then his head.

Bella had barely risen to her knees before Niall dropped his sword and lifted her up into the air against him. His arm tight around her middle, he buried his face in her neck. She smelled of snow and spice and freedom.

She was murmuring incoherent words between sobs as she clung to him, trembling. All the fight went out of her as she lost control. "Mary, where is Mary? They tried to kill her! I think she's dead."

"Mary is not dead," Niall soothed, stroking her back and pressing his lips to her temple. "I promise, sweetheart. She is safe."

Bella let out a shuddering sob and then glanced down at the blood-ied, dead warrior.

"He...he said they would kill me after their laird had his way with me."

Fury rose inside him once more. If—nay, *when*—he got his hands on MacGregor, he was a dead man. "No one is going to take ye away, lass. No one is going to hurt ye. I willna let them."

Niall met Walter's gaze. This meant war.

Not only did he want to battle MacGregor for what he'd done here today, if he didn't seek retribution, any other bastard who got it into their head that Niall was fair game would come looking for a fight.

With his blood still running hot, Niall forced himself to set his wife down. But he couldn't stop touching her. With his sword in the scab-bard on his back, he held fast to her hand. More than ever, he wished he had two arms to sweep her up into them and not put her down. Then again, his wife was not the type of woman who wanted to be carried. And that made him smile. At least by holding her hand, he could keep her beside him, right where she belonged.

"I'm so sorry," he murmured as they walked.

"This is not your fault." Her voice was resolute.

"Aye, 'tis."

"I will not allow ye to take the blame for it, Niall. MacGregor is a madman. And ye canna carry the burden of a madman's choice."

Still, he seethed. "What if he'd gotten ye?"

"I'd have fought, and ye'd have fought."

"But what if we lost?"

"We didna." She stopped walking and turned to face him, her eyes searching his. "We canna worry over what if, only on the future, Niall."

"Ye sound like my brother."

"Ye fought bravely. I've never seen a man run as fast as ye did. I've never seen a man take on so many at once. Your strength and power...'tis godlike."

Niall laughed softly. "Ye'll give me a big head."

"I but want ye to realize all that ye are. Your men respect ye. Leaders in Scotland respect ye. *I* respect ye. Ye saved me. I dinna know how I can ever thank ye."

Niall was hesitant to tell her that if it weren't for him, she wouldn't have needed saving at all. Instead, he let himself believe for a moment that she was right, and how good it felt to have her support, her respect. And he vowed to never let MacGregor hurt her again.

He leaned down and pressed his lips to hers, closing his eyes tightly against the torrent of emotion that flowed through him. He was finding it hard to breathe. So he just stayed like that, still and connected, breathing in her scent and trying to calm the surging in his blood of a dozen or more different emotions.

When he was able to regain his composure, he pulled away. "I promise that for the rest of our days, I will do whatever it takes for ye to keep looking at me like that. To believe in me."

Bella smiled. "Just be yourself."

Niall nodded, his throat tightening again. Her natural acceptance of him took his breath away. But they'd already taken too much time on the way back. They needed to hurry and get the hell out of here before reinforcements arrived. There was no telling how many other men MacGregor had with him wherever the meeting point was. Soon enough, that traitorous bastard was going to come looking for his men himself, and while Niall would love to be there waiting for him, he had to get Bella to safety first.

At camp, his men had already made a pile of the dead bodies and were readying the horses for departure. Two of their mounts had sustained life-threatening injuries and were put down, which only added more fuel to Niall's ire.

As soon as Bella spotted Mary sitting on the trunk of a fallen tree, she ran to her maid and crouched low to make certain she was indeed still alive.

Niall ordered Philip to take Mary up on his horse again, the women would not ride on their own for the remainder of the journey now that they were down two horses.

"We'll take a different route home. Get off the main road. 'Tis too easy to follow us in the snow."

Only when he had Bella in his lap and they were on their way did he allow himself a moment to breathe. But it didn't matter, his ears were pricked, his eyes wide, and every gust and howl of wind had him on edge.

This was not the end. MacGregor would be back, and this time, Niall was going to be ready.

WHEN THE BRIGHT winter light faded to purple, making the diamond-like sparkling in the snow fade, they reached Dornoch, a Sutherland holding on the border of their lands and the Dornoch Firth.

Out of the way, and farther east than the route Niall had originally planned to take, it was the safest. They were admitted into the castle, currently inhabited by Bella's older brother Magnus, who was still at Dunrobin. Everyone called her brother Strath—his nickname, shortened for his title Lord Strathnaver, so he wasn't confused with their father. The servants made up beds, warmed the horses, and fed the warriors. The guards of Dornoch Castle were warned to be on alert for MacGregor's men.

"Should we stay here for a few days? Until he is off our trail?" Bella asked, looking worried as she sat on the edge of the bed in her robe.

Her toes curled into the rug, and she bit her lip over and over, stopping only when she seemed to realize what she was doing. The lass was making a mighty good attempt at not looking worried, but all the same, he could see it. Despite her fidgeting, she was still incredibly enchanting. Her long locks had been brushed out and shined like spun gold in the light of the fire. Niall found it hard to take his eyes off her. It was hard to concentrate on anything other than taking her into his arms and hearing her sigh against his neck, her body melting into his.

"We'll stay one day." Niall lifted a boot onto a bench against the wall and untied the laces, then the other. "Then we'll be on our way. I'll send out scouts in the morning to see if they can find MacGregor's trail."

"Why would he have done such a thing?" Bella shuddered, rubbing her arms in the sleeves of her thin night rail. The movement made her breasts jiggle beneath the filmy fabric and had him instantly hard.

Niall cleared his throat, worked on tugging off his boots and hose.

Then, for good measure so he didn't accost his wife, he went to the wash basin and splashed cold water on his face.

"This is my fault, sweetling. I suspect the man seeks to humiliate me because he lost on the battlefield." No longer able to resist the desire to touch her, Niall sat beside her on the bed and pulled her onto his lap, kissing the top of her head.

"But that's just poor sportsmanship." She toyed with the ties at the neck of his shirt, making him ache to tear it off and press his skin to hers. But he was not yet ready for her to see him in all his scarred nakedness. "If every man attacked another and stole their wife when they didna win a tourney, the entire country would be in an uproar."

"There's more to it than that," Niall admitted. He told her about what had happened that morning, with MacGregor waking him with a kick to the back, and how MacGregor had been angry when the Bruce had chosen Niall over him to marry his daughter.

"Ah, so he's holding a deeper grudge." She was no longer playing with the ties of his shirt, but untwining them until his shirt fell open and the skin of his chest was exposed to the air.

"Exactly."

Bella splayed her hand on his skin, and Niall worked hard not to hiss in a breath at her bold touch.

"I just dinna understand though, husband. He will make enemies of so many powerful people—including the king. Why would he risk that?"

Because of the way he held her with his hand around her back, Niall could not remove her hand from his chest, and he was now finding it hard to concentrate on their conversation as she danced her fingertips over his skin. "A man like that is ruled by his ego and not his mind. He is not thinking ahead, only for the temporary satisfaction of seeing me in pain."

"I hate this." She leaned forward and pressed her lips to the dip in his throat.

"Aye, sweet lass. Battling is never fun."

"And he interrupted our kiss." She dipped her tongue out to tease him further.

Niall groaned. The little minx was seducing him—and doing it very well. "What makes ye more mad? That he came right when I was about to ravish ye, or that he stole ye away from me?"

She giggled and threaded her fingers in his hair, giving a firm tug. "Well, that is a hard thing to answer, husband. For I desperately wanted to be ravished."

Niall chuckled, brushing his nose over hers before kissing her gently. "Well, we are alone now and safe. And ye're doing a good job of reminding me just what I missed. How about I make good on that promise?"

"Oh, aye, I suppose I could allow it this once."

"Just this once."

"Aye, but ye're really going to have to show me that it's worth it."

Niall laid her back down on the bed and moved over her, and in a swift move of his knees between hers, he settled his hardness at the apex of her thighs. "Och, I'll show ye 'tis worth it."

He kissed her gently, then more demandingly, sending sparks of pleasure ricocheting through her. Bella was certain that no matter how many times he kissed her, she would never cease to wonder at the magic of it. The touch of his lips on hers made sparks of fire shoot through her limbs, making her weak and strong all at the same time.

She wrapped her arms around his neck and let her legs fall wider apart, trailing her feet up over his powerful legs and allowing him greater access to her center.

Niall kissed his way between her breasts, using his teeth to tug at the collar of her night rail, tugging it lower to expose her nipples. She ran her hand through his hair, tugging as he sucked one pink tip into his mouth and drove her wild.

"I want ye, I need ye," she crooned, gripping her night rail and hauling the fabric up over her hips, knowing she was acting like a wanton and not caring in the least.

Niall growled, the vibration against her skin enough to make her keen with pleasure. He moved lower, sliding down her body, his tongue wetting the fabric of her gown.

"Niall?" she asked, uncertain of what he meant to do but too curious to ask him to stop.

"Lift your gown up higher."

She did as he asked, distracted long enough not to see exactly what he was doing but feeling it all the same as liquid heat touched her very core.

Bella fell back on the bed, her gown wrapped around her head, as she was too shocked to pull it off when his tongue stroked that very wicked part of her.

She could barely breathe from pleasure—and from the gown suffocating her. In fact, she lay there in a state of pleasured shock for several hard breaths before her fingers figured out what to do. At last, she wrenched off her night rail, arching her back on the bed and crying out. The erotic sensations were intense. Indefinable. How in the world...?

And then that fatal explosion she'd felt before on their wedding night ripped through her in powerful pulsing waves.

"Och, my God, Bella, that was beautiful." Niall slowly crawled up the length of her body, kissing her until he came to her mouth. "I want to feel ye come on my tongue over and over."

"I would be more than willing to oblige ye, but please, first, I want ye inside me." Bella reached between them, yanking his plaid out of the way to feel the velvet hardness of his cock in her palm. She gasped at the heat of him, moaned as she placed him at her entrance and cried out as he drove in hard.

Niall owned her then. He was in complete control of her body, and yet she knew without a moment's hesitation that he would be her biggest champion in anything she did—had proven that so many years ago.

She clung to him, riding the waves of pleasure crashing down around her, and basking in the glow of his encouraging words and shuddering body as he too found that pinnacle moment.

When the weight of him became too much, she nudged him over onto his side and curled up next to him.

"Bella...ye're my light."

She snuggled closer, pressed a kiss over his heart, knowing how hard it must have been to say those words, and knowing just how deep they were in meaning. In the darkness he'd endured, she was the light that brought him home.

Chapter Fourteen

Niall woke before dawn, reaching over to the other side of the mattress to pull his wife against him only to find the bed empty. His eyes popped open. "Bella!" He was frantic as he tore from bed and searched the room, confirming he was indeed alone.

Bloody hell! He'd lost her. Again. In the night, she'd been stolen while he'd slept soundly beside her, so sated from their lovemaking that he'd allowed her to be taken. Even now, she could be halfway across Scotland with that jackal.

Niall ripped open the chamber door, prepared to storm through the castle half-naked, rousing everyone and anyone to help him get his wife back, when he startled to see his wife in the corridor carrying a tray of food and a pleasant smile.

Bella laughed. "Get back inside the room, ye rascal, else everyone see what ye've got hanging below your shirt."

Niall jumped back into the room, seeing that his unmentionables were indeed hanging beneath his shirt, as he'd not fully tugged the fabric down when he'd leapt out of bed in his panic.

"Ye nearly gave me a heart attack," Niall admonished. "Dinna leave me alone like that. Not after what happened with MacGregor."

How the hell had he slept so soundly that he'd not woken when she slipped from the room? Hell and damnation, he was losing it. Marriage was softening him. He was losing his edge, his ability to sense movement in a room.

Bella's face turned serious as she took note of his wide, no doubt crazed eyes.

"I'm sorry, husband. I thought to fetch us breakfast. Ye slept so soundly, I'd not the heart to wake ye. I was starving." She set the tray down on a table and came to stand before him, pressing her hand over his heart where it thudded a little too fast. "Dinna worry, we are safe here. I'd not have left the chamber if I thought there was any possibility of me being in danger."

He clenched his jaw and pressed his hand to hers, not wanting to upset her further. "Thank ye for getting us the morning meal, but please, dinna let your guard down, lass, wherever ye are. We're never fully safe. Please, dinna walk about alone."

Bella tugged her hand away and ran it through her hair. "I dinna want to be made a victim for life, Niall. A woman should be allowed to walk from her bedchamber to the kitchens alone."

He nodded grimly, knowing this and wanting that for her. "Aye, but maybe not just yet?" He took her hand back in his and brought it to his lips. "I promise, as soon as we're back at Dupplin, I'll not be as...overbearing."

Bella wrapped her arms around his neck and leaned up to kiss him, a smile on her lips. "Ye're not overbearing. Your concern for me is endearing actually."

"Is it?" He raised a questioning brow, certain that if he had to deal with himself, he'd be more than annoyed.

"Aye. But if ye're going to lay such ground rules for me, I'll have to do the same for ye. Ye're not to be alone."

Niall chuckled softly. "How about I have ye with me always?"

"That is all well and good until one of us wishes to do something alone and not have company."

Niall frowned. "And what would that be?"

"I'm a lady, I dinna discuss such bodily expulsions." Her skin pinkened.

"Ah." Niall laughed. "All right, the both of us can be alone for *that*."

"Good." She wiped her brow in an exaggerated manner and then kissed him again. "Do ye want to eat?"

"Aye. I'm starved."

Bella took the cloth napkin from overtop the food she'd scrounged in the kitchen. "Some cold mutton, I think, though I canna be certain without tasting, and some oatcakes that are a day or two past their prime, but beggars canna be choosers. And this, I do know, is ale, and it tastes decent enough."

"I see the cook here has his priorities straight." Niall laughed as he sipped the cool ale.

"Aye, ale before food, and everything will be good." She snickered at her little rhyme, and Niall felt a twinge in his chest.

She was truly enchanting. Playful in a way he'd not been in longer than he could remember.

"I'm sorry, Bella," he murmured, tucking an errant golden curl behind her ear.

Big blues eyes looked up at him questioning.

"About what?"

"Yesterday. I should have protected ye."

"Och, Niall, ye did. I'm here now am I not?"

"I know it. And I know I apologized for it already, but ye have to let me do so again. I should never have allowed him to take ye away to begin with."

Bella sighed. "It couldna be helped, Niall. Ye had half a dozen men trying to chop ye to pieces, and only one way in which to defend yourself. 'Tis a wonder ye were able to come to me at all. Ye're a wonder." She touched his cheek as she spoke the words softly and then tucked a piece of meat between his lips. "Ye need not be sorry for it. I am grateful ye came for me."

Grateful was not how he wanted her to feel. It was his duty to protect her, and he'd failed.

"Stop," she said, as though she could read his thoughts. "Let us eat. Let us be happy. We are safe. We are together."

He nodded, though he didn't agree. They weren't completely safe. They would soon leave this castle to continue their journey, and

MacGregor was likely lying in wait. Aye, they'd taken a different path, but once MacGregor realized he wasn't on their trail, he'd likely think of Dornoch Castle and circle back until he found them.

There wasn't any way in hell Niall was going to let MacGregor win that battle. But it didn't mean that Bella wasn't going to get hurt in the meantime.

Niall ate mostly quiet, listening to Bella chatter away about a summer visit to Dornoch when she was little. Mentally, he made a list of every potential place of ambush from here to Dupplin, and then another list of ways in which he and his men could hide their trail as they made their way south.

Luckily, he responded at the appropriate moments, letting Bella believe he was in the jovial mood she wished him to be. He didn't want her to worry. He'd already said too much. What good did it do for her to have to worry over him being worried over her? Besides, mayhap if she were oblivious to the danger, she'd be better off. Aye, he would simply let her be oblivious—and ignore the voice inside that told him that was complete rubbish.

After they ate, they washed in the basin and dressed, separating in the great hall as Niall went to speak with his brother, his men and the guards at Dornoch. Bella went with Mary to the kitchen to talk with the cook about preparing supper for the men.

"Any signs of the MacGregors last night?" Niall asked.

"None," the Master of the Gate said. "All was quiet. But we've not let our guard down. We've doubled the men on the wall and everyone has been informed that there could be an attack. Those in the village were warned and are prepared to light the warning fire if need be. I've sent several men to the village as well to keep them safe."

"Good. Precautions dinna hurt. It is my fervent hope they dinna come. And we'll be gone at first light tomorrow, so the threat to Dornoch will come to an end."

"Are ye certain ye dinna want me to send a messenger to Dunrobin asking for more men to escort ye?" the warrior asked.

Waiting for more men would take time they didn't have. "Nay. If ye can spare a half-dozen, I'd feel better. We dispatched at least half the men MacGregor sent to ambush us. Their numbers are down, and I'm certain we can take them on ourselves, but bolstering our numbers where theirs are lower will be an added protection."

"Aye. We can do that."

"Good. My thanks. Mind if I stand watch?" He was eager to look out over the moors himself and see where they stood.

"Nay, sir, by all means." The Master of the Gate led Niall up the stairs to the top of the ramparts where he could see the firth, the surrounding moors and the mountains in the distance. All was quiet as the sun rose, lighting the nighttime shadows in a pinkened haze that reflected off the ice and snow. The air was crisp—colder than the day before, so perhaps it was a good thing they would remain here for another day. The frigid temperatures meant anything that might have melted the day before was now likely iced over.

He stood there for perhaps two hours, until his fingers and the tip of his nose were numb, then he felt the slight heat of a body at his side and turned to see Bella standing with a steaming mug.

"I thought ye might be able to make use of this," she said, handing him the mug.

"What is it?" Niall wrapped his fingers around the mug, his skin immediately prickled with pain at the heat, but it passed quickly and soon felt only pleasant. It looked like ale with herbs floating on top.

"Warmed cider. Does a warrior's body good."

Niall chuckled. He breathed deep of the spicy drink, his nose feeling similar tingles from the warmth, and then he took a long sip. It warmed him almost instantly.

"A wee bit of whisky in it, too?"

Bella nodded. "Aye. What's a warmed cider without it?"

"Not as good." He winked.

She giggled, and the sound warmed him more than the cider. "I thought ye'd say as much. Are ye hungry? Can I get ye anything? An extra plaid?"

"I'm fine, sweetling. Thank ye."

Bella leaned against the stone and looked out over the moors. "I used to stand up here with my Da. He'd ask me all the things I could see. Made a game of it."

"Did ye ever see anything out of place?"

Bella shook her head and glanced up at him before flicking her gaze back to the moors. The cool air had reddened her nose, and she looked excited and happy. "Once. A lad was running across the field with a white ball of fur chasing after him."

"A wolf?"

"Nay. A sheep." She let out a burst of laughter. "'Twas bleating and bucking, and when it caught up to him, it knocked him clear six feet into the air. He tumbled down and landed on his back, and the sheep walked away as though it were an ordinary occurrence."

"Was the lad all right?"

"Oh, aye." She waved her hand. "But he begged my da to give him a position in the stables or with the chickens. Said he wasna much good with the sheep and feared for his life."

Niall grinned into his mug. "Did your da allow it?"

"For a time, until the chickens started pecking at him, and the horses all kicked and nipped him." Bella shook her head. "A mystery really."

"Where is he now?"

"I dinna know, but after the chickens, me da sent him to work in the fields. He might still be there, unless the wheat roots decided to give him a good whipping."

"Why do ye think he was no good with the animals?"

"Well, he was a wee thing, maybe seven or eight. Turns out he was a might bit too curious, poking their eyes, looking too deep in their ears, trying to see their hooves. He was always muttering about trying to find the toes." Bella shrugged. "He might not have been the brightest candle in the chamber."

Niall chuckled. "Poor lad."

"Aye." She sighed wistfully as though reliving the moments of her childhood right then and there. "What about ye? Have ye seen anything while standing here freezing your arse off?"

Niall was momentarily taken aback by her language, but judging by the way she was flashing him a mischievous smile, she'd expected as much and had done so on purpose to get a rise out of him.

"Just the beauty that surrounds me." He caught her side-eyed glance. "And the beauty beside me."

At that, she turned full around, tapped him in the chest with the tip of her finger and giggled. "Ye're a terrible flirt."

"A fact I well know." He took the last sip of his cider, feeling warm from both the drink and his wife's joviality.

"But I like ye anyway, Sir Niall Oliphant, savior of my person."

"And I like ye too, Lady Bella Oliphant, savior of my sanity."

She checked his cup and seeing it empty, took it from him. "Another?"

"In a little while, aye, thank ye."

"Mind the chill. Come inside soon. At least for the nooning?"

"Aye." Niall brushed his lips over hers, marveling at how they remained warm despite the chill. As much as he longed to pull her into his embrace for a deeper kiss, he had to let her go, else the men on the wall might mock him once she was gone. What was it about her that made him behave like a lovesick lad? Everything about her made him want to be a better man. To behave differently. To be different. He liked the way she made him feel—happy.

He watched her retreat, the gentle sway of her hips. The way the light of the sun shone on her golden hair, and he caught himself when a sigh was ready to escape his lips.

Ballocks. Married for two days and he was already turning soft.

Turning soft would only be dangerous for Bella—case in point not hearing her wake that morning—and he vowed never to let anything else happen to her. Which meant he had to pull back some.

Niall decided to skip the nooning inside and keep watch with the men until night fell, and then he slept a few hours in the barracks beneath the wall before coming back to the watch stand again. Bella did come looking for him, but he ducked away before she spotted him and felt instantly guilty. But avoiding her was the only way he was certain not to be distracted.

When dawn broke on the horizon, he went and woke his wife with a warm tisane, apologized for not coming to bed. He explained he'd wanted to remain with the men in case anything happened, which she easily understood. She smiled up at him with the face of kindness that made him grit his teeth. The woman had some sort of hold on him. One smile, and he was melting despite having been away from her for hours. How was it possible? Wasn't being away from her and denying himself the pleasure of sleeping beside her and making love to her supposed to cure him of the soft spot he felt for her? Clearly not.

Niall cleared his throat and frowned. Luckily, she'd turned away and didn't witness it, because he didn't want to hurt her.

"Come now. Dress. We must be away. Your brother's Master of the Gate is giving us six extra men. The skies look clear, and I'd like to get ahead of any weather. We've still nearly a sennight's ride before we reach Dupplin."

"All right, husband."

All right, husband. So agreeable. He raised a brow at her, thinking there must be something up her sleeve for her to react in such a way. Bella was amiable, friendly, loving, but she was also a schemer and a fighter, he knew that firsthand.

"What are ye up to?" He eyed her as she sipped her tisane, the picture of innocence.

She gave a dainty shrug of her shoulder. "Nothing. Why do ye ask?"

She stood from bed, set her cup aside and turned to face him. The violet of her eyes darkened, her pupils dilating slightly. Then she opened her dressing robe and let it fall to the floor, leaving her naked in the center of the room. She coiled a tendril of hair around one finger. And when he slid his gaze toward her breasts, she seemed to toy with him, absently brushing a trail between the two soft globes.

Niall cleared his throat, feeling all the blood rush from his limbs and straight to his groin. This was a cruel joke, presenting him with her body when he just wanted to escape her spell. How could he resist her? Good God, he was in trouble. Bella was a temptress. And he had not the power to resist her.

"Bella—"

She cut him off with a shake of her head as she sauntered forward, her breasts swaying in rhythm with her hips. "Dinna say anything."

Dropping to her knees in front of him, her eyes locked on his as she ran her hands along his calves, to the backs of his knees. There was a teasing smile on her lips, and every time he opened his mouth to say something, he found himself speechless. And then she ducked beneath his kilt. She pressed her lips to the tip of his cock, and from beneath the fabric, he heard her say, "I want to make ye feel as good as ye make me feel."

Niall groaned, reached for her, threading his hand into her hair. He wanted to tug her away and push her forward all at once. And then her tongue, hot and sweet, was on him, and he lost the last shred of his will to fight when she took him fully into her mouth.

FOR THE REMAINDER of their journey, Niall barely spoke to his wife. Not because he was angry with her, but because he was disappointed in himself for having been talked into marrying her. She was the best wife a man could want, there could be no doubt. She was everything. And he was certain there was no other woman like her in all of Scotland, perhaps the world.

And he didn't deserve her.

He barked orders at his men, was hyper-aware during their daily rides of any outside noise. He stood guard while his wife and her maid made use of the bushes, and hovered over her like a brooding nurse-maid the rest of the time. He did not allow her to ride her own horse, even after they borrowed two more from Dornoch. She didn't seem to mind all of this, and at night, when they were lying beside each other, he let all of his emotions out on her body as he made love to her over and over.

For Bella's part, he could tell she knew something was wrong. But she let him be, perhaps understanding how he might be feeling, or even expecting that when he was ready, he'd share with her. She seemed to have a sixth sense when it came to him. It was just as well, because he wasn't certain he'd be any good at sharing his feelings with her anyway.

Fortunately, they seemed to stay ahead of MacGregor. Scouts did not see any signs of them being followed.

They arrived at Dupplin in the dead of night, with Bella snoring softly against his chest. He asked Walter to carry her up the stairs to what would be their shared chamber. Niall tucked her in and made sure the hearth was lit before he went back down to the bailey to inform his men what had transpired on the road, and that they'd not seen any MacGregor men since.

"'Haps they will not come," Walter said. "Mayhap he just wanted to scare ye. To get even after the tourney."

"Mayhap," Niall acknowledged, but he didn't think so. The man held a deeper grudge than just being bested on the field, and he'd said as much when he'd kicked Niall in the back. Soon enough, he'd have to go after MacGregor himself.

If anything, Walter might also be in danger, since he was going to wed into the royal family.

"He has a vendetta," Niall said. "Against us both. He wanted to marry Princess Elizabeth—and now that ye've taken my place, we're both in danger."

Walter's jawline hardened. "I see."

"Watch your back, brother. If he's willing to attack us on the road and attempt to steal my wife, there is a chance he's willing to do more. He's reckless. Dangerous."

"I'll send a messenger to the Bruce. He'll want to keep the princess extra guarded as well."

"Aye. 'Tis a good idea."

"How is Bella?" Walter asked.

Niall glanced toward the stairs. "Well. She doesna seem overly disturbed by what happened. I dinna know how to take that. The lass is daughter to one of the most powerful earls in Scotland. She's likely seen a battle or two before, but I still want her to be cautious."

"Take it as a good thing."

"Is it?"

"Aye, she's not a whimpering mess." Walter laughed. "The princess would be up in arms."

"This is true." Niall chuckled.

"Get some rest. I'll take first watch with the men."

Niall patted his brother on the shoulder. "Ye know me well."

"I do. Ye'd be up all night and day keeping an eye on everything, but ye canna be everywhere at once. Allow me to help where I can. I'll be here until spring, and then the castle will return to your command once more."

"Ye've been such a huge help to me for so long already, Walter. I couldna have done it without ye." Niall did something he rarely did—he hugged his brother. "I canna thank ye enough. And I will be loathe to see ye go."

"I'd be lying if I didna say I was going to miss ye and everyone else. But pretend I didna say it, else the men will have my ballocks." He squeezed Niall's shoulder. "And we are family, Niall. Blood. Ye needna thank me for doing my duty. I couldna have lived with myself, nor forgiven myself if I didna help ye through the darkest days of your life. I only hope when I'm gone that Bella can do the same."

Again, Niall glanced toward the stairs, thinking of his lovely wife and all the ways she'd attempted to care for him so far. "I dinna think ye have need to worry over it. Bella is...verra capable."

"I'm glad. Now go and sleep beside your wife. I'll wake ye for next shift."

"Thank ye."

Niall climbed the stairs and snuck quietly into the room. He tossed off his plaid, leaving his shirt on as he always did, and then crawled into bed beside Bella. She murmured something in her sleep and rolled over, tucking herself around him as she did most nights.

And he sighed, thinking there was nowhere else he'd rather be.

Chapter Fifteen

"My lady? May I enter?"

Bella stirred at the sound of a maid knocking on the door. How long had she slept? It was clearly well into the morning judging by the way the sun burst in through the window. She bolted upright in bed, stared hard at her surroundings and not recognizing them at all. She called for the maid to enter.

"Where am I?" Bella wiped the sleep from her eyes and watched the maid set out a bowl of porridge and a cup of milk on a table by the hearth.

"Dupplin Castle, my lady." The maid did a good job of keeping the confusion from her tone, but Bella could tell by the slight narrowing of her eyes that she thought Bella might be asking her a trick question. She was not much older than Bella, with dark hair tucked into a bun at the nape of her neck and a belly that looked to be round with child.

"Ah, aye," Bella said, waving her hand in the air as she climbed from bed and tugged on her robe. "I was so sleepy last night when we arrived, I seem to have forgotten. What is your name?"

"I am Annie." She wiped her hands on the front of her apron.

"Thank ye for breakfast, Annie. Might ye know where my maid, Mary, is?"

"Nay, my lady, but I can find out for ye."

"Please, if ye would."

Annie left the room. Famished, Bella approached the table. She sipped the milk and shuddered. Goat's milk. Not her favorite. The porridge had been ladled thick with the goat's milk, too. Well, perhaps she wasn't that hungry after all.

Besides, what she really wanted to do was explore her new home, meet all the servants, the clanswomen and find the perfect place to set up her targets.

With that in mind, she hurried to dress and plait her hair. Mary had not arrived, and neither had Niall. She couldn't wait all day, so off she went. The corridor was empty, but she could hear the sounds of a bustling castle below. She found the stairs easily enough, still rolling her eyes at not having woken at all when she was brought up to bed. Who'd carried her?

In the great hall, she found several women at work. One was weaving rushes, another was sweeping the floors, shooing out about four large wolfhounds that didn't seem at all inclined to listen. Yet another was wiping down the long trestle tables that sat in the center of the hall, parallel to each other.

"Good morning," Bella said cheerfully.

The women stopped their work and glanced at her, perhaps in shock, she couldn't tell. They were all around the same age—a little older than the maid who'd come to her room that morning. They wore white aprons over their *arisaid* dresses in the Oliphant colors, and each had their hair pulled back in the same tight bun as Annie.

"I'm Lady Bella Suth—" She drew in a breath, correcting herself. "I am Sir Niall's wife, daughter of the Earl of Sutherland."

The three women dropped into a curtsy. "My lady," they murmured.

"And ye are?" Bella prompted.

They told her their names, and all three of them were called Sarah.

"How fascinating," Bella said. "Have any of ye seen my maid, Mary?"

They glanced at each other uncomfortably and then shook their heads vehemently, suddenly very interested in their work once more. That did not bode well. Typically, when she'd seen that type of avoidance before, it was because whoever she was speaking with knew exactly what she'd asked and didn't wish to relay the information. Where was Mary? It wasn't like her to simply disappear.

"What of my husband?"

"Minding the wall, my lady." The words from one of the Sarahs was clipped, and Bella could tell when someone wasn't interested in speaking with her. Perhaps Niall knew where Mary had gone off to. She just had to find him.

Right when she was about to open the door, Niall burst through it, his cheeks red from the cold. She was fairly certain that no matter how much time passed, she would continue to be taken aback by how handsome he was. His light hair was wild from the wind and his bronzed skin was flushed and had a shadow of a beard on his cheeks. Cheekbones and jawline looked to be carved from granite, and his green eyes made her want to melt into them. Bella craned her neck as she looked up at him, resisting the urge to wrap her arms around him and pull his body flush to hers, just so she could feel the contrast in his hard muscles to her softer body.

"Ah, ye're awake. Good. I want ye to meet my parents."

Her heart did a flip then. Meeting his parents was necessary, but she was not entirely prepared. She had to make a good impression, and she wasn't wearing her finest dress. Her hair was simply styled, and... and... None of that mattered, because he looked excited for her to meet them, and he didn't seem to think she needed to change. "Oh, aye, I would love to. Are ye certain I should not..." She glanced down at her gown. "Put something better on?"

"Nay, of course not. Ye look beautiful."

Bella nodded and took his offered arm as he led her down a long corridor toward the left tower. Before they climbed any stairs, he knocked on a door, and they heard the faint sound of a woman beckoning from within.

"My da's chamber is here," Niall whispered. "Sometimes he feels strong enough to go outside, but not enough to make use of so many stairs."

The room was dark, the shutters drawn, and a fire was built up in the hearth. The scent of the room was strong with herbs and tinctures, but they didn't quite mask the odor of illness.

"Da, Mama, I wish for ye to meet my wife, Bella, daughter of the Earl of Sutherland."

A lady sat in a chair beside the bed, frail with age. Her dark hair shot mostly with gray was worn in a tight bun, the same as the female servants of the castle. The man who lay upon the bed was also frail and propped up on many pillows. His skin was nearly as pale as the linens, and his eyes were droopy with sickness.

Lady Oliphant did not stand and waited for Bella to approach her, which she did with grace.

"My lady, it is a pleasure to join your family."

His mother did not respond, and instead turned her gaze to Niall. "What happened to the princess?"

Bella felt the slight like a slap, but she kept her emotions hidden, and instead waited to be acknowledged. Not once did she think this would be how she'd be greeted, but she supposed it was a shock to his parents to find him no longer betrothed to the king's daughter, and instead to a much lesser bride of value.

"The princess preferred Walter, and I agreed, preferring Lady Bella for myself."

"That," his father started and then fell into a fit of coughing that sent his wife for a cup of tisane by the bedside table. "That was *not* your choice to make."

"The king agreed, and seeing as how I aim to please my king, I did as I was bid."

"I am still chief of this clan." The older man's bellow was followed by yet another fit of coughing, which earned them both a glower from the lady of the castle.

Leaning over her husband and holding a cup to his trembling lips, she seethed. "Get out. Both of ye. And in case ye're looking for the dull-witted lass ye brought with ye, I had her sent to the kitchens to peel turnips."

Mary.

"Thank ye, my lady," Bella managed, relieved that Mary had not gone too far. "Please let me know what I can do to help ye."

"I dinna need your help," she spat. "All I need is for ye to get out."

Bella felt the tug of Niall's grasp on her arm, and she allowed him to pull her from the room, even as the breath was leaving her body.

Never before had she been treated as though she were nothing more than rubbish.

"I am an earl's daughter," she said when he'd closed the door. "Why is she treating me as though I were..." She tried to think of the worst thing he could marry. "A leper?"

"I'm sorry, sweetheart. They are in shock and aggrieved by my father's illness. While that is no excuse, I beg ye to forgive them for their unkindness. They will come around. I promise." But Niall himself didn't even look convinced.

Bella's feet felt heavy, and she leaned up against the wall, fearing maybe this had been a rash mistake. That choosing to marry each other so quickly hadn't allowed time enough for them to discover what the repercussions of such a decision would be.

"Bella..." Niall stroked her cheek. "Please, dinna fash. Ye're my wife and nothing can change that."

"I know." Still, she couldn't make herself meet his gaze. She'd not been so humiliated in quite a while.

"They will grow to accept ye. I promise. What can I do to make ye feel better?"

Bella perked up at that. Aye, she could wallow for the rest of the day, or she could move forward and hope that his parents did accept her as he said they would. Besides, Niall had enough to worry over. She didn't need him worrying over her hurt feelings. Her ego would heal. "Well, there is one thing I was hoping to do today?"

He wiggled his brows and gave her a wicked grin. "Oh, is there?"

She playfully nudged him in the ribs. "Not that, ye rogue, well, perhaps that, but I meant something else."

Niall chuckled and tickled her ribs. "Well, what is it? 'Haps I can help."

"I believe ye can. At home, I used to practice every day, and I was hoping to find a place where I could set up my targets out of the way. I wouldna leave them up, but 'twould be a place I know I can go when the mood strikes."

"Practice?" Niall cocked his head in question.

"Aye, archery."

"Och, right." Niall pursed his lips. "I think I've a good place, safe, and no one will bother ye. But before we gather your things, I'll take ye there to see what ye think."

"Thank ye, Niall." She laid her forehead against his chest, the steady beat of his heart calming her.

"Ye need not thank me, Bella. I'd do anything to make ye happy. Ye've had nothing but torment since becoming my wife, and I plan to make it up to ye."

Bella smiled up at him, her hands on his shoulders, and leaned up to kiss him. But before her lips touched his, the door handle to his father's chamber rattled.

She leapt away and hurried down the hall like a child about to be caught stealing sweets.

Behind her, she could hear the low timber of Niall's voice as he spoke to his mother, but she didn't wait around to hear what the women's reply might be to whatever it was he said. There was only so much humiliation a woman could take.

Instead, she hurried through the castle, trying to place the kitchens, ducking in and out of various rooms and using her nose as a guide. She was getting closer, judging by the scents of roasting meat and baking bread. The bustle of work grew louder, until she was finally stepping down into the heated kitchens of the castle. The elevated temperature of the room was the first thing she noticed, and then the scents and sounds. Dozens of people were at work. Lads turned spits of meat, women chopped, and scullions churned. The smells were heavenly. The ceiling was lined with drying herbs. The whitewashed walls were blackened near the fires, and the floor was swept clean. Cook shooed three cats from the kitchen and out a window, where they screeched as a hound leapt up to chase them.

Bella searched out the chaos for Mary. Kitchens weren't foreign to her. Her mother loved to cook, and her father even joined her sometimes. As such, all five of the Sutherland children had spent time in the kitchen helping their mother make her famous mushroom tarts and apple pastries.

"What are ye doing in here?" Cook shouted, brown eyes glowering in her direction.

It took Bella a moment to realize the cook was speaking to her. Shaking off her startle, Bella smiled, hoping to disarm the woman from her temper.

"I'm Lady Bella," she said. "Sir Niall's wife."

"Ohhh..." Cook breathed out, wringing her hands, and likely afraid she was about to be berated for having shouted at a lady. "I do apologize, my lady, I didna know. I should have by the looks of ye, but I was... Never mind, please accept my humblest apologies. I assure ye if I had realized, I'd not have spoken to ye in such a way."

Bella waved away the woman's worry, needing more people of the clan on her side than against her given the reception she'd had from Lady Oliphant. "'Twas an honest mistake. Perhaps ye can help me. I'm looking for my maid, Mary."

"We've no Marys here that would be your maid." Cook glanced around as if half expecting to see someone new in their midst.

"Her ladyship said she sent her here to peel turnips."

Cook frowned, wringing her hands in front of her. "Ye wouldna be speaking of the dull-witted lass, would ye?"

Bella felt her anger rise. Mary might be mute, but she was the furthest thing from dull-witted. "I assure ye, she's just as clever as anyone else, she simply canna speak. Where is she?"

"Och, my lady, I sent her on her way. I thought she was a beggar."

Bella felt as though she'd been slapped. Mary was one of her dearest friends. She'd been injured in the woods and now treated so horribly at their new home that she'd been sent *away*? The idea was unfathomable.

Trying not to show her panic, or react in anger, Bella calmly asked, "Where exactly is *away*?"

"I had one of the lads take her outside the gate." Cook was sweating and redder now more than from the heat of the kitchen, clearly understanding she'd made a grave error.

Now Bella could not help herself from exploding. *Out the gate indeed. Into the cold to die.* "How dare ye," Bella seethed. "Even if she was a lonely beggar, rather than helping her, ye'd toss her out? Is that how ye treat the less fortunate at Dupplin? Because where I'm from, we help those in need."

"Aye, my lady, I'm so sorry, my lady. If I'd known—"

"There seems to be a lot ye dinna know." Bella couldn't wait around to argue more. She needed to find Mary before something worse happened to her. "Which lad saw her out?"

"That one." Cook pointed to a lad by the door hauling in a sack of wheat.

"Take me to her," Bella demanded.

The lad looked to cook who nodded. "The beggar lass?"

"She's not a beggar." Bella was aware of her voice rising in pitch and the flinch from several servants, and she regretted shrieking this last bit. "Please, she is my maid, and I need to find her before someone else mistakes her for a vagrant and causes her harm."

"Aye, my lady. Follow me." The lad led her out the kitchen door, through the gardens, pigpens and chicken coups toward the wall and a door there.

"Out here."

"Ye just tossed her out the side gate?"

"Aye, my lady. I'm so sorry."

Bella pressed her lips together, refusing to yell at the lad for doing what he was told. She surged forward, opened the door and stepped out onto the snowy grass. Footsteps imprinted in the snow led to the left, and she followed them around the front of the castle where she found Mary cowering by the lowered portcullis, the guards at the top of the wall shouting insults at her.

"Shame on all of ye!" Bella bellowed, pointing at them and wishing she had her bow and arrow. "Shame!" Tears stung her eyes.

The men were at once silent. "My lady!"

"Open the gates. Now."

"Aye, my lady."

Bella knelt beside where Mary crouched shivering in the snow, tears staining her face.

"I'm so sorry, Mary. I didna know what had happened to ye. I promise, nothing like this will ever happen to ye again, my darling. Come inside. I will see that ye're warmed and fed."

Mary nodded, her teeth chattering. The skin on her cheeks and hands had turned blue, and tears froze on her eyelashes. Just how long had she been outside? At least she had her cloak, but there was still no excuse for how she'd been treated. Bella's chest burned with anger.

As they ducked under the gate, Philip rushed from the outside of the barracks toward them.

"What's happened?" he asked, alarm written over his features.

Mary squeezed Bella's arm and shook her head, perhaps embarrassed at what had occurred.

"She got lost," Bella said, unable to implicate the cook without implicating Lady Oliphant.

"Allow me, my lady. I will see her warmed up and fed." His arms were outstretched, and the look on his face said if Bella denied him, he might just wrestle her for control.

Mary nodded emphatically, signing to Bella and then grabbing hold of the warrior's arm and allowing him to lead her into the castle. He'd wrapped his arm around her and rubbed her shoulder and murmured close to her ear.

"What's this?" Niall found her staring after them in the center of the bailey.

She had no problem telling Niall what happened. "Mary was tossed out by the cook after your mother had her sent to the kitchen. They didna know who she was and so sent her away."

"This is an outrage. I will have them all flogged." He started to march away, but Bella stilled him with her hand.

"Nay, I think she'd rather everyone forgot about it." She nodded her chin toward the couple who were disappearing behind the castle's main door. "I think she might...have an admirer."

"Philip?" Niall looked shocked, then understanding dawned in his eyes. "Aye, I think he is sweet on her."

"Is he...safe for her?" Bella found herself leaning closer to Niall, wanting to feel his warmth. She had not gone back to her room for a cloak, not having the time to do so.

Niall grinned. "Aye. I trust him with my life."

"Then I shall, too."

"I took the liberty of fetching your bow and arrows," Niall said, shifting to show her where they were slung over his shoulder.

"I was so wrapped up I didna see. Thank ye." She shivered and rubbed her arms.

"But I didna realize ye were without a cloak, how remiss of me. I will go and fetch it for ye."

Bella was about to deny him when the doors to the castle burst open to reveal the hurrying figure of Philip.

"My lady." Just then, Philip came back through the doors with her cloak. "Mary insisted I bring ye this before seeing to her own care."

Bella shook her head and smiled. "Tell her I insist she rest the remainder of the day."

"I will, my lady." Philip rushed away, a sure sign he was definitely smitten.

Niall helped her into her cloak, despite her protestations.

"Come, let me show ye where ye can practice." He led her around the back of the castle, through the gardens to the postern gate, their footsteps crunching in the snow. They walked across the whitened moors, passed men training, sweat glistening on their skin despite the frigid temperatures. They stopped when they reached the river which was frozen along the edges. "I know ye practiced by the beach at Dunrobin, and while this is no beach, 'haps the water will bring ye peace."

"Oh, Niall, 'tis perfection. Thank ye." Bella gazed over the river, admiring how it trickled in the middle, skating along the frozen edges and swirling when it danced past a boulder. She could imagine that in the summer months, she would be able to sit by the bank and slip off her boots and hose to dip her toes in the water, just as she used to do in the sea at Dunrobin.

"Give it a go." He handed her the bow and quiver, surprising her from her reverie.

"Thank ye."

Setting the quiver on the ground beside her, she pulled out an arrow, nocked it and then picked a tree that had the perfect knot in its center, like a heart. Raising the bow, she set her mark and let the arrow fly, landing it right in the center of the heart-shaped knot.

"Still an incredible shot," Niall said with a slight shake of his head and a smile on his lips. "Ye amazed me back then, and ye amaze me now."

"Would ye like to try?" Bella asked.

Niall glanced at her sharply, pain wiping away his jovial features. "I canna, Bella. Ye must know that."

Bella wanted to turn the arrow around on herself. How could she have been so foolish and cold-hearted not to remember?

But then again, she found herself less often thinking about Niall's disability. It wasn't him. He was more than the sum of his parts, he was everything. And the way he'd fought the men in the forest, she assumed he could overcome his disability with a bow, too.

"I'm sorry," she murmured, biting her lip. "I think ye can do anything ye set your mind to."

"Dinna apologize. I'm flattered ye think me so capable. But this, I canna overcome." He shrugged his left shoulder. "But I do want to watch ye."

Bella nodded. "All right."

Niall leaned close and kissed her softly, melting away her embarrassment and showing her he did not resent her for asking.

She continued to practice on the various trees, with Niall cheering her on, until she ran out of arrows. Niall was pleasant enough, but she could tell that underneath his enjoyment, his encouragement, something bothered him. The way he longingly looked at the bow, she was fairly certain he wished he could shoot with her.

Well, this couldn't be the end of it for him. He'd loved archery as much as she did. Men without the use of two arms had to be able to still shoot, and she was determined to figure out a way to see it happen.

Chapter Sixteen

"Brother, I've a missive from the king." Walter strode into Niall's study bearing a sealed message. "He awaits your reply."

Niall turned from where he'd been staring out the window. In just about an hour, the sun would set. The sky had been mostly white all day, but it had now taken on a hazy gray, soon to be very black with little light from the moon.

There was a reason he'd chosen that specific spot for Bella to practice shooting beyond the water. He'd chosen it because if she went out without him, he could always stand and watch from here. Not that he'd let her go out without him until MacGregor was dealt with.

Niall cleared his throat and glanced back toward his brother. "Thank ye. Did he say it was urgent?"

"He didna say."

Niall opened the letter while Walter helped himself to a heavy pour of whisky.

"I'm hoping 'tis not that I'm needed to serve my bride by making our marriage official before the spring." Walter tossed back the glass before refilling it.

"Ye can slow down on the whisky, 'tis not that bad." Niall read over the letter. "There is a meeting of the chiefs and lords at Arbroath Abbey to discuss Scotland's independence. The king is asking if father is well enough to join him, and in case he's not, if ye and I will go in his stead."

"Da's in no shape to go," Walter said.

"I agree." Niall tossed the missive onto his desk. "Which means the king will expect the two of us." That he didn't agree with, but how could he argue an order from his sovereign?

"Och, but I pray the princess is not there." Walter refilled his cup as if anticipating an execution.

Niall chuckled. "As I recall, ye didna argue against my request for ye to wed her."

"Aye, I want to help the king. But, ballocks, she drove me crazy at Dunrobin. She has her moments, and I think beneath the cool exterior lies a passionate woman, but she was very intense in regards to what she expected from me and her place in the royal household. 'Twas enough to make a man...well, drink."

"'Haps she'll calm when the vows are said—hopefully before ye drown yourself in my whisky."

Walter shrugged. "And mayhap not. She's not as...calm as your Bella."

"Calm?" Niall chuckled. "Are we speaking of the same lass?"

Walter smirked. "Well, she's docile as a lamb compared to the princess. I believe I will have my hands full."

"That I dinna doubt." Niall wrote out a note to be returned to the king, letting him know that he and Walter would be present at the meeting. Fortunately, Arbroath was only a few hours' ride away, or else he would have had to devise a way to deny his king without making the man angry, because any further away would be too far from Bella in this tumultuous time. Walter took a seat, leaning his head back, eyes closed as if asleep, but his fingers tapped on the arm. Niall cleared his throat, took a seat in his own chair and blurted out, "Ma and Da dinna approve of Bella."

"What?" Walter sat up straighter, instantly alert.

Niall rubbed the spot above his eyebrows that suddenly pinched.

"They expressed displeasure at my having married her. With the poor lass standing right there."

"That doesna make sense." Walter frowned. "I told them I was now betrothed to the princess and they were pleased, even going so far as to say it was a good move."

"Aye, it doesna make sense. Do ye recall if our family has had any issues with the Sutherlands?"

"Da himself sent me to ask for Lady Bella's hand a few months back," Walter continued. "Why would he care if we switched brides?"

Niall shrugged. "I dinna know. But they were both unkind to her this morning when I brought her to them, and I canna for the life of me figure out why."

"'Haps they are simply expressing their displeasure at not having been a part of the decision making. Ye know how hard it must be for Da now that he's bedridden. A man with so much power but too weak to wield it. He spends so much of his day lamenting his failing limbs and doesna let mother leave his side."

"Aye, but she was even cruel, sending Bella's poor maid to the kitchens."

"I did hear about that fiasco. How is she now that Philip has her under wing?"

"Good, I suppose, I've not heard, but judging from the way he was coddling her, and the sweet look of love in her eyes, I'd say 'twill not be long afore my wife finds herself without a maid." And without her oldest friend. Niall was certain it would break her heart to be without Mary. He didn't think Bella would begrudge her friend a love match or a happy future, but from the sounds of it, she'd never been without her.

"Och, but she could still be her maid. Love has never stopped a woman from working." Walter shrugged.

Niall raised a brow at his brother. "What would ye know of love and a working woman?"

Walter wriggled his brows. "I dinna know if ye want me to answer that question."

"I dinna." Niall rolled his eyes. "Mary is more than a maid to Bella.

She's a dear friend. I dinna think they'd be happy to part from one another, even if Mary does wed."

"Ye're likely right. Did she ever mention why Mary doesna speak?"

"Nay." Niall happened to glance outside in time to see three riders on the moor. "Riders."

"Ballocks."

His immediate thought was of the MacGregors. He left the return missive on his desk while he and Walter ran from the study, leapt down the stairs and then outside to the bailey. As he approached the gate, he saw that the men standing guard did not appear to be alarmed. Niall flew up the stairs to look out over the wall himself.

Now he could see why his men were not alarmed. Three of the four scouts he'd sent out had returned. He'd not expected to see them until the morning as he'd specifically instructed them to keep a night watch. Where was the fourth? They drew closer and he could see they were covered in muck and barreling toward the castle as though the Devil was on their heels.

"Open the gate," Niall bellowed. Men tugged on the ropes, cranking the portcullis up as the thick wooden beams were removed from the iron holds on the wooden doors, and the iron lock disengaged.

The men sailed into the bailey, their horses foaming at the mouth and lathered in a mixture of sweat and muck from the hard ride. Niall was there to greet them, looking them over for injury.

The scouts looked haggard as they slid from their mounts and handed off the reins. Their breathing was heavy, and their skin was pale where it showed through the muck. Their eyes were weary as they bowed to Niall.

"What's happened?" Niall demanded.

"We each went our separate ways as ye instructed. North, south, east and west, meeting at the river before we were to start our night rounds."

"Where's Hammond?"

The three riders glanced at each other and then back at him, shaking their heads and looking toward the ground with sorrow. "He didna make it."

Niall gritted his teeth, waiting for them to tell him exactly what happened.

"We circled back to the meeting spot," Adam, the shortest of the three said, "When I arrived, Hammond's body was there, stabbed multiple times. He was still warm. It hadn't been long. If only I'd gotten there faster, I could have helped."

"Or ye too could be dead," Niall said.

The lad shrugged, and Jasper continued.

"I drew up close after that, Adam was still bending over Hammond's body, and we drew our weapons waiting for men to ambush, nearly killed Francis when he arrived. We stood there like that, maybe an hour or more, the three of us guarding Hammond's body. When no one came, we started to take him up onto my horse. His horse was gone. That was when the arrows came. But not one of them landed on us. All of them surged into Hammond's body."

Niall shuddered. Who would do such a thing to a man already gone?

"They came from everywhere," Jasper said, "as though the bastards lived in the trees. We ran. And we didna stop."

"Ye left Hammond?"

The men hung their heads in shame, and Adam's shoulders started to shake. "I've never seen anything so vicious, sir, not even in battle."

"'Tis the devil's work," Francis said, crossing himself, which created a wave of crossing among the crowd that listened in.

"There wasn't a way to carry him with so many arrows in his body. We'd have to break them off and risk getting shot ourselves," Jasper explained.

Niall gritted his teeth. "Aye, ye're right. But this not the work of the Devil. This is the work of a coward."

"More than one, sir."

Niall cracked his neck, feeling his blood surge with the need to thrust his sword into his enemy. "MacGregor has to be behind this."

"We didna see anyone, nor a sign of clans."

Niall turned to Philip, who'd come to stand beside him. "Gather the horses. We'll ride out now and retrieve Hammond and track down the bastards who did this." He glanced up at the sky. "Pack some torches in case we need them. 'Twill be dark soon."

Within minutes, he was mounting, then he heard his name called from the front stairs of the castle.

Ballocks, in his urgency, he'd forgotten about Bella. She ran toward him, worry on her face.

"Where are ye going, husband?"

"My scouts were attacked. We have to retaliate."

He expected her to wail or beg for him to stay, but she nodded solemnly, grabbed his hand were it lay on the pummel and pressed it to her lips. "Godspeed. Make them pay for what they've done."

Niall couldn't help but smile. His wife was a bloodthirsty wench. "I'll ask ye to pray for us while we're gone."

"Aye, for a swift and safe return."

It was only after he'd left her and they were barreling across the moors that Niall realized something else—he had chosen to go into battle and not once had he thought about what he'd lost in the last one.

BELLA STARED after Niall's retreating figure, and then at the darkening sky. As soon as he'd gone beneath the gate, her hands had started to shake. She'd not wanted him to know how scared she was, or how much she worried for him. She'd only wanted to impart her support, and that she believed in him. And now he'd gone off to fight an enemy neither of them knew, and she might never see him again. That seemed hardly fair at all.

They'd only just begun their lives together. And even though she'd been worried about coming here and leaving her family behind, the hope she'd had at a life she could build with him had been strong.

Of course, she was a fanciful, naïve lass, and she would do well to remember it. Head always stuck in her stories. Tales of love and happily ever afters. The real world wasn't like that. How many times had their own mother worried that their father wouldn't come back?

How many times had the great Magnus Sutherland been on his deathbed from battle?

With the trembling that had started in her hands moving up to her jaw and making her teeth rattle, she retreated inside to the chamber she shared with Niall and watched out the window as he and his men grew smaller and smaller until they disappeared into the woods.

Still, she remained there, staring toward the trees, keen for any movement that might mean their return. From what she'd gathered, the men had not been too far. Perhaps they would be back sooner than expected.

Mary entered the room quietly, bringing her a warmed cider with a splash of whisky. She indicated Bella should drink it when she wrinkled her nose at the smell. Then Mary made a show that she would force her to do so if she didn't drink. Dutifully, Bella sipped the cider, admitting it did make her feel a little better. Without words, Mary's eyes showed sympathy. She put her arm around Bella's shoulders as they stared out the window together.

"How silly of me, Mary, ye should also be having cider as Philip went with Niall."

Mary shook her head vigorously, grabbed Bella's hairbrush and began unplaiting her hair. She stroked the brush through Bella's long hair the same way she'd done since Bella was a lass. It had always helped to relax her in the past

But this time, it didn't.

IN JUST UNDER an hour the men arrived at their destination. The ominous gray of the sky had deepened, but thankfully, darkness was held at bay for a few moments longer. Hammond's body lay where the scouts had left him. Though not a single arrow was left in his body, it was so riddled with holes it was clear to see dozens had once pierced his skin. All around the body were boot prints smearing the snow with blood. Whoever had killed him had returned to gather the evidence.

The men stood over Hammond, whispering a prayer for his soul, and then they wrapped him in a plaid.

"Load him up," Niall ordered the scouts who'd come home to report the incident. "Take him back to the castle and see that his body is cleaned and prepared for burial. The three of ye will inform the family and help around their croft anyway they might need. See to their comfort, be the son they lost."

"Aye, sir." They gingerly laid Hammond over a horse brought just for that purpose.

"The rest of ye, fan out. We'll find these bastards."

The first place Niall looked was toward the trees. If the scouts had been ambushed by an invisible enemy, the natural thought was that the men had been perched above, unseen. The forest was a mixture of lush firs and barren oaks. The firs were likely too weak to hold a man at the top, which meant they'd climbed the thick trunks instead.

Just as he suspected, he found boot prints around half a dozen trees. A small party sent to menace his men.

They inspected the trees for any trace of plaid threads or fabric that might have come off, but they found them all to be clean, or at least it looked that way in the fading light. He didn't want to light any torches in case the men still waited. With the snow still covering the ground, it would be hard for their enemy to hide their tracks, though they'd made a valid attempt. The prints went off in six different directions, but all of them lead the same way, circling back around toward the river.

"The light will not hold out much longer," Niall said, muttering an oath. "But if we dinna look now, we could lose them."

"Aye," Walter agreed.

As if fate agreed, the clouds overhead parted, allowing a sliver of the moon to come through and reflect off the white snow on the ground.

"Let's make haste and give thanks for small favors." Niall led his men to a shallow spot in the river to cross over with their horses, but there were no prints on the opposite side, nor in the woods beyond.

The only way to have disappeared like that was if they'd been on a *birlinn* or another small boat. Even on a watercraft, they would have had to get off at some point. Niall split the group into two, sending men south and taking a group north. They traveled for about an hour, until they came to a part of the river that would not have allowed a boat to pass, and there still had been no footprints on either side, at least none they could make out. They turned around and met the men who'd gone south in the middle. They too said they'd come to a waterfall. The men would have had to get out and swim to the shore or else fall over the edge. And there'd been no footprints.

What the bloody hell?

"They canna have simply disappeared." His brother blew out a frustrated breath.

"Aye, we've missed something." *But what?* The sun was starting to set, and soon it would be impossible to keep looking. "We'll go back to the castle for now, send more men out on the morrow when the light is good."

Back at the castle, the mood was somber. One of their own murdered, the rest of them terrorized, and seemingly by a ghost. The villagers were all warned, and those who couldn't protect themselves were brought within the castle walls for sanctuary.

Niall sat brooding in the great hall, nursing an ale with his brother sitting silently in front of him. They'd arrived back late enough that most of the servants had gone home or to sleep. Bella, too, must have gone to sleep. Niall didn't want to wake her or disturb her. To tell her he'd once again failed. That he couldn't protect his people.

"My sons." The sound of their mother's frail voice rattled the two of them into sitting up. "What did ye discover?"

"Mother." Niall sat up straighter. "I'm sorry if we woke ye."

She waved away his words. "I couldna sleep for fear of what might happen. Tell me, what did ye discover?"

"Nothing." Niall sat back, still brooding over what they could have missed.

"Ye dinna have to hide it from me," she said bitterly. "Your father asked me to find out. He is still chief of his clan."

"We tell the truth, Mother. We found nothing but Hammond's body. We go out again in the morning."

She shook her head. "Nay. Your chief has forbidden it."

"What?" Walter asked while Niall sat silently staring.

Perhaps there was more to what Walter had alluded to in the study earlier in the day. That his parents, feeling the threat of age and the loss of power, were becoming unreasonable in the interim.

"Mother," he said, standing up and leading her to his chair where he gently forced her to sit. "Listen, Walter and I are doing what is best for the clan. I am to be laird after Da goes to his reward. Walter is my heir."

She grumbled something about the Sutherland chit not being able to bear children. For a moment, he thought she might have found out the truth, but then realized she was only being as sour as she'd been the day before. That because he'd alluded to Walter being his heir, she'd assumed Bella wasn't capable.

"'Tis not fair the way ye're treating my wife, my lady mother. I'm proud of her, and I want ye to be proud of her, too. Nothing is going to change in that respect, but what can change is that I will call a meeting of the clan elders and tell them Da is no longer able to lead his clan, ask them to take a vote for me to become laird now instead of at his death. They'd be mighty displeased to know that Da and ye dinna think it important to find out who murdered our scout. Who terrorizes our clan."

Their mother pursed her lips. "Ye wouldna dare."

"I would."

"I'd back him," Walter piped in. "Bella was good enough for the two of ye some months ago when Da informed me I was to ask for her hand. She is the reason Niall is not still upstairs in his room brooding."

Niall clapped his brother on the back. "Not entirely. Ye did get me out of there."

"If only because I mentioned the chit."

"True enough."

Still, their mother sat there contemplating. "I will endeavor to be nicer to the gel if ye will allow your father to remain in power."

Niall shook his head. "Ye misunderstand me, Mother. I willna allow Da to put our clan in jeopardy, even if ye are cruel to my wife, though I never pegged ye for bitter woman."

The lady sat back hard enough that Niall feared she'd knock her head into the seat.

"Niall, how dare ye speak to me this way?" Tears gathered in her eyes and he felt instantly guilty.

"I do apologize for offending ye, but I canna allow the clan to falter, nor my wife to be abused at your whim. I love ye, lady mother, but ye have to know that holding on to whatever anger or grudge ye have seems ridiculous."

She crossed her arms over her chest, swallowing hard as she glanced up at him.

"Please, convince Da to let us do what needs to be done, else we will take that choice from his hands."

Their mother stood, and for the first time, he noticed how stooped her shoulders were, how tiny she'd become as her body grew older. The last year had not been good for her.

Niall pulled her into his embrace, and though she resisted, he hugged her still and then kissed her cheek.

"For the clan, Mama."

Without answering, she turned away from her sons and walked back toward the stairs. She stopped at the foot of them and said without looking back, "I will speak to him...for the clan."

Chapter Seventeen

Over the next two days, Niall and his men scoured the surrounding area for any signs of MacGregor, his men, or possibly another culprit, but they continuously turned up empty. Bella waited each night for him to come to their chamber, but each time fell asleep before he arrived. When she woke in the morning, he was gone, but she had a sense of him having slept beside her, and his woodsy scent lingered on the indentation on his pillow. The man was almost like a phantom in the castle. One she could feel and was aware of but rarely saw.

By the fourth day, Niall and Walter could wait no longer to comply with the king's summons. She'd been waiting anxiously for this moment and hoping there might be another message from the king saying they were no longer needed. But such a message never arrived. An anxious knot formed in her belly, for Niall and Walter to journey to Arbroath meant possible danger, and her father had always told her there was a risk any time there was a gathering of lairds, chiefs and the king in one place. On more than on occasion, an enemy had struck out then, causing maximum damage. It also meant that those at home were in more danger, because their castles were left without their leaders.

Of course, Bella was not unused to this. Her father was often away on clan or royal business. Their mother had defended the castle more than once against invaders. And Bella would do the same. That didn't mean she dreaded him leaving any less.

A messenger had left days ago with the reply that Niall and Walter would be there, and if he put it off any longer, he was in danger of angering the king. So he made arrangements with Philip to make daily searches of the surrounding lands and to keep all the men on high alert. All of this she'd overheard when she listened in on various conversations, as her husband had told her none of it outright.

"Be safe," she said, trying to hold a smile on her face, though she didn't feel at all jovial.

"I will. And ye, be safe here. Dinna practice your shooting without an escort. And if ye can, please, dinna practice at all until I get back."

Bella nodded, surprised that he was even giving her the choice. Niall could very well have told her she must remain within the walls, which her father had done many times when he left.

"I mean it. Use caution and never go alone." He took her hand in his and brought it to his lips. "I'd forbid ye from leaving the castle, but I know ye too well."

"Aye, it would seem ye do." She grinned up at him, this time the smile going all the way to her eyes. "I am going to miss ye."

"I will miss ye, too. But I shan't be gone more than a sennight, 'haps a little less."

"Can I not come?"

"Nay, love, not this time. If we were going to court, aye, but from what I gather, 'tis a secret meeting, and I couldna put ye in danger. Your da will be there, and if he sees ye, he'll likely take my head for putting ye in danger."

"This is true." And with those words, he'd all but told her that joining the leaders at Arbroath was a dangerous mission. Her mind whirled with all the terrible possibilities, but she forced herself to put on a brave front for Niall. "Well, then ye must be sure to come back to me. I'll have a surprise for ye when ye return."

"A surprise?" He winged a brow and eyed her skeptically. "I dinna think I like surprises."

She shrugged. "Well, ye'll have to pretend then."

Niall pulled her against him and kissed her tenderly, the touch of his lips warm and fleeting. "I will come back then, if only to appease my curiosity."

"Aye, come back."

She wanted to tell him more, to tell him that if he didn't return to her she'd be devastated, that she'd gotten used to the feel of his warmth beside her at night and tripping over his boots in the dark when she searched out the chamber pot in the middle of the night, though she could have done without that, it wouldn't be the same in any case. She liked his smile, the teasing glint in his eyes when she caught him watching her, the sound of his laugh and the taste of his lips. To think that just a month before, she'd been certain never to marry and would have missed out on all of these things.

Bella watched Niall, Walter and a few of their warriors leave from the bailey to head to Arbroath and then made the climb to her chamber to watch them disappear from the window, the same routine she'd had since Niall started his daily searches in the surrounding lands. Afterward, she made her way down to the kitchens, where she'd made friends with Cook, who allowed her to help with meal preparation. The staff of the castle had warmed to her, and the few times she'd seen Niall's mother, the woman hadn't glowered at her. Instead, she'd made a smile that looked half like a grimace. But it was something, and she'd take it.

Soon enough, she'd find her place and settle completely.

After showing Cook how to prepare her mother's famous mushroom tarts, which would be served at the nooning, she went out to the fletcher's workshop to work on Niall's surprise.

"Have ye got what I asked for?" She smiled wide, folded her hands in front of her and rocked onto her tiptoes with glee. "I am excited to see it."

"Aye, my lady."

The fletcher pulled a wool blanket off of a back table to reveal the special bow she'd had commissioned for Niall. He'd been with the family for years and had made Niall several bows before his accident so knew the specifications for his height and arm length. Though this bow had special modifications that Bella had created after spending hours with her arm tied behind her back and seeing just how she could use a bow that way. She prayed her design would work. If it didn't, she'd just try again.

"He'll have a time of it training to shoot from the opposite side, given he was used to holding the bow with his left arm. With the mechanism ye requested, however, I think he will get the hang of it. I tried it myself, and it works." The man's smile was genuine, and there was hope and pride in his eyes.

"That is my fervent hope. Sir Niall and I met during an archery competition when we were children."

"So I heard."

"May I?" She stepped farther into the fletcher's shop and reached for the special bow.

"Aye, my lady."

She took the bow and smoothed her hands along the arched face to the tip. This was the first place where Niall's bow differed from others. Rather than only the bowstring connected at the notch, there was another long, finger-length thick leather loop. This attachment would be looped around Niall's left shoulder, to help him anchor the bow against his body, essentially acting as an extra support. In the center of the bowstring was a thick braided rope, about an inch wide and two inches long, which he would bite to pull the string back in place of his missing fingers. At the center of the cording was where the arrow would be nocked.

"Ye said ye tried it?" she asked.

"Aye. Works just like ye thought it might, my lady," the fletcher beamed.

"Mind if I give it a try?"

"Please." He motioned for her to follow him behind his workshop where a makeshift target area had been set up.

"Thank ye."

At first, she looped it over her shoulder, tightened the strap to fit her frame, and held her left arm behind her back. But nocking the arrow like that was too difficult. So instead, she held the bow between her knees, nocked the arrow, slipped the loop over her shoulder. Using her right arm, she held the bow up, steadying it, then let her elbow relax so she could bite the cord. Teeth clamped on to the corded rope, she tugged with all her might, finding it a lot harder to pull the string back with her teeth than she would have expected, but she eventually got it and locked her arm. Holding on to the rope with her teeth was uncomfortable, but not impossible. She lined up her sight, and let it go.

The arrow flew through the air and hit the target, but several inches to the right and up a few.

Bella laughed. "It works! I didna hit my target, but with practice, I could."

"Aye, my lady. Took me a few hours to get close to the center, and still I'd need more time practicing to get it perfect. Ye designed a good bow, my lady. But ye and Niall shall have an easier time of it as your skill surpasses mine."

"Not by much I imagine." She grinned. "Ye didna become a fletcher because ye canna shoot."

"True." His cheeks reddened.

"May I take it now?"

"Well, there was one more thing I wanted to run by ye."

"Aye?"

"I had thought it might be a nice touch to carve his name into the wood. I used to do that when he was a lad, but I didna want to overstep if ye wished it to be plain."

Bella handed him back the bow. "Please do. And also your brand. Ye must have a brand, so anyone who sees it will know ye're the one who made it."

"Aye, my lady. And what of ye, shall I carve something special on it from ye?"

Immediately, an idea came to her, and she suppressed a giggle as her heart soared. "Aye." She leaned closer and whispered to Fletcher what she wanted him to carve. "But do so on the inside, so it's not so visible to anyone taking a look."

"Aye, my lady."

The day might have started off in a somber way, but it was quickly looking up. Bella couldn't wait for Niall to see what she and the fletcher had created and to see him try it. No longer would he have to simply watch her when she was practicing with her bow. He could join in. They could compete once more. She could show him that being without a limb did not mean he could shoot.

The following days passed the same way, with her going about the duties she'd slowly started to acquire since being at the castle. Bella was starting to get into a routine, and though she missed her family, writing letters to them in the evenings helped while away the time. Mary was also good company, and they penned back and forth, Mary telling her all about Philip and how he'd stolen a kiss the day before in the gardens.

She'd also been visiting the fletcher's workshop and practicing with Niall's bow. She wanted to be able to show him it could be done, and with precision, which meant she needed to practice with it—she had not used her own set in as many days, which was just as well, since she didn't want to worry Philip and the men by having them escort her outside the walls.

But it had been many days since Niall had left, and the scouts had not seen any sign of the MacGregors. It was likely that the vile laird had moved on from his vendetta, or in the very least, he wasn't going to strike when Niall wasn't here, as his intention was to hurt her husband.

"Mary, will ye tell Philip I wish to go to the river today to practice my archery."

Mary nodded, departing after she'd brought Bella some porridge to break her fast. The cook had started to make it the way she liked it—with milk, cinnamon and a tab of butter in the center. It was divine, just like home.

By the time she finished and made it down to the bailey with her things, Philip was already giving precautionary instructions to the men.

"Should we go another day?" Bella asked, chewing her lip.

"Nay, my lady, all is safe. The scouts returned this morning to report that all was clear. But it doesna hurt for the men to be prepared."

"All right. We will not stay out long."

They made their way through the back gardens, barren in the

winter, through the gate that creaked with the cold and echoed across the snow-covered fields where the men were at work training. They bowed as she passed, and she offered them all cheerful greetings. Though it was cold still, the sun was out today, which always brought out the best in her moods.

"Where shall I set this up, my lady?"

"Just there is fine." She pointed between two trees and then backed up fifty paces.

After he set up the target, Philip stood off to the side to watch, and Mary sat on a log with a blanket wrapped around her.

"Are ye not going to shoot?" she asked Philip, knowing Mary wouldn't. The lass had tried a few times with her, and each time, the arrow had somehow backfired into her poor forehead.

"Nay, my lady, not today."

She nocked her arrow and lined up her sight, but every time she was about to let it go, she felt their eyes on her.

"This is very odd. I've practiced with an audience before, but I feel...different today."

Philip looked at Mary, who shrugged. "No different than a tournament, my lady, or any other time ye've practiced."

"That is true." Perhaps she was only feeling off because Niall wasn't here, or because she'd not shot with her arrow in days. With the thought of a challenge in mind, she lined up her arrow again, blew out a breath and fired.

One inch to the left of her target.

"Unacceptable," she murmured to herself while Philip and Mary clapped.

Bella shook out her arms, blew out several more breaths. She stomped her feet and worked out whatever kinks were in her body and whatever nerves were holding her back. The next dozen shots she hit dead center.

Philip clapped. "Sir Niall said ye were good, but I'd not realized how good."

"He is my equal, Sir Philip."

"Not according to him, my lady. He has nothing but praise for ye."

Bella blushed. "Well, there have been many years between the match that named me superior. I think we are due for a rematch, and I intend to see it done."

Philip was silent, but she could tell by his furrowed brow he did not agree, and since he did not know about her secret bow, she couldn't blame him. Given his position as her escort, and a warrior in her husband's army, he would not contradict her out of courtesy and etiquette. No matter, even if he didn't, she wasn't going to tell him about the bow. She'd sworn the fletcher to secrecy so it would be a complete surprise for Niall when he returned.

"Trust me, Philip," she said, putting her bow tip on the ground. "He will shoot again."

Mary nudged him in the ribs and gave him a look she'd seen her mother give her father on many an occasion.

"I believe ye, my lady." When Philip said it, there was a conviction in his tone that showed her he actually did believe her.

"Good." Bella smiled and returned to her target, firing off another dozen arrows in quick succession and hitting multiple targets beyond the one they'd brought. Just as she would if she were in battle.

"Impressive."

But before she could respond to Philip's compliment, a stray arrow whizzed past her to land just behind where she stood.

Bella whirled in confusion, thinking she'd somehow misfired, even though it was impossible. Another arrow and then another landed next to her, until she was standing in the center of six arrows, all with plaids of green and red tied round their middles.

"MacGregors," she murmured.

"My lady!" Philip was shouting, had been shouting, and he ran forward and crushed her to the ground where he lay on top of her. Poor Mary cowered beneath her blanket as though the fabric would make her invisible.

"We must run, Sir Philip! Lying here will only get us killed."

Philip grunted and let her up. Bella ordered Mary to run and slipped and skidded in the snow before catching herself upright.

Her lungs burned as they charged across the field. The men who'd been training had not been close enough to witness what occurred, but they saw them running and heard Philip's bellow of attack, they charged forward to form a protective circle around Bella and Mary as they retreated inside the castle walls.

It was only when they were behind the safety of the twenty-foot high stone barrier that Bella realized no one had run after them. No one had given chase. No one had even revealed themselves after firing the arrows. Whoever it was had watched with sickening pleasure as they'd ducked and then run.

Like the attack in the woods on the scout, the tactic had been to cause fear. Induce terror.

"'Twas the MacGregors," she panted, placing her hands on her knees. "They...they shot at us. Their plaids were tied around their arrows."

Philip had had the temerity to take one of the arrows from the ground and showed the men the plaid tied around the middle. The warriors were loud in their disdain and desire to charge the enemy and cut them down.

Up on the wall, the men called out what they saw—which was nothing. No men approached. Nothing stirred in the trees. The MacGregors were as good as phantoms.

"My lady, I think it wise ye dinna leave the castle until your husband returns," Philip said. "'Tis not safe."

Bella didn't argue. Besides, if she were to leave, whoever escorted her would only be in danger. She couldn't allow that. Nay, she'd stay right here. Dretch, but when would Niall be back? She needed to feel the comfort of his arms around her.

Philip ordered the men to mount up as he led a charge beneath the portcullis. Bella prayed they caught the MacGregors and that none of the Oliphant men were harmed.

IT TOOK them two days to arrive at Arbroath Abbey, and just as long for the men to come to somewhat of an agreement. Gaining independence was priority number one for the king, and Niall was one-hundred percent behind him. Freedom was something their king had been fighting toward nearly his entire life. A cause the Oliphants had upheld and fought for. Many Scotsmen had fallen, and still they fought. How many battles now? How many lives in total lost?

The Wars for Scottish Independence had been going on since Niall was a bairn. He could not think of a time when they were not at war with the bloody *Sassenachs*. When he was a wee lad, he'd pretended to be William Wallace when he played with his mates. They'd mourned his death when the English had beheaded him. Niall and Walter both had begged their father to let them go with him when he fought for the Bruce. That had been the first time Niall had seen battle, and he'd been proud to be a Scot.

Now, here in this grand abbey, he had the chance to become a part of something even bigger. Grander. To change history and the course of the nation.

"We'll petition the Pope. Make him see that excommunicating our king for the past several years was punishment enough. That we as a people want to be free from English tyranny. We will all sign it. He canna excommunicate an entire nation."

There was a round of cheers. "Aye! Never surrender!"

Niall glanced around the room, taking stock of all the men present. He stood between his brother and Magnus Sutherland. Bella's older brother, Magnus, and his youngest brother Ronan were also present.

There were perhaps fifty men in all, accounting for the majority of Scotland.

The doors to the abbey opened with a creak, drawing everyone's attention to the back of the nave.

Eòran MacGregor was attempting to sneak in but was seen by everyone present.

Niall stood straighter, and a thousand prickles stabbed into the back of his neck. MacGregor had not been present the past two days. In fact, Niall hadn't even expected to see him given the meetings had started and no one else had dared come late. Why was he late? Ice gripped Niall's spine.

"I dinna like that he was late," Niall murmured to Walter.

Walter's expression mirrored Niall's. Lips straightened into a flat line and brows narrowed, assessing. They both were stiff with tension. Nostrils flaring. "Aye. What do ye think he's been up to?"

Magnus Sutherland looked their way. "Is something amiss?"

"We were attacked by MacGregors on the way home from Dunrobin."

"Aye, my men told me." Sutherland flicked his gaze to where MacGregor stood on the opposite side of the chapel.

"And again less than a sennight ago," Niall said. "They fled without a trace."

"They are known to do that. Ghost tactics." Magnus shook his head. "Cowards, truly. Did ye kill any of them?"

"A fair amount when they ambushed us, aye."

"Ye want me to speak to MacGregor? Bring the peace?" Magnus asked.

"Nay, not yet. I..." Niall swallowed around the rising panic. "I need to go."

"Where?" Magnus asked.

"Back to Dupplin. Something doesna feel right. He was two days late. Enough time to have attacked the castle while I was gone."

From across the nave, MacGregor stared at them, a dark look on his face as well as something hinting at triumph. Niall didn't like that look. It did not bode well.

"I need to leave now. He's either done something or is planning to."

"I'll have our horses readied," Walter said.

"Nay, ye remain behind. At least our presence will be noted."

"Take my oldest son," Magnus said. "Your brother-by-marriage. Let Strath help."

Niall nodded. "Let us go."

They quietly left, and within a quarter of an hour were on the icy road. They rode hard for two days, and every time they had to stop, Niall felt the rising panic all the more. How many times was he going to fail Bella?

Chapter Eighteen

Niall and Strath crossed into the bailey of Dupplin Castle at dawn two days after leaving the abbey. They were covered in sweat that had frozen and unfrozen on their bodies.

The men had seen them coming and raised the gate. They cheered his return but then looked oddly at Strath, who was most certainly not Walter. Where the Oliphant lads were golden-haired, Strath had a nearly black tone to his long hair.

"Niall!" Bella rushed from the castle and flung herself toward him before he had a good balance on the ground. Luckily, his horse had not moved much, and he was able to steady himself with his back to his mount. When she had kissed him all over his face, she jolted at the sight of her brother. "Strath?"

"The one and only," her brother teased, pulling her from Niall's grasp and into his own embrace with a teasing grin. "I missed ye."

"Is that why ye've come? Where is Walter?" Her eyes widened. "Oh, nay, he's gotten married hasna he? Just as he thought he might."

"Nay, nay," Strath answered before Niall could. "We came—"

"Walter had some other things to attend to." Niall gave a slight shake of his head. He didn't want to worry Bella unnecessarily about MacGregor and the reason for their abrupt return.

"Sir," Philip approached. "I dinna want to interrupt your home-coming with your wife, but there is something that needs to be brought to your attention."

The same prickle that had shuddered its way up Niall's spine at the abbey did so again. "What is it?"

Philip nodded to Strath. Bella let go of her brother and went to stand beside Philip. "We were attacked some days ago."

Niall's blood went cold. Hell and damnation, this was exactly what he'd feared. "Casualties?"

"None, my laird. I had Lady Bella and Mary out by the river while she practiced her archery. Arrows started to fly all around us—with the MacGregor plaid tied to the shafts. They didna hit us. We ran back to the castle with the training men at our backs. No one came out of the woods to show themselves, and when we searched, they seemed to have disappeared again. There's been no sign of them and no more attacks since."

"The same way they attacked the scouts in the woods and killed Hammond, only this time, they didna kill anyone," Niall mused. "But they did aim to scare my wife."

"Aye, sir. We've been on heightened alert, continuing the searches that ye tasked us with before ye left, and doubling the guard on the walls. No one has left the castle unless it was absolutely necessary, and the crofters have been warned to remain locked up tight."

MacGregor. Ballocks. The man was hiding in plain sight, and showing up at the abbey had given him an alibi. Which meant either he didn't believe they knew him to be the culprit, or he thought them too stupid to figure it out. But leaving the plaids on the arrows as a way of identi-fying them was an idiotic move.

"MacGregor came late to the meeting with the king. Likely because of what he was doing here." Niall's hand fisted hard enough he could have crushed stone. He knew he should not have gone to the meeting. But how did a man choose between the orders of his king and protecting his wife?

The Bruce could have Niall arrested for not following an order, possibly even toss into the dungeon as an example to anyone else. Even if Walter was soon to marry the Bruce's daughter, he wouldn't play favorites. Not in this tumultuous time. And with men turning their backs on each other, he wouldn't blame the king for thinking yet another had betrayed him. Bella was safer with Niall not in a dungeon. Even if that meant he had to be away from her for short periods of time. As soon as he got to his study, he would write a letter to the king. Glancing down where she stood beside him, he said, "I promise ye, lass, I'll not leave your side again until MacGregor is buried deep in the earth."

Bella took his hand in hers. Her fingers were delicate and cold from the winter air. He rubbed his thumb along the calloused pads of her fingers she used in archery. Touching her brought him a sense of calm he didn't feel otherwise.

"Is there a chance it could be someone other than MacGregor?" Strath asked.

"Nay." Niall relayed the incident on the morning of the tournament and the ambush in the forest, which had been MacGregor without question. The two subsequent attacks had been less defined, but the fact that the arrows had been deliberately tied with MacGregor plaids, and Eòran himself had been missing from the meeting during the time of the latest attack. It seemed like there was no question about who was responsible.

"I see. Ye're right. That's motivation in itself."

"Aye." Niall brushed a kiss on top of Bella's head.

"Come and break your fast," she urged, tugging at his hand.

"We'll be along shortly. I want to speak with the men."

A flicker of disappointment crossed her features, but she nodded with a slight smile and turned to go back inside.

"Wow." Strath watched his sister's retreating figure with a gaping mouth. "What have ye done to my sister?"

Niall frowned and flicked his gaze after his wife. She was climbing the stairs, her skirts wishing around her ankles, long blonde hair cascading down her back. Gorgeous as always. "What?"

"That is not my sister. My Bella would have raged at ye for making her go inside while ye talked with the men."

Niall chuckled, fully understanding what he meant now. "No doubt she'll rage at me later."

"Ah, well, if ye know it's coming, then, aye, she's the same old Bella. 'Haps she has something else up her sleeve. We'd best be quick about talking with the men and getting inside to breakfast."

Niall grinned. Her brother would pummel him into the ground if he knew what Niall was hoping she had up her sleeve.

"Och, will ye stop looking after her like that," Strath said with disgust. "Ye're making my gut rebel."

Niall chuckled, slapped Strath on the back and led him toward the gatehouse so he could speak with the men on watch.

BELLA PACED THE GREAT HALL, nervously awaiting Niall and her brother. Set upon the dais table was the bow wrapped in two woolen sacks she'd sewn together for extra measure so that no one would be too curious and take a peek. Would he like it? Would he think she'd overstepped? Would he be angry at her for making the presentation of her gift such a public display?

Her knuckles were white and her fingers raw from gripping them so tightly. Goodness, if he didn't come inside soon, she'd wear a path through the rushes and perhaps even the wood plank floor below.

The servants were all looking at her nervously, seeming uncertain of her mood. No one moved. They eyed her as though she were a rabid dog ready to pounce. Speaking of dogs, the wolfhounds that normally loitered in the great hall and lounged by the hearth were sitting up alert and inching closer to the door. They'd yet to put the morning meal on the table as she'd ordered them to hold off until she'd presented Niall with his bow.

Fletcher stood in the corner. She'd invited him to watch his master open the carefully made gift as soon as she'd seen the men riding closer. In another corner stood two squires ready to bring out the targets, also covered in woolen sacks, for Niall to give it a try.

Now she was thinking that was a mistake. He wouldn't want to be put on the spot. His skill on display. Or lack of skill, as he would see it. He hated having attention drawn to his injury, and now she was making a spectacle of him.

Bella ceased her pacing and was about to tell them all to leave when Niall and Strath came marching through the door. Her brother looked so much like their father, save for his dark hair and eyes, and side by side, her husband and brother looked like night and day. Golden and dark. Just the sight of them together chuckling in camaraderie brought a rush of warmth through her—and a sudden pang of homesickness.

"What's this?" Niall paused a few feet away from her, taking in the servants, Fletcher and the lads with what he would perceive as giant woolen sacks very obviously covering something in the corner. "I thought we'd come to break our fast, but it seems ye have something else in mind. What's under those sacks? What have ye got there, lad?"

"Not yet," she rushed. "Ye recall I said I had a surprise for ye." Licking her lips, she tried to form the words, but her mouth kept opening and closing as though she'd suddenly gained Mary's affliction. *Oh, dretch, why is this so hard?*

Bella stared around the room in mounting horror, not knowing what to say. She'd been so sure of her gift before... Now, every uncertainty washed through her. Everything that could go wrong, including hurting Niall, which was not her intention at all.

"Sir Niall," Fletcher said coming forward. "Your gracious wife commissioned me to make a gift."

Bella smiled gratefully at the man, inclining her head.

"A gift." Niall's eyes brightened as they danced toward her. "My surprise is a gift, lass? But I have nothing for ye in return."

"This was something I wanted to do for ye. I need nothing in return, husband." Heat flooded her cheeks, and she twisted her hands in front of her. "And perhaps now is not a good time..."

"My, ye certainly want to keep me in suspense do ye not?" He chuckled. "Will ye let me open it?"

"Nay, 'tis just, I'm no longer certain—"

Strath cut her off. "Come on, Bella. Everyone loves your gifts. Let us see it."

With her brother there for support, and deciding that if Niall hated it and her for having it made, she could always go home, Bella backed toward the dais. She lifted the large sack with both hands and carefully carried it forward to present it to her husband in one awkward thrust.

"Here."

Niall took the sack, held it out and curled wrist up to inspect the edge. He raised a brow. "Ye sewed it shut."

Oh God. Holding it with one hand, he wouldn't be able to cut the threads. But her brother saved her before she could say anything by tugging out his *sgian dubh* and cutting the threads with a jovial, "'Tis just like home with me unwrapping everyone's gifts afore they get a chance"

Bella laughed. Her brother did have a penchant for sneaking into the great hall where their parents left a stash of gifts at the end of every year to celebrate their children. He would open each one, and then attempt to put the wrapping back together, but they all knew what had happened.

Bella tugged off one sack while her brother tugged off another, leaving the bow in Niall's grasp.

The polished yew wood gleamed in the light of the candles. The room was silent, and Niall was staring hard at the bow, perhaps trying to figure out just what she thought he would do with it. Bella stood frozen for a moment, fearing what he was thinking with no outward expression to give her a clue.

"This—" she touched the looped leather strap, "—goes here." Gently, she brushed his left shoulder. "And this—" she pointed to the corded knot of roping on the center of the bowstring, "—ye put between your teeth to pull the bowstring back. When ye're ready to launch your arrow, ye let it fly."

"Ye had this made for me?" His voice was quiet and still did not give away how he felt about it.

All smiles had left her now, and her fingers were cold, slowly losing sensation. She noted he took sight of what she'd had carved inside. *Ye will always be my knight.*

"Aye," Bella answered, her voice stronger. "Ye're the best archer I know. And people that are good at things should never quit. There's no amount of hardship that should hold ye back, Niall."

When Niall met her gaze, his eyes glittered with emotion, but he quickly blinked it away, handed the bow to Strath and tugged her up against him. Bella was shocked at first, not expecting that, and when he pressed his lips hard to hers for an all-too-brief kiss, her knees buckled. Luckily, he held her up, his smile enough to melt every bit of fear she might have had.

"I take it ye like it?" she whispered.

"Och, aye." His voice was tight, as though he were trying to hold back his emotions.

"Will ye try it? I can show ye how 'tis done. Fletcher and I have been practicing."

Niall seemed taken aback by that. "Ye truly are an extraordinary woman."

Bella's face heated, but she tried to act as though what he said didn't affect her as much as it did and ran her fingers over the wood and string. Why had she fretted so much about whether he would like the gift? He clearly did.

"A demonstration by your lady," Niall called out to those in attendance, holding the bow up in the air.

The lads who'd been waiting in the corner brought forth the targets and set them up, three in all, at different lengths from where they stood.

"First, adjust the strap to make certain it holds tight with your arm extended." With her arm behind her back, Bella slipped the strap over her left shoulder and adjusted the chord with her teeth and right hand. Once it was secure, she held on to the curved grip of the bow and thrust her right arm out, taking note that the strap was snug. Niall watched her intently. "Then ye'll tuck the bow between your legs, and clip your arrow at the notch here where the corded rope is. Then ye'll reposition the strap and grab the rope with your teeth." Biting the rope, she straightened her arm, jaw clenched securely to hold the string and arrow extended. "Aim," she muttered around the rope between her teeth. "And fire."

She let the arrow go to the shortest target, not wanting to show off that she could hit the farthest target in case it took him a while. After all, she'd been practicing for days.

"Incredible," Niall said.

"That is amazing," Strath said. "This could change the way we fight."

Bella glanced at Fletcher, and they shared a triumphant smile. "Your turn, husband."

Niall followed her instructions exactly, raised the bow, took aim and hit the edge of the target.

"Incredible! Especially for a first try. I knew ye still had it in ye." Bella clapped. "Do it again."

Niall frowned, nocked another arrow, aimed and fired. This time he was much closer to the center, but not quite perfect. Those in the great hall were cheering, stomping their feet and encouraging him to do it again. Each time he nocked the arrow, Niall's speed increased, and with each shot, he was closer to the center. He beamed at her, at the target, at his people, and there was a confidence she saw in him that matched, if not exceeded, the way he'd looked on the battlefield brandishing his sword.

When he hit the shortest target and split her arrow, the crowd shouted so loudly the rafters literally shook with their pride.

Bella shrieked. "Ye've beaten me!"

Niall let the bow slide to his side, grabbed her around the waist and lifted her up to twirl her in a circle. "My God, lass... My God..."

He was bending to kiss her when the sharp, reproachful sound of his mother interrupted. "What is going on here?"

Niall set Bella down, and she stepped in what she hoped was an appropriate distance away from her husband.

"I am using my new gift, my lady mother. Come and see."

Lady Oliphant frowned, lifted her skirts and marched toward her son, taking note of the targets and arrows.

"What is this?" Her long fingers thrust toward the targets. "Who would set this up in my great hall? What is that?" She jabbed toward the bow.

"A new bow," Niall said. "Bella had it made for me, so I can shoot again."

The normally bitter lady's eyes widened and filled with unshed tears. "Show me."

Niall nocked an arrow, reset the leather strap and shot it into the center of the first target.

"Do the second," she whispered, her hands coming to cover her mouth. They were shaking, and tears were visibly rolling down her cheeks as Niall fired into the second and then the third, farthest target, hitting the center each time.

"A miracle," she murmured, visibly shaken. "A bloody miracle."

"Nay, Mama, not a miracle. 'Tis Bella."

Lady Oliphant turned to face Bella, reached for her hands and squeezed them. "Ye...ye did a wonderful thing for my son. I...I must apologize for how I treated ye before. I was... Well, it doesna matter. Ye've given me my son back. Made him happy."

And then she was tugging Bella into her arms, squeezing her as tightly as she could, until Bella coughed from the strain of trying to breathe but didn't push her away all the same.

"Mama, ye're supposed to thank her, not kill her," Niall teased.

Belle watched him over his mother's shoulder. There was such joy on his face. A mirthful glint shone in his eyes. He was almost an entirely new man. The clan could feel it. The tension in their shoulders relaxed, and they were laughing, smiling and chattering away.

"Can I try, sir?" One of the squires who'd obviously had to work up the courage to come forward and speak with Niall.

"Of course, lad." Niall bent to give him instruction.

Never again would she question her decisions when it came to knowing her husband and what he needed. Her heart soared, and she realized watching him jest with her brother and pound Fletcher on the back that she was deeply in love with him. More so than when she'd been a lass, more than what she'd built him into over the years. This man, this true Niall right here in front of her, she *loved* him. Truly and deeply.

HOW AM I SO LUCKY? Niall met Bella's gaze, taking in the emotion in her eyes, the secret smile curving her lips. No one had ever done something like this for him. Aye, there had been pep talks, and there had been pushing. His brother and Philip had forced him to pick up a sword again. But to design something for him to use, to know how much he loved archery and want to make it a part of his life again...

Thanking Bella would not be enough. He could get down on his hands and knees and crawl over flames shouting his gratitude, and it would not be enough. A weight seemed to have been lifted off his chest, and immense pleasure radiated through his veins. There were no words he could use to describe what was happening inside him. He felt...*alive*. More than that, he felt invincible.

Once more, he glanced down at what was carved on the inside of the polished wood bow.

Ye will always be my knight.

Suddenly, an idea came to him. Though he would spend the rest of his life cherishing her for what she'd done today, he knew the perfect way to thank her sooner rather than later for this precious gift.

With that, Niall laughed, and challenged his wife to an archery contest.

Chapter Nineteen

T he following morning, Bella woke to a gentle nudge on her hip. She smiled, stretched out the kinks in her muscles from all the archery she'd done the day before and then blinked open her eyes to find a hideous ogre of a woman standing beside the bed. Face covered in soot or something else equally appalling, the woman was tall enough that she might be able to reach the rafters. She was as tall as Niall, as broad even, with breasts the size of Bella's head. Her hair was wrapped up in a rag covered in the same dirt that was on her face.

"Good morn, my lady," she said in high-pitched voice, yet oddly deep, if that was even possible given the sounds should negate each other. 'Twas disturbing.

Bella looked away, feeling entirely uncomfortable. She'd never seen this woman before.

"Can I help get ye into a bath?" the ogre woman asked, wiggling her fingers at Bella in a way that seemed almost...lecherous.

"Nay, I'm quite all right." Bella scooted to the other side of the bed, suddenly worried the behemoth might just lift her up and toss her into a cold tub like her old nursemaids used to do when she'd refused long enough that the water had lost its warmth.

"Come on, dearie." The older woman started to climb onto the bed, and Bella screeched when she grabbed hold of her ankle beneath the blankets giving her a tug.

What in the bloody hell? The woman had the strength of a warrior.

"Do ye not recognize me?" With a tug, Bella was pulled all the way across the bed, legs spread wide and her night rail riding up to her hips, with the woman looming over her.

For a split second, Bella was utterly horrified, and then she saw him —the beautiful emerald of his eyes, and the laughing smile beneath the muck.

"Ye rascal!" She swatted Niall, burst out laughing and grabbed hold of the large breasts he was bouncing near her face. Rolled up linens she was guessing. How had she not seen him before? "What are ye doing?"

"Isna it obvious, lass? I once asked if ye'd make me be your lady, and ye said aye. Now here I am playing the part. And from the look on your face, ye fell for it for a short time."

Bella laughed so hard her belly hurt. Then she leaned up and pressed her lips to his. "I've never kissed a lady until now."

"Och, lass. If I get a kiss from ye, I'll be your lady any day." Niall tumbled her back down to the bed, yanking the stuffing from his dress and pulling it over his head to reveal he wore nothing beneath.

Bella stilled. Never before had he come to bed with her fully nude. In fact, he'd always worn a shirt, and she'd respected his wishes to do so. But there he was now, kneeling between her legs, his hard body on display.

Rippling abdominal muscles led down to a shaft thick with desire that jutted from curls a shade darker than the flaxen hair atop his head. Bella leaned up on her elbow, flattened her palm to his middle and circled her thumb around his navel. She felt the hardness of his body, the corded muscles that bunched and flexed with his movements. Aye, she'd touched him in the dark when they'd lain together, and always he'd worn his shirt. Seeing him fully undressed was something altogether different. The blood whistling through her veins started to hum, and the places that tingled when he touched her burst to life. She pressed her other hand to his stomach and slid them both up to his chest, pausing over his nipples and feeling them harden beneath her palms. His breath hitched, and though she stared at his skin, she could feel the heat of his gaze on the top of her head. They were both silent, intense.

Had he meant to take off his shirt when he took off the gown? To fully show himself? Did he realize how much that would mean to her?

Bella met his gaze, licked her lips and said, "I love ye." That wasn't what she'd meant to say. Not at all, but the words had slipped out before she could say anything else. Scrambling to her knees and facing him so they both knelt in the middle of the mattress, she kept touching him.

Niall stared hard at her, as though her words were still percolating in his mind and he was trying to make sense of them.

"I love ye," she said again, sliding her fingers over to his left collarbone and down the knotted scarring from where his arm had been taken just below the shoulder. The pain he must have endured made her heart ache.

Niall hissed a breath at her touch but didn't move away. Didn't ask her to stop.

"Does it hurt?" she whispered, yanking her fingers back, afraid she'd caused him pain.

"Nay." His voice was tight, and he gently pressed her searching fingers back. "I've never had anyone..."

Bella leaned forward and kissed his shoulder, kissed his scars.

"Ye're the first to see me. To touch me, beside the healer," he said. "Ye're not... It doesna scare ye?"

Bella met his gaze, shook her head and pressed her lips to his. "Nay, my love."

"I have this ache in my chest." He twirled a lock of her hair around his finger and tickled her cheek with it. "I didna know what it was until ye said the words. I love ye, too, Bella. Deeply. Ye're all I think about. I worry over ye night and day. Not just about your safety, but about your happiness. Whether or not I deserve ye."

"I wouldna, couldna have any other man, Niall. Ye're all I've wanted since I was a lass."

"So ye'd say I ruined ye for all other men."

Bella giggled. "Aye, most definitely."

"'Tis the same for me. Every woman I've ever known, I compared to ye. When Walter came back to Dupplin months ago telling me he'd asked for your hand and ye'd turned him down, claiming ye were in love with another, I was enraged with jealousy. Every woman I saw with hair like a golden halo was ye, and every man she was with was the man ye'd fallen for. Who was that man?"

Bella bit her lip and scooted a little closer. "'Twas ye, Niall. When I came into my da's study and saw the back of Walter, I thought it was ye. Then he told me ye were engaged to another, and I thought my world would crumble. I declared then and there that I would never marry, and for a few months, my parents let me believe they were on my side."

Niall chuckled. "Are ye not glad they changed their mind?"

"Extremely."

Niall ran the backs of his fingers over her shoulder, sliding the fabric down to expose her flesh. He pressed his lips to her skin, sending shivers running through her.

"I love your skin." He flicked his tongue over the line of her collarbone. "The way ye smell, the way ye taste. How soft ye are compared to me."

Bella lifted the hem of her night rail, raised it over her head and tossed it to the floor so she, too, was naked.

"I want to feel my skin on yours." Aye, she'd lifted his shirt to feel his stomach rub against hers when they'd made love before, but chest to chest—nothing in between—that would be different. Limbs entwined with nothing between them, that would be completely new.

She scooted closer on her knees, feeling the hardness of his shaft press hotly to her belly, her knees knocking his, her breasts rubbing against the crisp sprinkle of hair on his chest. A shiver rushed through her at the contact, and Niall, too, shivered.

"Every day since I spied ye in the bailey getting your ears chewed off by a princess, I've given thanks that ye agreed to be mine." Bella twined her fingers with his and raised his hand to her lips, flicking her tongue over the tip of his pointer finger.

When Niall met her gaze, his eyes had darkened into twin pools of green. His jaw ticked mercilessly, and when she sucked his finger into her mouth, he let out a low growl, tackling her to the bed. He pinned her legs beneath his powerful ones, his hand holding both of hers above her head. He loomed over her, his raw, passionate masculinity sending another shiver coursing through her.

Bella's entire body vibrated with anticipation.

"Ye dinna know what game ye play at, love." Niall gently bit the side of her chin before sliding his tongue down her neck and finding a nipple, and mercilessly tormenting her.

"Oh," she gasped, "but I know exactly."

She raised her legs up around his middle, tilting her hips at an angle that allowed his throbbing shaft to slide along her folds and the head tease her center. One more twitch from her, and he'd be close to slipping inside.

Niall chuckled. "So I see."

She shuddered, gasping as he took her invitation and surged forward all the way to the hilt. Would she ever get used to the feel of him filling her? Claiming her? Zounds, but he was massive, hard and powerful. Once inside her, he pulled back out, teasing her as he remained on the brink, capturing her mouth for a demanding kiss.

Bella writhed beneath him, trying to pull him back inside by pressing her feet to the backs of his thighs, but he held steady, taunting her with the nearness of him, the pleasure that built within her.

"Niall, please," she begged. "I want ye. I want...all of ye."

Niall's forehead fell to hers, and he groaned, sinking back inside her. She squeezed her hands in his large one, moving her body with the force of his thrusts. She melted for him, begged for more as the pressure built within her, that delicious spine-tingling pleasure that layered one shudder on top of another, until her entire being broke apart.

Bella cried out, intense white heat exploding inside her. Niall increased his thrusts, pounding deep, until he, too, cried out his pleasure and shuddered, his hand that held her still shaking.

He pressed his forehead to hers, kissed her gently on the lips, and murmured, "Ye are my everything."

Chapter Twenty

Three days later, not a single sign of MacGregor or his men had been found. The frustration he felt at the continued chase of a man who wouldn't make himself known left Niall in a murderous mood each night.

Niall had sent a missive to Walter following their return, letting him know that there had been another attack while they were gone, and that the MacGregor and his warriors still eluded him. He'd also asked his brother to inform the king on the matter. If MacGregor was going to continue to antagonize the Oliphant clan, there was every possibility of a brawl breaking out between them and their warriors at the next meeting of the clans.

Strath and Philip had been taking daily shifts, searching out the surrounding lands and ensuring that no MacGregors were in sight. So far there had been nothing. The blasted men were like ghosts, and short of Niall taking a band of warriors to the MacGregor castle and declaring war, there was nothing much he could do about it, save protect his lands, his people, his wife.

But that would be his next step. The only thing that made him waver was the gut instinct that MacGregor would be back. And if the man was going to come back to fight, it would be better for the

Oliphant warriors to fight on their own grounds. They'd have more provisions, a better understanding of the land, and a castle to fall back against in case the MacGregors gained the advantage.

In fact, Niall went so far as to send a scathing missive to MacGregor's castle, with express instructions to his messenger to send it over their castle walls with an arrow in the dead of night and then flee. If that wasn't a call to war, he didn't know what was.

That had been days ago, and MacGregor still hadn't shown his face.

Which was why Niall needed to do more to draw him out.

And the only way to do that was to put himself and his wife in possible danger. When he'd broached the topic with Bella, she'd immediately agreed. But he still didn't feel right about it. So for the next several days, he'd cautiously laid his bait. First, he'd gotten the idea from their childhood challenge—he'd dressed as a woman and ridden the moors alone. He had several of his warriors do the same, so any MacGregor ghost scouts would see the women riders and believe that the Oliphant clan were no longer on their guard.

The men had made a great game of it, teasing each other about their dress and asking to court one another. But all jokes aside, today was going to be the final test, to see if MacGregor was indeed going to attack.

After spending a morning making love, and assured his men were set around the perimeter of their lands, Bella and Niall took his new bow not quite all the way to the river. He wanted to have a bigger lead time should their enemy approach.

It was a gorgeous morning, and the first signs of spring were starting to show. The snow had melted, and the temperatures had come above freezing. In another couple of weeks, Niall would not be surprised to see some flowers sprouting in the grasses. And he would be here to see them despite the battle that was brewing. He was not going to lose.

Bella twirled in a circle, delighted to finally be outside the castle walls, even if it was as bait to their enemy. Her face was turned up toward the sun, arms outstretched, her bow and quiver full of arrows slung crossways over one shoulder. Soft golden curls fell down her back, moving gently with the breeze, and the delight he saw on her face brought an instant smile to his lips.

To be that carefree...

A raven cawed from one of the trees, sending a flock of them jolting from a tree beside the riverbank.

Niall was immediately on alert, eyes scanning the river and the trees for anything unusual. Were the MacGregors already in place, ready to attack? But he saw nothing out of the ordinary.

Bella rushed up to him, circled his waist with her arms and leaned up to kiss his chin. "Ye worry so much. It has been a sennight or more since they last attacked, and with your men riding around the holding dressed as women for days, dinna ye think the MacGregors would have attacked by now if they were going to?"

"I canna say what goes through the mind of a madman, love. In fact, I want to go back to the castle. I dinna like this. 'Twas a bad idea, and I never should have suggested it."

Bella clucked her tongue. "Nothing is going to happen to us. The men have been searching for days with no sign. Perhaps even now, Walter has spoken to the king and MacGregor is being chastised for what he's done. He could be rotting in a dungeon, and we might never have to see him or his men again."

Niall let the set of his shoulders relax, but he didn't let his guard down completely. "He deserves more than a chastisement."

"Aye. He does. But he is a powerful chief with a strong army that the king needs. With King Robert trying to gain independence for Scotland, he'll not risk losing an ally over a clan dispute."

Bella spoke the truth, which didn't make it any sweeter going down.

"Och, but ye're right, my lovely wife. I still loathe the bastard, and if I ever catch sight of him, 'twill take every ounce of self-control I have not to run him through. And if he baits me, if he so much as twitches in my presence, that will be the end of him."

Bella kissed him again. "Ye're the better man in every way."

Niall let himself cave to her kiss, wishing he could convince her to go back up to their bedchamber instead. If he kept kissing her like this, they'd end up making love on the cold ground. Reluctantly, Niall pulled his lips from hers. "Dinna flatter me, lass. We came here to shoot. I still aim to best ye."

"Do ye? For ye've not been able to yet."

"And ye dinna want to best me?"

"Nay, it doesna bother me that we're equals."

Niall wrapped his arm around her middle and hauled her up against him once more. Would he ever get over how good it felt to have her flush to him? "It doesna bother me either, love. Honestly. I am proud of your skill. Have been since ye were a wee heathen."

Bella laughed. "I know. How about we forget these targets and see if ye canna try and hit all the marks I've made on the trees."

Niall let her go, and they each readied their bows, taking aim at the knots in the trees that she'd used for target practice before.

After an hour or so, they set their bows down to give their arms a rest. They'd tied in every shot, even when Bella had chosen a tree across the river. Niall had insisted on getting the arrows himself each time, muscles taut as he jogged, waiting for the moment his enemy would strike. He could feel it in the air. Feel their eyes on him.

"Let us return now," Niall said as he tucked their arrows back in their quivers.

"Nay, not just yet." She spread out a blanket on the ground and pulled out the picnic Cook had packed them. Cold pieces of chicken, hunks of cheese, bread, dried fruit and a wineskin full of wine. "I know it's not truly spring and a wee bit chilly out still, but I thought it might be fun to have a picnic." Bella flopped down and tucked her feet beneath the fur hem of her cloak. She patted the place beside her. "Come and sit. I'll feed ye like lovers do in stories. And when we're done, we can go back."

Niall wavered a moment, glancing back toward the castle where men stood on the walls. His archers were prepared to fire at his signal or the first sign of the enemy approaching. Other warriors were training in the fields nearby, pretending to be absorbed in that, versus what they were truly doing, which was scouting the area. "And will ye tell me a story, lass?"

"Aye. What kind of story do ye want? One of adventure? Tragedy? Love?"

"Hmm…" He settled beside her, lying on his side, propped up on his elbow so he had a good sight of the river behind her. "How about all three?"

"Och, a challenge. Well then, I shall begin. 'Twas the coldest winter in the Highlands that had ever come to pass. Lord and Lady Goathead were—"

"Lord and Lady Goathead?" Niall chuckled and raised a brow.

Bella stuffed a hunk of chicken into his mouth with a grin on her lips. "Dinna interrupt, else ye'll miss the best parts."

"Aye, my lady, whatever ye say."

"Lord and Lady Goathead were verra proud of their three daughters—Muddyhose, Crinklynose and Bumblows."

Niall chuckled, grabbed a hunk of bread and said, "Ye'll not be in charge of naming any of our hounds." He quickly shoved the bread in his mouth and laughed around the bite as she gave him a warning look.

Bella, sweet as pie, kept going with her story, face as serious as though she hadn't just spouted the most ridiculous drivel. She picked up a slice of dried apricot and pinched it between her fingers. "The snow had fallen so thick, it was nearly as tall as a man. In fact, it made it possible that their enemies could climb the snow and scale their walls." She bit into the apricot and tugged until the piece popped into her mouth. Chewing, she looked around with consideration. "When the men climbed the walls, ready to attack, they came upon—"

An arrow hit the edge of their blanket, pinning it to the ground. From across the moors, they could hear the shouts of warning from their men.

Niall shouted an expletive, and they were both quickly on their feet. Bella grabbed hold of her bow and quiver, nocked an arrow and searched out the enemy. Warriors from the mock training were running toward them and from across the river MacGregors were melting from the woods, charging through the icy waters and coming to shore. Niall bypassed his bow in favor of pulling his *sgian dubh* from his boot. He threw it across the field and watched it sink into one man's neck. Without hesitating, he grabbed for the second one in his other boot and threw it at the closest approaching enemy warrior, while Bella shot one warrior and then a second.

Arrows flew down around them from where the MacGregors must be perched in trees.

Niall strapped on his bow, prepared to shoot, but it slipped off his shoulder. There wasn't time to right it. They needed to run, to get Bella to safety.

"Run, Bella!" he shouted, yanking on her arm and forcing her to quit shooting and to escape from the bastards' quick approach. His plan had worked. Too well.

They started to run, legs stretching far. He held on to her arm, practically dragging her as he charged toward his own men and the safety of the castle walls. But then Niall heard a terrifying sound behind them.

Hoof beats.

They might have been able to outrun the warriors with the head start they had—but a horse. Not a chance in the world.

Bella heard it, too. She turned around, nocked two arrows and fired them off to take down two men. She did it again, shooting down one man on a horse but missing the other.

Niall felt like everything was moving in slow motion. His wife, acting the part of a warrior and trying to protect them both from an enemy that was destined to win. The horses drew nearer, and then they were upon them. Niall grappled one of the warriors, tossing him to the ground, but it wasn't enough. Another lifted Bella off her feet, tossed her weapon and swiftly retreated.

"Bella," Niall bellowed her name, feeling helpless, foolish.

How had he convinced himself this was a good plan? Baiting the enemy...what a bloody idiot he'd been. MacGregor had outsmarted them, found the weak point in their line and crossed it.

There was only one way he could protect Bella now. Niall grabbed his bow, nocked an arrow, aimed, and said a prayer as he let it fly. The arrow shot through the air, whistling as it went. It glided in slow motion and zeroed in on its mark. His mark. The back of the bastard who had his wife. A breath later, the arrow struck.

The MacGregor rider cried out, arching his back and letting go of the reins.

"Jump, Bella!" Niall shouted, running toward her, dodging the

MacGregors who'd finally made it to where he stood. A second later, his own men were there, the clashing of steel on steel echoing in the serene afternoon.

But Bella didn't jump. With the man now slumping over in the saddle and the horse still barreling toward the woods beyond, she managed to somehow knock him from the horse and take her seat astride the saddle, skirts hiked up around her thighs.

Niall had not known she was an excellent rider, but he supposed he should have, as she seemed to master everything she tried.

Bella gained control of the mount and turned around and headed back toward Niall. She barely slowed down as she came upon him, reaching out an arm as though she would take him up.

Fortunately, Niall was also a good rider. He ran alongside the horse, grabbed hold of the pummel and took advantage of her strong grip on his forearm as he launched his body in the air to settle behind her.

The horse's stride increased as they rushed toward the castle.

Neither of them spoke, both were out of breath and frantic to get to the walls, likely for different reasons.

Strath passed them as they went, bellowing a war cry as he engaged the MacGregors that swarmed the land like ants.

As soon as Bella was near the castle, he shouted for the guards to open the gate. He was going to send her through, call for a sword and go back out to protect his men.

Through the gates, he tugged the reins to halt his horse. He wrapped his arm around Bella's waist and lifted her from the saddle, shifting her to the ground as he scooted forward to take her place.

"Philip! Protect my wife."

"What are ye doing?" she asked, terror on her face as she reached for him.

"What I have to do, lass." He bent down and kissed her swiftly. There was no time to linger.

"Nay, Niall, ye canna go back out there."

The anguish he saw on her face was enough to make him falter, but there was no other choice. If he didn't take care of MacGregor now, what was the likelihood that Bella would survive another attack? He could not do this to her again. This was the battle they needed to settle once and for all.

"I will come back. If ye must, take your bow and arrows to the ramparts. Ye can fight from there." Never would he have thought to say something like this to his wife before, but Bella had just proven herself more than capable on the battlefield, and he'd be a fool to suppress her. He was also fully aware that should he tell her to go inside, she'd likely do just the opposite.

Before he could say more and hear any protest from her, he called out to one of the men, "Sword!"

A claymore was tossed through the air, and he caught the hilt. With one last longing look at his wife, he nudged the horse back out onto the battlefield. Across the moor by the river, the melee continued. Men struck and clashed. But it was clear the MacGregors were losing men and energy fast.

With his calves holding tightly to the middle of the horse, Niall crashed into three MacGregors, his sword slicing one, the horse running over another, and the third leaping out of the way. Niall circled back around, arcing his sword toward the man who'd narrowly escaped him the first time. Their swords cracked together, but with the other man being on foot, he was no match for Niall on the horse.

By the time he finished with that man, the one who'd fallen was climbing back to his feet and lunging at the horse. Niall blocked the blow to the horse's neck when he realized the man's intent and kicked him backward.

"Bastard!" Niall shouted.

The other man shouted something much worse in return and made a vulgar remark about Niall's wife.

That was the last straw. Niall leapt from the horse, his knees hitting the man in the chest as he took him down and sliced through his neck with the massive sword.

"Oliphant!" Niall turned to see that Strath was beckoning him. The men were retreating to the walls, the MacGregors that had not perished were running back toward the river.

"Nay!" Niall ordered. "There will be no mercy here today!"

He leapt to his feet and ran after the MacGregors. Would they lead him toward Eòran? Cowardly bastard that he was. He'd not dared to show his face, once more sending his men to do his dirty work for him.

They reached the river, the MacGregor men crashing through the water in an effort to escape the madman that Niall had become, as well as the dozen warriors charging behind him. He dragged one man down into the depths, his knee on the man's chest as he sputtered. Then a man standing on the opposite edge caught his line of sight.

Eòran MacGregor.

The bastard was smiling, such a cruel look upon his deranged face that Niall was momentarily stunned. He let the man he'd been trying to drown up, only to find himself falling backward at the hard shove of his opponent.

MacGregor laughed on the opposite side.

Niall pushed to his feet and used his sword as leverage by stabbing it into the shallow bed of the river. But that moment of weakness was enough for his opponent to recover and lunge toward him, prepared to slice him open.

Thankfully, Strath was there by his side to dispatch the man as Niall recovered. He'd almost died by acting so rash, by rushing into battle without a plan.

Niall pointed his sword at MacGregor. "I challenge ye. Just the two of us. We end this today."

MacGregor's smile grew. "I accept."

Chapter Twenty-One

From Bella's viewpoint on the ramparts, she had a clear sight of the river. The warriors had come to a sudden halt and were standing opposite each other and appeared to be in discussions. Oliphant and MacGregor warriors lined the river bank, fully armed, their shoulders heaving from the exertion of their fighting. Niall stood in the river, water that had to be ice cold mid-way up his calves.

Why have they stopped?

The sight of them at a complete standstill when moments before they'd all been intent on killing one another made no sense. What could they possibly have to say? In all the tales of battle she'd heard from her father and brothers, not once had this situation arisen.

The look she'd seen in Niall's eye had been deadly. When he'd galloped out of the gate, she'd been certain he was going to massacre every one of the MacGregors by himself.

Bella let her bow drop to her side as she blinked, trying to make out what she saw before her. "What is happening, Philip?"

"I dinna know." He shook his head, and Bella, chancing a glance at the other warriors on the wall, saw they looked just as confused.

"Guess," Bella challenged Philip. He knew Niall better than she, perhaps he had a good idea what was happening.

"If were to guess, I'd say Niall has challenged him."

"What?" Bella pressed her hand to the cold stone of the ramparts, leaning closer to the edge as though that would help her see the men better. At this distance, she could barely make out their faces, only knew her husband by how tall and golden he was. "Why would he do that?"

"To cease the fighting. To save his men. To take down MacGregor once and for all." With every word, Philip sounded more convinced he was correct in his determination.

"And MacGregor will be arrogant enough to agree." Bella's stomach did a flip, falling somewhere toward her feet.

"Aye, my lady."

Bella swallowed around the lump that had formed in her throat. She tried to remind herself that when Niall fought MacGregor at Dunrobin, he'd won in a sweeping victory. She didn't want to think that when he'd turned his back on MacGregor, the man had taken advantage of a coward's victory. But he had failed. She had to remember that, too. And Niall had men at his back, including her brother, that would protect him should MacGregor try a cheating tactic.

But...what if the rules were that no one could step in? "We have to do something, Sir Philip. I dinna want Niall to do this. MacGregor doesna fight fair. I need to go down there."

"Nay, my lady, we canna interfere. 'Tis about honor, and ye'll strip Niall of his if ye tried to impede what he has planned."

Bella turned to face her husband's long time friend and personal trainer, hands fisted at her sides. "Philip! How can ye say nay? How can ye watch this happen? Will ye not let a wife comfort her husband?"

Philip looked her in the eye, his face full of sincerity. "Nay. Because I know that if ye were there, Niall would not be able to concentrate on the fight. He'd be worried about ye. Just as I would be should I be in his place and Mary was standing nearby. Because he has tasked me with protecting ye, and I'd not be doing my duty. Because he can fight MacGregor if he knows he need not worry about ye."

"Ye need say no more. I understand." And she did, but that didn't mean she liked it. Everything Philip said made sense, especially the part about her companion. She flicked her gaze briefly on him and then back to the river. "Ye love Mary?"

Philip laughed softly. "I do. Never thought I could fall in love, but she's changed me."

Bella smiled lovingly at the back of her husband's head, recalling how many times she'd threaded her fingers in those locks. "Love will do that to ye."

The logical side of her knew if she were to go out on that field in an attempt to help her husband, she'd be in the way, a deadly distraction. But the part of her that was ruled by her heart wanted to rush out there and put an arrow through every one of their enemy's hearts.

"Ye were valiant on the battlefield, my lady. A true warrior. And ye saved your husband's life. Now he needs to save yours." Philip must have been reading her thoughts.

"But I am safe here behind the wall." She tried to calculate the distance between here and the river. Could she fire an arrow into MacGregor's heart? She'd never attempted to shoot from this distance. It had to be well over five-hundred feet maybe more.

"Aye. But ye havena been before now, my lady. Ye've been attacked more than once now, and Niall must prove to ye, and to himself, that he can protect ye."

Bella nodded, watching as the MacGregor and Oliphant men made a wide circle around Niall and Eoran, who both now stood in the water. Her brother was at Niall's back, which gave her confidence. Should Niall go down, her brother would bring him back to safety. Protect him.

If she couldn't be there, at least he was.

"Ye wish to be there, too, do ye not?" Bella said.

"Aye, my lady. But I am honored to protect ye."

"I'm sorry." As Niall's trainer, Philip had also acted as his bodyguard when Walter wasna there. He must be feeling a similar tightness in his chest at not being down by the river.

"Dinna be sorry. Niall has entrusted his wife to my care. There is no greater honor than that."

Movement by the river had them both going silent. They watched the two warriors circle each other in the water with their swords raised. The men were silent. No cheering or insults being thrown, just the wind and the flowing river. MacGregor had the use of a targe on his arm, and he would not doubt take advantage of Niall not having one.

Then, all of the sudden, there was a rush of movement that had Bella jumping. The sound of their swords clashing rang out across the moor, ricocheting off the castle walls with the strength and power the men had put behind their attacks.

With the men surrounding them, it was hard to see what was happening. They chanted, blocking the sounds of the weapons connecting, as if that first hit had given them permission to now open their mouths. Bella tapped her fingers on the rampart wall, stood on tiptoe as if that would help her get a better view. She bit her lip until she tasted metallic, but all it did was increase her frustration at not being down there. *Doing* something. She lifted her bow, nocked an arrow and took aim, but Philip pressed his hand against her arm and forced her to lower her weapon.

"Sir Philip, I need—"

"Nay, my lady. Ye canna fight this fight for him. It will never end. If I must, I will have the guards take ye to your chamber."

Bella shook her head vehemently, abhorring that idea more than watching a man try to kill her husband. The view from their chamber's window was of the front of the castle, not the back where Niall was fighting. She ground her teeth together, gripped the stone and waited.

MACGREGOR DIDN'T WANT to fight fair. That was evident from the way he tried to hit Niall in the head with the targe while he stabbed with his sword. Niall ended up taking many blows to the side of his head in order to block the blows of the sword. Just above his temple was warm, trickling with blood, and he knew it was because the iron studs on the face of MacGregor's targe had torn the flesh of his scalp.

But he wasn't giving up. Just like at the tournament, Niall was determined to win. MacGregor was a ruthless bully, and one that needed to be put down.

Niall used his feet to kick at MacGregor's kneecaps. At one point, the other man's legs buckled, and he dropped to the water. Niall moved to strike, but MacGregor's sword arched up to block him at the last minute, and he slammed his targe into Niall's own knee with a bone-jarring crunch that made his eyes dance for half a breath.

Niall stumbled backward, not willing to go down. If he went down, it would be his death. He had to work through the pain. Work to stay upright. Work to fight. When he'd fallen before, Strath had been there to block his enemy, or he wouldn't have made it. But in this fight of honor, no one would be able to step in to help him.

Falling meant death.

The men around them cheered and stomped. The water churned. Niall tried to zero in on the sounds of the wind and the blood rushing through his ears. To wriggle his toes that had gone cold in the frigid waters. He tried to keep himself focused on his opponent rather than his wife, whom he hoped had followed his direction to stay behind. His breathing was heavy as he sucked in air and forced the pain and discomfort all over his body to dissipate.

Bella... She was the reason he was out here. Protecting her. He couldn't let her down.

This had to end now. They could pick at each other all day until they were both exhausted, or he could put all the energy he had left into one final blow.

Niall opened his mouth, drew in a deep breath and let out a battle cry that tunneled up and out of his throat with the force of a gale wind. MacGregor leapt to his feet as Niall charged forward arching his sword. The vermin was prepared to protect himself from the forward-facing attack, but at the last second, Niall dodged to the left and sliced deeply through MacGregor's side. Blood gushed from the wound and swirled in the churning waters, but MacGregor did not go down. A crazed look came into his eyes, as though he would cheat death or take Niall with him. Niall backed up out of reach as MacGregor swung wildly with his sword. But it was no use, for the harder he fought, the more his wound bled. The water around their feet was already red, murky. Niall just had to outlast him... The wound gaped wide, showing the white of his ribs, the sleekness of organs that attempted to hold their place despite their casing being ripped apart.

MacGregor dropped his sword, eyes wide, and fell to his knees. His breaths were shallow, weak. He stared up at Niall with anger and defeat. Niall stumbled back a step, exhausted, in pain. He, too, let his sword fall.

Neither of them had the energy to continue, and MacGregor's wound was fatal. The fight was over.

Niall turned around to trudge toward the bank, tired, his head pounding. A sharp pain stabbed him in the back below his right shoulder, and he fell to his knees. He heard a loud splash behind him as MacGregor fell all the way forward, his body finally giving out. Niall reached behind him, but he couldn't feel whatever it was that had run him through. His men were shouting, and chaos reigned around him.

The battle was over, and even though he'd killed MacGregor, the man might have killed him, too. The sharpness of the wound emanated somewhere around his right side, halfway up his back. The pain was intense, but he'd felt worse. Niall tried to get to his feet, but each time he tried, he stumbled forward again. His breathing came in ragged pants.

Ballocks, but he couldn't decide if his head or back hurt worse.

With Niall down, the Oliphants made quick work of dispatching the rest of the MacGregors. The king would not be pleased it had come to this, but he would have known in advance from speaking with Walter that MacGregor had instigated the fight. That Niall had no choice.

In any case, he'd had to protect Bella. His people. He'd had to avenge the poor lad who'd been killed in the forest. Had to make certain that whoever else MacGregor had a vendetta against did not suffer the same fate. Aye, he'd done his duty.

Strath knelt before him, met this eyes and said, "I've got ye." Then he hoisted Niall over his shoulder as though he weren't a six-and-a-half foot-tall warrior weighing at least sixteen stone.

"Just...let me down. Let me...fight." If he could just have someone there to hold him up, he'd be fine.

"Dinna be stupid," Strath said. "Ye'd not last a minute with that dagger in your back. Ye're bleeding something awful, and if I dinna get ye back to the castle, my sister will have my head."

"Must...protect...Bella."

"Aye. But I've a thing for self-preservation as well, and ye didna grow up with the lass. She'll cut me from neck to sternum, I've nay doubt."

Niall agreed but found his tongue had gone numb and he was unable to answer.

"I'm glad we're in agreement. If ye were willing to see me killed, it might make it hard for the next family gathering." Strath chuckled, and though it seemed he meant to make light of what was happening, Niall could sense the tension in him.

Niall ground his teeth against the pain in his back, the worry for his men. Warm, sticky blood flowed from the side of his head where he'd been bashed a dozen times by the iron-studded targe. The blood now found its way into his eye, blinding him on one side. His vision came and went on the other side, mostly from loss of blood as the pain had eased into a dull ache. Strath put him on a horse stomach first and led it back to the castle at a jog, shouting for the men to open the gate.

Behind him, the sounds of battle ceased as the Oliphant men came to their victory.

"Walter... Need to tell him..."

"He'll be here soon. Ye can tell him yourself," Strath said. "Strength. Ye've been through worse. Ye came out of it strong. Ye'll do it again."

They made it through the gate and into the bailey. He was pulled from the horse and laid on his side on the ground, the knife still in his back.

"I didna want to remove it as he might lose more blood," Strath explained. "He took a nasty beating to the head. And after he delivered the death blow to MacGregor, the man threw a *sgian dubh*."

Ah, so that was what happened. Niall had thought they would fight with honor. Once a cowardly cheat, always a cowardly cheat.

Niall blinked open the only eye he could see with to find what seemed like a hundred faces loomed in front of his, but none were the face he needed to see—Bella's. He closed his eyes, feeling a chill take over him. All he wanted was to see her one more time. For her beautiful face to be forever ingrained in his mind, floating before his eyes.

Saints, but he was tired. Men were lifting him again. And then he heard her shouting. He imagined her shoving her way through the men to get to him. Niall forced himself to blink open his eyes and saw her anguished face loom over him. He smiled. "Bella..."

"Och, Niall." Her long slim fingers covered her mouth and tears glimmered in her eyes. "What did he do to ye?"

He closed his eyes, the world swimming all around him in muted sounds. "I love ye, lass. Ye're safe now."

Then Bella's soft warm hand was on his face, stroking his cheek. He leaned into her palm, remembering the joy and mirth in her gaze as she told him a funny story, the passion in her eyes as she fell into his embrace. "I love ye, too." She choked on a sob and then spoke again in a stronger tone. "Dinna leave me, Niall. That's an order."

Bossy even when he was like this. Niall smiled, wanted to laugh, but he no longer had the energy. He felt so heavy, and yet he was floating. Nay, that was his men carrying him.

They jostled him a little as he was carried up the stairs to the keep. The men questioned where to go, thinking to take him to the great hall. The chamber off there was already occupied by his ailing father. And then his mother was shrieking. There was a calming word from Bella. She was taking charge. She was his hero to the very end.

God, he'd loved her from the first moment he'd seen her, bossing all the warriors around with her hands on her hips.

The last thing he heard before all went black was his wife's commanding voice. "Take him to our chamber! Fetch the healer! Go, now!"

Chapter Twenty-Two

"I will not." Bella crossed her arms over her chest and glowered down at the healer who'd requested for her to leave. She was an aged woman with creases so deep in her face they might have been a map of all the injuries and illnesses she'd treated throughout her life. "He is my husband, and I will remain by his side."

The healer shrugged, her thin lips turned down with distaste. "Suit yourself, but stay out of my way."

Bella nodded, wondering why the woman would even consider that she would put Niall's life at further risk by getting in her way.

The old woman ordered Strath and Philip to hold Niall in place while she removed the dagger. Bella cringed, forcing herself to remain where she was when she wanted to climb onto the bed and sooth her husband for what was surely going to be a painful procedure.

Set on a table beside the bed was a pot of steaming water, linens, whisky, ointments, herbs, and a thread and needle. Bella kept her gaze there while the woman gripped the slick handle of the *sgian dubh*. She gave one tug, but it didn't budge. She had to brace her foot on the bed and wrap her hand in the hem of her skirt to keep her fingers from slipping. With a mighty yank, it came out, and with it the gush of blood that Strath had warned about.

Bella did get in the way then, but only to catch the woman as she stumbled backward. After righting the healer, she removed herself back to the corner to watch.

Blood oozed from the wound, and Niall howled as though he'd been stabbed all over again. Her heart ached, and she kept losing her breath. She backed toward a chair by the hearth to sit before she fell to the ground unconscious.

"Are ye well, my lady?" the old woman asked as she poured whisky on the wound, eliciting yet another wretched howl.

The men held Niall to the bed, not allowing him to come up off it as he seemed to want to do.

Bella cleared her throat. "I'll be all right."

"'Tis fine if ye wish to wait elsewhere," the woman said, softer now. "Many a lady does."

"Nay. I'll stay," Bella said firmly, feeling her breath and heartbeat begin to settle. She gripped the sides of the chair as though the wood cutting into her skin would help to steady her. "I need to stay."

The woman continued her work. "The wound is deep, but given his howls, I dinna think his lung is punctured." She cleaned his wound with the warm water and then packed it with herbs and ointments before sewing it closed. The men helped her to maneuver Niall as she wrapped a linen bandage around his torso to protect the stitching and hold her poultice in place.

"Keep an eye on him. If he wakes, give him this tincture in whisky." She handed Bella a tiny vial. "And if he is hungry, give him a broth sprinkled with this." She gave her a small pouch of herbs. "Have someone fetch me if he catches a fever. I'll be back tomorrow to change the dressing on his wound."

Bella nodded, her numb hands taking hold of the items. She watched absently as the woman made her way to the door where Niall's mother spoke to her softly and handed her a pouch of coins.

Lady Oliphant entered the room, touched her son's forehead, kissed him and murmured something in his ear. She came to stand beside Bella and enfolded her in her arms.

"He'll be well, my dear. Dinna fash. He went through far worse before."

Bella jerked back, shaking her head. "'Tis my fault. The MacGregor was trying to get to me all this time. If only I'd been able to convince him that baiting the man was a bad idea..."

"Shh... MacGregor was looking for an excuse to attack. Niall gave him one. It would have happened one way or another, lass. Dinna blame yourself. We must live our lives. We canna remain sheltered because someone has threatened to do us harm every time we step outside our walls. We have to protect ourselves. To prove to others we will not allow them to do us harm or make us scared. Niall put an end to weeks of terror."

Bella heard the words Lady Oliphant was saying, knew that she meant well, and that they were even words she might impart on someone in her same situation, but she couldn't help but shake her head. She couldn't help but say nay, to blame herself still.

"Come, let me get ye a tincture that will help ye sleep. Ye'll be no good to my son in this state."

Bella took a step back, gripped the bed post as if that would somehow help her to remain where she was. "I canna leave him."

"He'll not wake, my dear. Not for a little while at least. And if he does, one of the men can come and fetch ye."

Bella shook her head, planted her feet firmly on the wooden floor. "Nay. I canna leave."

Lady Oliphant sighed. "All right. I know how ye feel. I rarely leave my husband's side. All the same, I will have Mary bring ye the tincture, and perhaps it will help to calm your nerves as ye keep vigil."

Bella stood there numb for an uncertain amount of time. The men had cleared the room, leaving her alone with her husband, whose breathing was ragged and shallow. Bella set down the supplies the healer had left her. The bloody sheet he'd lain on when first put down had been replaced by a clean one, and a wool plaid had been tugged up around him. If she didn't know what had happened, she might have thought he was simply sleeping.

She placed a hand on his cheek, feeling the warmth of his skin. His head had been bandaged too, another poultice tucked against the mangled flesh. The man had taken a serious beating for her. And won.

Bella leaned down and kissed his cheek. "I love ye. Dinna leave me." Tears stung her eyes, and with no one present, she let them fall. Then she climbed onto the other side of the bed and curled up beside him. "I canna imagine a world without ye in it." She reached forward to trace his brows, his jawline. "Ever since I was a little girl, there ye were. And ye've been with me ever since."

"Bella," he murmured but didn't open his eyes. "Dinna leave me."

"I'm not leaving ye. I'm going to stay right here. Help ye get better. Ye will heal, and ye will be strong again. Ye must wake soon. Fight through this. I've still to tell ye the end of the story of Lord and Lady Goathead."

His lips quirked up into a smile, or at least she thought they did. She felt like she was staring at him so hard, she might have imagined it.

Bella felt beneath the blanket for his hand and held on tight. "I'm not letting ye go."

He woke screaming.

Niall sat up straight in bed, grabbed at the pain in his arm only to find it missing and then panicking all over again. His head pounded, his vision was blurred, and ballocks, but his insides hurt like the devil. He felt like he'd been stabbed in the bloody back.

"Shh..." A soft, feminine voice worked to soothe him.

Niall turned blindly toward the sound, seeing the outline of an angel. He reached for her but felt only air, and then she was on the other side of him, floating about the room. He tried to widen his eyes, to follow her path, but no amount of widening or rapid blinking made her come any clearer into view.

"Lay back," she crooned, her warm hands firmly pressing on his shoulder.

Niall did as she directed, not wanting to upset the sprite. "Where am I?"

"In your chamber at Dupplin Castle."

"What happened...?" He felt for his arm, touching only the mattress where it should have been.

"Ye dinna remember?" she asked.

He shook his head, but that only made his stomach rebel. Grabbing at his head, he felt linens overtop of the pounding. Before he could stop himself, he was leaning over the side the bed gagging, but nothing came up. The angel held a pot beneath him, crooning and stroking his shoulders.

"Please," he murmured, suddenly feeling his body on fire, so hot. Sweat broke out on his skin. "Tell me what happened. Tell me..."

When his body finally realized there was nothing to purge, he lay back down, feeling as though a boulder had been dropped on him, rolling back and forth from head to toe and crushing him everywhere.

"There was a battle." The bed dipped as she sat beside him. Just the nearness of her brought him comfort. "About a year ago. In it, ye were injured, but ye are alive."

"Have I been in this bed for a year."

"Nay, love, ye were well."

"Love? Ye love me?"

"Aye, verra much." She brushed a kiss over his forehead. "Ye're burning up."

She disappeared for a moment and then pressed a cool wet cloth to his forehead. The rim of a cup touched his lips. "Drink." The taste was bitter, burning a path down his throat, but a few minutes later, he felt his pains begin to ebb, and he asked for more.

"Why do ye love me?" he asked. "I am a broken man."

"Broken or not, ye are mine, and I see ye for what ye truly are. A warrior. A lover. A friend."

"What is your name, angel?"

"Bella."

A smile crossed his lips. "Aye, Bella. I have loved ye for so long. Are ye really mine?"

"Always."

Niall's eyes closed, and Bella stroked his cheek until his muscles relaxed with sleep. Though he had a fever, his breathing had grown stronger. Where it was once ragged and harsh, it was even now.

He'd been having nightmares and waking up confused for about three days now. She'd been able to soothe him most of the time. The previous morning, however, he'd thrashed about and threatened to kill everyone in the room. Strath and Philip had to hold him down and force the healer's sleeping drought into him.

Bella had started out sleeping beside him, but he'd become so restless that she'd moved to the chair in order to avoid injury. Secretly, she feared he wouldn't remember who she was, since each time he woke, he seemed to be reliving the battle injuries from the year before. One thing that never changed was that he continued to say he loved her. That he'd always loved her. So perhaps there was some hope.

When she questioned the healer about it, the woman said that sometimes with head injuries, such as the one he had, memories could disappear. Bella prayed it wasn't so.

While he slept, she washed him in cool water, tended to his injuries using the direction of the healer, and prayed hard that he would wake unscathed.

"How is he?"

Bella roused from her chair as her brother poked his head into the room.

"I think he's doing better. The fever seems to have gone down, and he's not thrashing about as much today."

Strath went over to the side of the bed and looked down at Niall, nodding as he did so. He reminded her so much of their father, the seriousness of his gaze, the concern for others. Strath was laird of his own holding, and one day would make a fine earl.

"Walter is getting cleaned up," he said.

"He arrived?" Bella sat up straighter. More than once, Niall had asked after his brother.

"Aye."

"I should take my leave, Bella, but if ye need me to stay longer, I can."

Bella crossed the room and embraced her brother. "Thank ye for all ye've done. I dinna know what I would have done without ye. What can I do to show my thanks?"

Strath chuckled, giving her hair a tug as he'd done when they were children. "I'm certain I will think of something."

Bella stuck out her tongue out at him. "I will be there for whatever ye need. And I'll see ye in the spring at Walter and the princess's wedding in any case."

"That is true." He glanced again at the bed. "I'm glad ye've found happiness, sister. I think he will be well. The man has a will of iron."

Bella smiled and stroked a lock of hair out of Niall's face. "He does."

"He's lucky to have ye."

Bella nodded and gazed down at Niall's sleeping form. She'd be happy if they never had a brush with death between them for the rest of their days. Was that too much to hope? "I'm lucky to have him, Strath."

"Now if only I could find such a match." Her brother sighed wistfully.

Bella tore her gaze from her husband to stare at her brother. He'd never expressed much interest in finding happiness within a match. He was betrothed to a lass in a neighboring clan but had not shared with Bella how he felt about it. The way he was looking now, as though someone had stolen his favorite treat, Bella thought he might not be exactly happy with the arrangements. The only way she knew how to cheer him up was by teasing him. "Ye wish to marry a man like Niall?" she teased.

"A man could only be so lucky." He chuckled, shaking off his melancholy. "Seriously though, I meant love. 'Tis but a fleeting thing, I think."

Bella shrugged. "'Haps. Ye're an amazing man, Strath. I think your betrothed will learn to love ye."

"Hmm. I didna tell ye...the match was dissolved after Da caught the man raiding our northern border. Maybe I'll accept a commission upon the border and find a way to steal a *Sassenach* bride as Da did."

"Well, ye certainly do like a challenge."

"I do." He chuckled. "I love ye, wee sister."

"And I love ye, big ogre."

Walter entered then, wishing Strath well on his return to his castle at Dornoch.

"How is he?"

Bella repeated what she'd told her brother, but then added, "I'm sorry."

"Why are ye sorry? Did ye put him in his sickbed?"

"I might as well have. MacGregor might have been the one to do the damage, but it is because of me he was able to get close enough to do so."

Walter put his arm around her shoulder and squeezed. "Dinna blame yourself. MacGregor was looking for a reason to strike at the Oliphants, and the coward found it. I could be as much to blame as ye are."

"How so?"

"I'm to marry the princess now, and that is the reason he was striking out at Niall to begin with."

"Get your hands off my wife."

They both jumped and stared at the bed as Niall's eyes opened wide, clear of fever.

Bella laughed with joy and leapt toward the bed, kissing Niall squarely on the mouth. "Ye've woken!"

"Aye." He glowered at his brother. "Did ye come back to steal her away?"

Walter chuckled. "Brother, all of Scotland knows she's yours, and trust me, no one would dare fight ye for her unless they had a death wish. Your bravery and skill is being sung at every castle by the bards."

"Is it now?"

"I may have embellished a line or two," Walter said with a wink.

Niall chuckled and wrapped his arm around Bella. "Ye're safe."

"Aye, and so are ye. Ye scared me to death." She pressed more kisses all over his face.

"I will protect ye always. Death canna have me."

She kissed him again, clutching at his stubbled cheeks. "Dinna test him so often, and perhaps he will spare ye."

Niall winked, sending a thrill of gratitude through her. "Bossy even now as I lie here cut apart."

"Ye knew what ye married. I'm no simpering lass."

"Aye, I did. The bravest, most beautiful, most intelligent lass in all of Scotland." He tugged on a lock of her hair.

Bella crawled onto the bed beside him as Walter crept from the room. She curled herself into his side and placed her hand over his middle gently so as not to jar him too much.

"I love ye, warrior," she murmured.

"And I love ye more than life itself, lass," he whispered. Their eyes locked then, and the depth of emotion misting in his gaze had her own eyes growing wet. There was a significance to that gaze, making her heart soar with gratitude. Oh, how much she wanted to say. "Ye've given me the greatest gift, a life full of meaning and love. A future I can grasp. Happiness."

Bella let the tears fall then as she brought his hand to her lips and kissed his knuckles. "And ye have given me the same."

Epilogue

Several months later...
Scone Abbey

Mary stood in the center of the abbey courtyard with a large turnip on her head.

"Wife, take that off your head," Philip demanded, marching toward the quickly growing gathering of people.

Mary shook her head adamantly, signing to him that she would most definitely not be following his orders. Bella bit her lip to keep from laughing at the determined hand gestures that accompanied her decline of his insistence.

"My lady," Philip begged, turning pleading eyes on Bella.

"I willna harm her," Bella said with a laugh. "Mary and I have done this trick many times. Sometimes, I'm even blindfolded. Do ye think I'd want to hurt my dear friend?"

"Nay..." Philip mused his worried gaze on his wife. He put his hands on his hips, and she could see from his expression that he was contemplating perhaps picking his wife up and absconding with her.

"Let me do it." Niall sauntered forward with his bow, a grin on his face that said he also wanted to add to his friend's torment.

Philip blanched. "My laird..." But what could he say?

Niall was now the chief of the Oliphant clan after the passing of his father two months before.

Mary was nodding again, and Bella stepped aside, pleased to have her husband show off his skill to everyone at Scone. They'd arrived the day before for the wedding of Sir Walter and Princess Elizabeth. It seemed like the entire country was now gathered in this one place in celebration.

The wedding vows had taken place that morning, and now everyone was celebrating, including the bride and groom. From what Bella could see, the couple looked to be mostly happy. They had been smiling and whispering every since, and when the priest had said Walter could kiss his bride, he'd done so lingeringly, enough so that the king had stepped forward and would have likely separated them had the priest not given a slight shake of his head.

Even now, they stood close together near the courtyard, chatting as though they shared a secret. Bella could not have been happier for Walter, who had expressed much concern about his upcoming vows.

"He can do it," Bella said cheerfully to Philip, putting her arrow back in the quiver and taking a step back. "There is only one archer in Scotland who can best me, and that is my husband."

Philip nodded, his face pale, but Mary had a wide smile on her face. She placed her hands on her hips and stood tall, keeping herself very still so that the turnip on her head did not move an inch.

The bailey was a rush of whispers as people worried about whether or not Niall would be able to make the shot.

"Silence!" Bella shouted. "Go on, my love, show them."

Niall grinned and winked at her as he nocked the arrow, slung the strap over his shoulder and bit down on the corded rope. The bailey was silent, the air crackling with tension, but Bella was proud and confident in her husband's skill. He drew back the bowstring, took aim and fired.

The arrow shot through the air, cutting every doubt from those in attendance as its point obliterated the turnip atop Mary's head, raining pieces over her hair and splattering its juice onto her face. Bella laughed and whooped, hugging her husband while Philip rushed forward to grab his wife up into his arms. He would likely not let go of her until they were all safely back at Dupplin.

The silence in the bailey quickly to exploded into a roar of cheers. No one here had ever seen Niall use the modified bow. Bella had wanted him to show everyone for more than one reason. Not just to prove to all that her husband was still a capable warrior—everyone knew that—but to show them that any man who had to go through the difficulties her husband had could heal and have options available to him. No one should have to suffer.

"Ye make me so proud," Bella said, grasping his cheeks between her hands and kissing him.

"I have ye to thank," Niall murmured against her lips and then bent her backwards, claiming her in a deliciously potent kiss that before now had only been experienced in their bedchamber.

Forgetting where they were, Bella wrapped her arms around his neck, clinging to him and ready to strip herself bare to claim the prize his kiss promised. When he finally ended the kiss, she could have fallen to the ground for all the strength she had left in her legs.

The sound of clapping slowly broke through the cobwebs of her mind. Niall righted her to face their king, who grinned and came forward.

Niall bowed low, while Bella curtsied.

"Incredible."

"My wife's design," Niall said, taking no credit.

"Truly?" The king raised a brow, swinging his gaze toward hers.

Bella blushed but straightened her shoulders with pride. "Aye."

"Well done." Robert the Bruce ran his hand over the polished wood. "Ye'll be hearing from my Master Fletcher."

Bella's belly did a flop, and instead of shouting with excitement, she managed to say in a calm tone, "I would be honored."

After that, they were drawn into the abbey where tables and benches had been set up in the refectory and a great feast laid out. On the dais with the royal family sat Walter and his new wife.

Bella's heart lightened at the conspiratorial wink Walter flashed his bride. Thank goodness Walter had not consigned himself to a lifetime of unhappiness.

Niall caught her staring at the table. "They look happy," he said. "Aye."

"I'm verra happy for my brother."

"I am, too. Everyone should experience love."

Niall stroked her spine as they approached her parents' table where they would dine. "I'm not certain they'll feel half the happiness we do, my love, but even still, half of it would be a good place."

She grinned up at him, about to tug him to her for another kiss when her mother and father interrupted them.

Her father grabbed her up in a tight hug. "The castle has not been quite the same without ye, but we see ye've been verra busy, and we're more than proud."

Bella blushed again. "I have missed ye both. Everyone."

When Bella hugged her mother, Lady Arbella glanced down at her middle, a broad grin covering her face. "Oh, my darling, ye've done it."

"What?" Bella glanced down to where her mother was looking at the small bulge of her belly. The one she'd been trying to forget she had.

"Ye're with child."

Bella whitened. "Nay, Mama." She looked back at Niall, making certain he wasn't listening. He was engaged with her father at the moment, so she whispered. "I fear I have...a tumor. I have been unwell, and there is a swelling in my abdomen. I didna want to tell Niall. I've been...living day to day and trying to make the most of everything."

Arbella laughed. "Oh, my love, I dinna think so." She listed off all of the symptoms Bella had been having—nausea in the morning, sore breasts, insatiable hunger and aversion to some of her favorite foods, exhaustion. "Ye're with child, several months if I were to guess."

"How is this possible?" Bella glanced at Niall, completely perplexed.

Arbella shrugged. "I dinna know. I sometimes only have a tiny amount of bleeding, insignificant enough that I have thought to have missed my monthly. Perhaps that has something to do with it."

Bella touched the small bump in her belly that she'd thought would be the death of her up until now. "A bairn."

"Aye."

She hugged her mother tightly. "I have to tell him."

Turning to Niall, she grabbed hold of his hand and ι‿ toward an alcove. She couldn't keep the news from him, and ι. didn't get him into the semi-private area, she'd shout it to the entire great hall.

"What is it?" Niall looked worried as he searched her face for answers.

"I've just discovered the most amazing news, and while I know I should wait until we were alone tonight, I couldna keep it from ye." She spoke fast, feeling flushed with excitement.

"Aye, tell me." He grabbed hold of her hand.

Bella met his gaze, locking her eyes with his. She licked her lips and then burst out with it, "I am with child."

"What?" Niall blinked as though he'd not heard her.

"My mother has just confirmed it. I am with child. We're going to have a bairn." She pressed his hand to her belly, and he splayed his palm over the ever-growing bulge. "Do ye feel that? It is our child."

Niall's eyes widened, a smile forming on his face as what she told him dawned.

"Together we make miracles, husband."

He wrapped his arm around her waist and hauled her up against him, kissing her tenderly. "God, I love ye."

"Am I dreaming?" Bella asked. "Is this real?"

"Och, aye, sweetheart. This is real."

"Never in all my dreams," she mused against his mouth, kissing him again and again.

"Och, but ye see," Niall said, his emerald eyes locking on hers. "That is where I did see it. In my dreams."

Bella laughed, and Niall let out a triumphant shout.

Those who stood on the outside of the curtain did not know exactly what was going on behind it, but what they guessed at left no question that Laird Niall Oliphant was indeed a whole man, and that his wife was heartily satisfied.

THANK you so much for reading! If you enjoyed **THE HIGHLANDER'S GIFT***, please spread the word by leaving a review on the site where you purchased your copy, or a reader site such as Goodreads!*

Do you want more of the Sutherland Clan? Did you know that many of the characters in this book have their own stories?

- Strath and Eva — READ *The Highlander's Stolen Bride*
- Roderick and Greer — READ *The Highlander's Hellion*
- Liam and Cora — READ *The Highlander's Secret Vow*
- Edan and Plaid — READ *The Highlander's Enchantment*

Don't miss out on the family line! Begin where it all started with the Stolen Bride Series!

Magnus and Arbella — READ *The Highlander's Reward* and *Wild Highland Mistletoe*
Daniel and Myra — READ *The Highlander's Lady*
Ronan and Julianna (m — READ *The Highlander's Warrior Bride*
Brandon and Mariana — READ *The Highlander's Triumph*
Heather and Duncan — READ *The Highlander's Sin*
Lorna and Jamie — READ *The Highlander's Temptation*
Samual and Catriona — READ *The Highlander's Charm*

Get them all and fall in love with the whole family!

"For fans of Highlander romance, this series is a must read!" ~ Night Owl Reviews, TOP PIC

Keep reading for an excerpt of the next book in the series ***THE HIGHLANDER'S STOLEN BRIDE***!

Excerpt from The Highlander's Stolen Bride

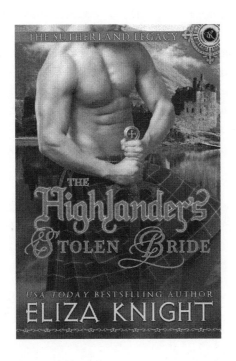

Spring, 1322
Northern England

Eva de Clare had been told that every English lady looked forward to her wedding day. But she was pretty certain that was a lie. In her case, her wedding day was fast winning out over her worst nightmare.

Standing in her father's study was her betrothed—a man who'd been blackmailing her family for at least two years that she knew of. Somehow, he'd managed to wheedle his way down to this—her hand in marriage.

Lord Belfinch stared down his nose first at her, and then her father. His thick brown hair was cropped close to his head and his face was as cleanly shaven as a sheep shorn too close to the skin, revealing pock-marks along his jaw line. Thin purple veins were visible at the plump parts of his cheeks, creating a map to his bulbous nose. Sharp, black eyes bore into her as he assessed her with a sneer of his yellowed teeth.

This man who made her physically ill was to be her husband. Her father might as well have sentenced her to death, for she wasn't only ill from looking at him, although he was extremely unpleasant, but rather because there was no blood pumping through his veins. Nay, a man that evil had to be filled with tar.

Eva tried to hold in her shudder. She wished her sister, Jacqueline, was here to talk sense into their father. More than anything, she wished her mother was here to hide her in the woods on one of their wilderness adventures. A gust of wind banged against the closed shut-ters, as though her mother spoke to her from beyond the grave, or maybe tried to scare away the vile beast about to force her into marriage.

Not a day went by that Eva didn't mourn the loss of her mother, her dearest friend and champion. Lady Northwyck had allegedly passed away from a sweating sickness some years ago—after being abducted by the father of the man who stood in front of her.

From what Eva had gathered, the *illness* had come about swiftly and ravaged her mother's once-strong body. No matter how many times Eva tried to escape to go to her mother's side, even if that meant she would be abducted as well, her father stopped her. She'd not even been able to say goodbye. Mother had never been sick in all the days Eva could remember. Imagining her wasting away and being helpless to do anything had only made Eva more aware of the fragileness of life.

Eva had always wondered if her death was real or not, because just last year she'd received a letter in her mother's hand saying that soon she would work out a plan to rescue Eva. But nothing had come of it. Her father had raged about falsehoods and trickery when he'd seen the letter. After that, any correspondence that came to her was opened and read by her father first.

And now, it was painfully evident how much she missed her mother's level-headedness.

Belfinch's blackmailing had started shortly after her mother's death.

With her sister married off to a lord nearer to London, and her mother gone, the only one she could argue her case with, and the only one who *should* protect her, was her father. But apparently, Lord Belfinch had a tight hold over her father.

She'd discovered her father was being blackmailed by accident. She'd seen Belfinch leaving her father's study two summers prior with a large jingling sack. Shortly thereafter, her father had levied an additional tax on their tenant farmers. Many were already struggling to make ends meet, and the tax nearly broke them. Eva had taken up the cause with her father, and when he'd stubbornly refused to back down, she'd asked about the coin he'd paid Belfinch. The look on her father's face had been all the confirmation she'd needed. When he then admitted he didn't have a choice, and he would not give her the reason as to why Belfinch was blackmailing him, Eva guessed it must have something to do with her mother's disappearance. But instead, her mother's disappearance had only been the beginning.

Despite her pleading, her father had continued to make exorbitant payments to Belfinch without explanation. As a result, their farmers were defeated in mind and spirit, and even in body. And so was Eva. Where was her mother? Was she truly gone?

Eva did all she could to help her people. She even wrote to her mother's family in Scotland, but when she never heard back she assumed either her father was taking the letters or they'd not written her back. Jacqueline, too, tried to write to their family in Scotland, but when her husband found out, he burned the letter.

After pilfering a few coins from the coin purse her father was supposed to give to Belfinch, she'd finally been able to convince a traveling bard to take a letter and send it out. Still, she'd not heard back.

Too keep herself from going mad, Eva continued her wilderness excursions, teaching women to forage for food in the forest, since they often went without even their own portions of farmed produce. Jacqueline sent money that Eva snuck to the farmers so their children wouldn't starve. But this couldn't go on forever. Belfinch had to be stopped.

But how? Was this it? Would spending the rest of her life with the lout be payment enough? And how would her people get on without her?

There would be a revolt. The people of Northwyck would be in danger and once again, she felt completely helpless.

Over the last few weeks while the negotiations were taking place, her father's hair had grayed completely and lost the luster it had once held. New deep grooves had etched themselves in his face, and the whites of his eyes had gone yellow. Was it the stress of Belfinch's noose closing around her father's neck, or the guilt for the wrongs he'd done himself?

"Papa," Eva pleaded. She grasped her fingers tightly in front of her waist, wanting desperately to tell her father all the reasons this was a bad idea, but the man standing two feet away held a power over her that made her tongue dry and brittle.

Even with the short distance between them, she felt like he was on top of her, suffocating her.

Lord Belfinch was twice her age, and where her father had gone completely gray, this man looked to be getting younger. Not a wrinkle marred his eyes despite his years, and not a single gray strand colored his hair. There was a gleam of malice in his dark eyes that frightened her, and the way her father's shoulders stooped as though the devil himself had given him a whipping was extremely disheartening.

It would seem the only one who could stand up for her in this situation wasn't her father, but herself.

Turning from her father, she faced Lord Belfinch head on. Shoulders squared, spine straight, her stance belied the fluttering in her belly.

"Lord Belfinch," she started, fixing him with a steady gaze. "While I confess I do not understand the arrangement you've had with my father—"

"You are correct," he cut her off, sounding strangled, as though it took all of his willpower to keep himself from shouting.

Eva pretended as though he'd not just interrupted. She was certain any reaction would give him the satisfaction he was looking for. "I am not chattel up for bidding. I must beseech you—"

The man held up his hand, interjecting once more. "That is where you are wrong, young lady."

Eva bristled at his tone and his use of young lady, as though a lass of twenty-two summers were a mere babe. Well, in his case, she practically was. Even still, her chest tightened with anger. She stood so erect her spine might snap. It was hard for her to hold her tongue. Her mother had believed that children or women should be seen and not heard, and she'd grown up voicing her opinions, much to the irritation of her father. Lord Northwyck had indulged his wife, but could not tolerate the behavior in his children. But with Belfinch... Her throat was tight, and she lost her senses and the ability to speak.

He rolled his eyes, disgust wrinkling his nose as he spoke low and nasally. "You see, you are chattel. Every daughter is."

Her belly threatened to upend its contents. Daughters were currency to him. Zounds, but if she were to actually marry him—which she swore right then and there she'd never do—Lord save her from having any daughters.

She *had* to get away from him.

"He's right, Daughter. You must do your duty."

Another gust of wind rattled the shutters. Even her father, who stared hard at her as though he were mentally willing her to be quiet, jerked up as though the rattle had been just for him.

"And this you must also understand," Belfinch said. "I am not *bidding* on you, quite the contrary. Your father *wants* me to marry you so badly he is willing to part with a small fortune in order to see it done. I am getting paid to take you off his hands."

Eva opened her mouth to respond, but no sound came out. Her tongue and throat were so dry, she was certain if she were to breathe, her insides would turn to dust. How had he done it? How could he make her feel like less than nothing with a few disdainful looks and hurtful words?

But perhaps it was not so much the power he had over her, but instead the lack of objection from her father. The fact he was allowing all of this to happen. Deep down, Eva questioned whether her father could truly want to get rid of her. In her heart of hearts, she just couldn't believe that he would pay anyone to take her. He was being forced. That had to be it. Her father was forceful, harsh sometimes, but he couldn't be completely without feeling, could he?

What hold did Belfinch have over him? If he'd only trusted her enough to tell her when she'd asked those two summers ago, she might have been able to stop it.

Feeling the telltale sign of tears prickling the backs of her eyes, Eva shifted her gaze to her father, who wouldn't look at her.

"Please, Papa..." She hoped her plea and the hurt she knew must be showing on her face would jar her father out of his decision.

Before her father could answer, Lord Belfinch was once more interrupting.

"The deed is done, my lady. The contract is signed. And I'll teach you a lesson in contradicting me."

"Contracts can be broken." The words escaped her before she had a chance to pull them back.

Before she even knew what was happening, there was a loud crack, and her face exploded with pain.

Eva stumbled backward, her mind a mushy jumble. Tears blinded her as the truth of what had just happened dawned on her. She caught herself, righting to her full height once more, the pound of pain in her face, the taste of blood on her tongue.

Lord Belfinch had *hit* her.

In front of her father. And her father had done nothing to stop it.

Eva brought her hand to her face, feeling the heat of where his fist or palm had connected. She shot her father a look of pure exasperation. He was no longer looking at the floor. His gaze held hers, and he shook his head. Was she imagining it, or was it sorrow making the grooves in his face even deeper?

"That is only a *taste* of what you can expect should you raise your voice to me again." Belfinch stood before her, puffing his chest, his yellowed teeth bared.

She hadn't raised her voice, merely contradicted him. Done only what she'd done all her life, which was to express her point of view.

But with a man like Lord Belfinch, any sign of disagreement would be seen as hostile. From this day forward, if the priest should give his blessing, if she was not able to escape, she would be his property, and all opinions she might have would be forfeit.

Eva would rather die.

And she'd just had a taste, as he said, of his temper—which was probably child's play compared to whatever his true rage must be.

She might actually die.

The way he was looking at her now, she wasn't so certain he wouldn't kill her on their wedding night. Or was he more sadistic than that, excited about the prospect of tormenting her for the rest of her life?

A fiery heat fluttered in Eva's chest. She couldn't decide whether to escape or to fall to the ground in a trembling heap. She'd never felt it before, this fervent, contradicting itch in her heart. Her hands started to tremble, and she had the intense urge to run. But where could she go?

When had her life turned to this? How had she not seen it coming?

Curses were on the tip of her tongue, demands that he never touch her again. But if he were willing to hit her with her father present, and now knew her father would not call the guards or tear up the contract, what worse thing would he do next?

Her mind raced as she waited to see.

She calculated the number of steps it would take to get to the door. How many seconds it would take for her to reach the stairs, the bailey, and what she could say to convince the stable master to give her a horse then demand the gates be opened without argument. How long would it take to ride to her sister's? Two weeks, at least.

But the odds were not in her favor. As soon as she reached the door, Belfinch's vile hands would no doubt grasp her and tug her back.

Then he'd likely beat her within an inch of her life and her father would just watch.

Mayhap the priest would see the red on her face, the slowly manifesting bruise, the swelling of the corner of her lip, and call off the wedding. Or maybe he would look the other way. She had to figure out how to get out of this. To escape. To help her father, else he be dragged to an early grave by the greedy bastard. Or by his rebelling peasants.

"Let's go." Belfinch didn't even wait for her. He turned his back and headed to the door, so confident that she would follow.

When her feet made no move to step forward, her father manifested beside her and took her by the elbow, tugging.

"Forgive me," he murmured, true anguish in his voice, but how could she take him seriously?

Anger now boiled inside her. Whatever hold Belfinch had, it couldn't be worse than giving away his own daughter.

How could she truly believe his anguish when he was for all intents and purposes leading her like a lamb to slaughter?

"Save me, Papa."

"It is done." His response lacked emotion, as though he'd already long ago resigned himself to this.

"Nothing is ever only one way. Please," she pleaded, her voice cracking. She dug her heels into the floorboards, refusing to move.

Belfinch returned suddenly, perhaps having taken note of their whispered words, and gripped her other elbow, his fingers pinching into her soft skin.

Instantly, her father let go.

A startled cry sounded from somewhere, like a wounded animal, and at the growl of her betrothed, Eva realized the noise had come from her.

All the saints above, someone rescue me.

But there was no one.

Her sister was far away and unaware of what was happening. For certes, if Jacqueline had a clue, she would have raised an army on her own to come and save Eva.

Belfinch dragged her down the stairs, his steps long as he skipped them two at a time. Without the use of one arm, Eva fumbled with her skirts to keep them out from under her feet, afraid if she told him she was having trouble, he would simply toss her the rest of the way down.

At the bottom of the steps, a priest in long black robes waited, as though he'd been summoned even before she had. But it wasn't their usual priest. Belfinch must have brought this man with him.

Which meant the priest would not help her. He wouldn't care about the ache in her cheek or whether she consented to this marriage at all. The man would do as he was told, likely fearing for his life.

A shudder took hold of her, and she hugged her middle, trying to tug free of Belfinch's grasp.

Eva looked around the great hall desperately, taking in the stunned expressions of the servants and the warriors that stood on the perimeter. Would one of them step forward? Would one of them question this farce? At some point in her short life, she'd helped every one of them. Given them food, coin, sewed their shirts, made a tincture for an illness, or comforted a wife when her husband went to battle. She had given them the very best of her.

But no one stepped forward.

One by one, they looked away.

Eva's heart broke then, shattering into a million tiny pieces. This was really happening; they would simply let her go, and there was no way for her to be saved. Holding back tears, she stared each of them in the eye as she passed, silently lancing them with her pain.

I have to save myself. Somehow.

"Take us to the chapel," Belfinch ordered her father.

With stooped shoulders and a slow, shaky gait, her father led them out of the great hall and into the bailey of their castle, the distant mountains looming up in the afternoon gloominess.

Overhead, the clouds covered the sun, making what should have been a bright day very dull indeed. Gloomy. As though Mother Nature knew exactly what was happening and somehow wished to warn the world of the impending doom.

"Wait," Eva said, stalling. "I am not dressed for a wedding. At least let me put on my best gown."

"What you wear doesn't matter," Belfinch said dismissively, yanking her along. "It is the deed itself."

If they were talking about anything other than a wedding she didn't want to happen, Eva might have thought his words wise.

"But every woman dreams of wearing a beautiful gown on her wedding day."

"Not my wife."

Eva bit her lip against the retort, still feeling the sting in her cheek. *His* wife wouldn't have an opinion or dreams.

"At least allow me to get my mother's necklace."

At this, Belfinch paused, and she could see the gleam of greed in his eyes. "Necklace?"

"Aye, she gave it to me before she... passed away. It is made of pearls and gemstones in the most brilliant colors." She was exaggerating, but it didn't matter, she just wanted to get away from him, lock herself in her room if she could, anything to put this wedding off.

"All right. I shall allow it."

He turned them back around, steering them toward the castle again. Once inside, he started to lead her up the stairs.

"I can go myself."

Belfinch let out a short, sharp laugh. "I don't trust you'll come back."

He wasn't a stupid man, that was for sure.

"I swear I will," she lied, her voice not even shaking, even though she was one giant wave inside.

Belfinch narrowed his eyes. "If you're not back in five minutes, I *will* kill your father."

Eva gaped at him but nodded anyway, because he was allowing her a few moments alone. As she climbed the stairs, she let the tears stream down her face. Because she wasn't going to lock herself in her room. Even if her father had betrayed her, she couldn't let him be killed.

Once in her room, she hurried to her wardrobe and unlocked the special chest her parents had given her as a young child to hide her most sacred treasures. Inside was her mother's necklace, the only thing she'd brought with her from her clan. It was indeed made of pearls, fine iridescent pearls that took on pink and purple hues in the right light. The clasp was gold, and there was a large sapphire in the center of the necklace. Scattered throughout the pearl strand were several other light-blue beryl stones. Not as glamorous as she'd made it out to the greedy monster, but it meant the world to her. Clutching the necklace, Eva raced from the room. She'd need help with the clasp to put it on, and there was not enough time to struggle with it herself. Taking the stairs with her skirts clutched up, and without someone dragging her, was a lot easier this time around.

But once she made it to the bailey, tension filled the air, and the men looked to be on edge. Eva stopped short, the pearls digging into her palm she gripped them so tightly.

"What is it?" she asked, looking toward her father, whose pallor had turned gray.

She'd only been gone a few minutes, what could have possibly happened?

"Get in the chapel," Belfinch ordered.

But he made no attempt to go with her. Instead, the priest took her arm and hurried her inside with several servants. Once inside, they barred the door.

Eva yanked free of the priest's hold. "What is happening?"

The priest stared gloomily toward a stained glass window of the Virgin Mary. "Riders were seen. They fear an attack."

*Want to read more? Check out **The Highlander's Stolen Bride** on wherever books are sold!*

About the Author

Eliza Knight is an award-winning and *USA Today* bestselling author of over fifty sizzling historical romance and erotic romance. Under the name E. Knight, she pens rip-your-heart-out historical fiction. While not reading, writing or researching for her latest book, she chases after her three children. In her spare time (if there is such a thing...) she likes daydreaming, wine-tasting, traveling, hiking, staring at the stars, watching movies, shopping and visiting with family and friends. She lives atop a small mountain with her own knight in shining armor, three princesses and two very naughty puppies. Visit Eliza at http://www.elizaknight.com or her historical blog History Undressed: www.historyundressed.com. Sign up for her newsletter to get news about books, events, contests and sneak peaks! http://eepurl.com/CSFFD

- facebook.com/elizaknightfiction
- twitter.com/elizaknight
- instagram.com/elizaknightfiction
- bookbub.com/authors/eliza-knight
- goodreads.com/elizaknight

Manufactured by Amazon.ca
Bolton, ON

4Q842546R00143